Keeper of the Mountain

A novel by
Nshan Erganian

Amazing Things Press

Book design by Julie L. Casey

ISBN 978-0615964652

Printed in the United States of America.

For more information, visit

www.nshanerganian.weebly.com
or
www.amazingthingspress.com

With Appreciation

This novel is dedicated to my parents,
grandparents, and the generations of Armenian
people whose spirit and supreme sacrifice
made my life possible. I am forever grateful.

Susan Clark is beginning a new chapter in her life as she drives to Auburn, Missouri, to begin her first teaching job. She's young, vibrant and has an engaging personality that the children will fondly remember long after they are out of school. She's thankful that Dr. Mark Sarkisian hired her for the job, and soon she'll be praying that he can save her life. If her chronic disease doesn't kill her, then her captors will...

Chapter 1

Dr. Mark Sarkisian did not have to wait for the buzz of his alarm clock on that August morning thanks to Quarter, the big Labrador. She was already barking at a flock of birds nesting in a large apple tree next to the bedroom window. It was one of many fruit trees surrounding the century-old farmhouse at Apple Hill Orchard. Mark and Marnie Sarkisian had purchased the orchard a year earlier in anticipation of Mark's retirement from the Auburn School District.

The school district's kindergarten through twelfth grade enrollment hovered near eight hundred students. It was relatively small in comparison to other districts in northern Missouri, especially those located in St. Joseph and Kansas City. However, Auburn's rural setting had a strong appeal for the man who had dedicated twenty-seven years of his life to various positions within the school district. Mark had joined the faculty as a language arts teacher and athletic coach. He was promoted to the high school principal's job in five years, and seven years later the school board appointed him the superintendent of schools.

Mark acquired the nickname "Sark" during his first year of coaching the high school basketball team. That same year, Coach Jerry Tarkanian had the "Running Rebels" from the University of Nevada-Las Vegas making a run for the NCAA basketball championship. Mark Sarkisian's team was also challenging for a high school conference championship, so the Auburn cheerleaders cooked up a skit for a pep assembly that spoofed the two coaches who shared the same nationality. That was as close as the comparison ever came. Jerry Tarkanian went on to even greater national prominence, but Mark Sarkisian stayed with the Auburn School District another twenty-six years. The nickname eventually lost its luster, due somewhat to a mediocre performance by the basketball team during the next two seasons. It was no secret that the Auburn patrons could be quite fickle when it came to packing the bleachers during a losing season or two. Nevertheless, the Sarkisians became comfortable with the community and, in time, added two children to the county population. After several years, Mark's career was firmly established with the Auburn School District and he had no desire to look for "greener pastures." This past June, however, the 52-year-old educator opted for early retirement in order to channel his energy into fulfilling a dream to own a commercial orchard. It was understandable that many of the local people scratched their heads and posed a simple question, *"Sark's going to be a farmer?"*

Why not? The Sarkisian's two children, Shawn and Kristin, were grown and Marnie was receptive to trying a different lifestyle. It would be a welcomed alternative to spending her evenings attending ball games, school carnivals, and hosting fundraising events for one worthy school project after another. In fact, during Mark's retirement reception, his loving wife politely announced that she would no longer be a nominee for an award given annually to the person who purchased the most fundraising items from the children. Marnie's message was brief as she announced that the cheerleaders and other organizations would have to find someone else willing to serve their family fund-raiser pizzas throughout the year. Months later, many of the patrons who attended Mark's reception had very little recollection of his lengthy retirement speech, but they vividly remembered Marnie's comment.

The Labrador's barking grew louder. Mark realized that Quarter was more than ready to begin their daily jogging routine along the roads and wooded areas that surrounded the

Apple Hill Orchard property. Mark loved running between rows of apple and peach trees as the fruit began to ripen. Quarter's preference, however, was the backwoods trails where she could dart after rabbits, squirrels, and deer that grazed on tender plants. Quarter never caught a deer, but she usually managed to keep pace and gradually close the gap to within a few yards of a whitetail's hindquarters.

Mark put on his jogging attire and a worn pair of running shoes. Marnie was beginning to stir in bed when the phone brought her fully awake. Mark was still brushing his teeth as he motioned for her to answer the phone. He could tell from the conversation that their daughter was on the other end of the line. The brief telephone call ended just as Mark stepped into the bedroom.

"Good morning, sleepy head," he said cheerfully as he reached into the bed, attempting to tickle his wife's exposed foot. "What did Kristin want this early in the morning?" Marnie delayed her response until the exposed foot was safely tucked under the covers.

"She called to say she would be here in a couple of minutes." Marnie yawned and stretched her arms above her head. "She wants me to go shopping with her later in the week, but I think she's coming now to talk with you."

4

Marnie noticed her husband give her a curious look. "She didn't say much, except that one of your new teachers seems to be missing."

"Hmm, I wonder what that's all about," Mark said while pulling on a hooded jersey to shield against the cool morning air. "I'm ready to head out now, so I'll just wait for Kristin at the bottom of the drive." He gave Marnie a quick kiss on the cheek and headed for the front door. She was pleased with the plan; it would give her ample time to get ready for their daughter's visit.

"Coffee and choereg, sweetie?" Marnie knew her husband would jump at the invitation to enjoy the Armenian sweetbread that Mark's mother had taught her to make. He had mentioned numerous times that in his childhood he delighted in eating the braided bread after dipping it into a cup of hot chocolate.

"You bet! That'll be mighty fine unless I get a better offer from someone else."

Marnie was used to the teasing after thirty-one years of marriage. They had parented two children, endured Mark's studies for university degrees, and managed to achieve a balance in their lives. She was very much aware that Mark's humor was his way of coping with the stress that comes during one's lifetime. She stretched in bed and thought about how life had been one adventure after another ever since they were college sweet-hearts. She had made a special effort to become close to Mark's family in the early years of their marriage. One of those adventures had involved being taught by Mark's mother how to prepare some of his favorite ethnic foods. Unfortunately, the loving mother-in-law cooked from memory, so "a pinch of this and a pinch of that" never seemed to appear as measurements in the Armenian recipe books.

Quarter jumped high in the air when Mark came out the front door of the renovated farmhouse. She loved to be with Mark and showed it by running in circles around the yard while he did stretching exercises. The ground was damp from a rainstorm that had passed through the region during the night, but now the air was fresh and sent puffy clouds across the sky. Mark finished his warm-up routine and the Lab joined him for the trek down the long driveway. Mark tactfully sidestepped pools of water that remained on the driveway from the prior night's storm, but Quarter stayed the course, content to slosh through the puddles. The two passed twenty rows of peach trees that had already yielded a golden crop to the fruit pickers. The apple harvest would begin in a few weeks and hundreds of trees would be freed from the weight that had forced their branches to droop. Mark slowed his pace in order to enjoy the beauty of nature. His life was nice and uncomplicated, but that was all about to change.

———◦◦———

Susan had been on the road for nearly an hour. The trip had been a very pleasant drive through rural farmland with late-summer crops and cows grazing in lush pastures. Rain was forecast for that evening, but Susan could already see darker clouds beginning to form in the distance. She hoped the storm would hold off long enough for her to get in a workout once she got closer to Auburn. A quaint road sign caught her attention:

Welcome to St. Joseph, Missouri
"Where the Pony Express began and Jesse James ended"

Susan was familiar with St. Joseph, a city of 75,000 residents. She had competed with some of the city's best athletes during her high school and college years as a distance runner. It was the "big" city for most people living in the northwest quadrant of the state. It was also the home of a university that maintained a friendly rivalry with Susan's alma mater in Maryville.

The final leg of the journey would be a simple thirty-minute jaunt to Auburn, but Susan wanted a break and a chance to change into her workout clothes. A gas station was just ahead. The car had plenty of fuel, but she needed a restroom and a snack to help regulate her blood sugar. It would help to fight off fatigue.

She pulled into the parking lot and retrieved her gym bag and an apple from the back seat. Once inside, she entered the privacy of a restroom stall and loosened her clothing. Quickly, she checked the insulin pump that had been feeding her system with life-sustaining medicine. So far, there was not a problem. Her energy level began to increase as she casually changed into her running gear and munched on the apple.

Susan returned to her car, feeling renewed. Thirty more minutes to go. Just thirty minutes, and Susan Clark would begin her hell on earth.

Chapter 2

Mark and Quarter had gone only as far as the entrance to the orchard when a vehicle with the bold lettering **Auburn County Sheriff** approached them. It came to a stop, and a smiling face leaned out of the driver's window.

"Hi, Dad. You and Quarter chasing rabbits again?" chimed the petite deputy sheriff sitting behind the steering wheel.

"Hi, Kristin!" Mark's response was accompanied with the broad smile of a proud father. "Yes, one of these days Quarter might actually catch a bunny and not even know what to do with it." He ran his hand over the Lab's smooth coat. "Honey, what brings you here so early in the morning?"

Kristin Sarkisian had been on Sheriff Larry Ray Garrett's police force for two years, but Mark was still getting used to his daughter serving as a deputy sheriff. Regardless of how snappy she looked in her brown khakis, Mark had a difficult time thinking about his petite daughter wearing a shiny badge and packing a .38 Special on her hip, but Kristin Sarkisian was not the typical daughter. Her parents had envisioned that she would become a teacher, but the former high school cheerleader and senior class president decided a degree in criminal justice might lead to a more exciting career.

"Actually, Dad, I'm here on official business, but I also need to talk with Mom about a shopping spree to spend some of your money. I was on stakeout last night because of the area burglaries, so I'm off-duty right now."

"Well, thanks a lot!" Mark feigned being disappointed. "I'm not invited?" Kristin noticed her father put his hand on his hip. His look seemed to indicate that his two favorite women were ganging up on him.

"Come on, Dad. You know you're way too busy with your little orchard hobby. I seem to recall that for about twenty years, you told Shawn and me about your desire to save the starving Armenians by growing thousands of bushels of fruit."

"It keeps me out of trouble," Mark quickly responded to the jesting. "After all, it would not look right having the former school superintendent handcuffed by his daughter and thrown into the Auburn County jail."

"Right, Dad. I'm sure there would be a lot of your former students you assigned to after-school detention posting bail for you." Kristin delighted in bantering with her father, but it was time to shift the conversation. "Actually, I did have another reason for coming this morning." Her tone became more serious. "Do you remember that teacher from Maryville that you hired for this school year?"

"Susan Clark, very nice young lady," Mark responded with enthusiasm. "She was a great athlete at the university and set records for distance running." He paused to reflect for a moment. "I think she even ran the Boston and Chicago marathons." He continued to provide Kristin with information about the new teacher who balanced academics and extra-curricular activities while helping her parents on the family farm. "I thought she would be really good with the children in the elementary school." Mark's curiosity was aroused. "What's Susan up to?"

"Dad, that's just it. We don't know." Kristin sounded bewildered. "She was driving to Auburn yesterday and no one's seen her since, at least no one that we've talked to so far."

"It does seem strange." Mark looked puzzled. "It's pretty hard to get lost between here and Maryville, Missouri." Kristin could tell her father was skeptical. "I think a young woman who trained on country roads for twenty-six mile marathons wouldn't have trouble navigating eighty miles of good highway."

Kristin gave an agreeing nod. "The state troopers spent most of last night checking the gas stations and convenience stores along the route, but so far there's no sign of her. One day she's everywhere talking to people, and then not a soul has seen her." The deputy shook her head in disbelief. "It's like she just vanished."

"I'm sorry to hear that, Kristin." Mark realized the visit was more than just to share the local news. "Can I be of some help?"

"Susan Clark's parents are coming from Maryville to talk with the sheriff today and he wanted to know if you would join him. He thought it might help since you met with their daughter when she interviewed for the teaching job."

Mark was pleased that his daughter was on Sheriff Larry Ray Garrett's force. He was a homespun local guy who had distinguished himself as the county's top law enforcement official for several years. He was unique, a throwback to the past era. While most lawmen had switched to automatic weapons, Sheriff Garrett preferred to remain a cowboy packing a .44 Colt six-shooter and wearing a ten-gallon Stetson. People had great respect for the congenial sheriff. They were comfortable in referring to him as Larry Ray instead of a more formal title. The sheriff never took offense to that casual relationship with the citizens. In fact, he once told Mark, "It really doesn't bother me, but I draw the line at being called Bubba."

Mark thought about Kristin's request. "I'm not sure how much help I can be, but I suppose I can meet with her parents. I have to go into town anyway to get chemicals for spraying the fruit trees."

Kristin smiled, knowing that her father wasn't likely to turn down a request for help from one of his good friends, especially his best friend, Larry Ray Garrett. "The Clarks wanted to stop at the school, and the sheriff thought it might be better to talk with them there instead of at his office. Is noon okay with you?"

"Tell Larry Ray that will be mighty fine," Mark replied as he knelt to calm down the black Lab that was now showing keen interest in a rabbit scurrying through the orchard. "Maybe there's nothing at all to be worried about, but I can understand how Susan's parents would be upset not to hear from her. Will you be joining us?"

"I'm afraid not, Dad. I'm going to meet with state troopers at the sheriff's office at about the same time." Kristin paused long enough to hear a transmission coming through on her two-way radio. She turned the volume down and refocused her attention on her father.

"We had another burglary in the eastern part of the county. We don't think it's juveniles or they would just take cigarettes and booze. These guys are hitting homes and businesses, getting into safes, and stealing some high-dollar stuff. I've been assigned to work with the state police to come up with a plan before this gets too far out of hand."

"Okay! My deputy daughter is finally doing criminal investigations," Mark cheered and showed his satisfaction by pumping a fist in the air. He had always believed that Kristin was capable of handling more responsibility than just dealing with misdemeanors and juvenile delinquents.

"Dad, you know you can only hand out traffic tickets for so long until you start to go bonkers," Kristin said as she gave an exaggerated look at Quarter as though the dog could understand. "I think it will be interesting to work with the state police on this case."

"Honey, I'm proud of you," Mark responded with a smile. "But, promise me that you'll be careful."

"It's a deal, Dad!" The spirited response was Kristin's way of letting Mark know that their special father and daughter bond was still intact.

All of the police talk had made no impact on Quarter. Mark released the dog and she immediately took a strategic position at the base of an apple tree. A squirrel began to chatter an alarm that the big Lab had once again interrupted the tranquil life in the orchard. Quarter rose on her hind legs and braced her front paws on the tree trunk as she began an incessant bark. The action antagonized the squirrel even more. Mark watched the two animals carry on a scene that had been repeated on many occasions and always with the same result.

"Okay, Quarter, I get the message," Mark said shaking his head. "The squirrel is quite aware that you can't climb trees." He realized that it was time to get on with the workout if he was going to meet with the sheriff at noon. "I better get going, Kristin. Your mom is in the house and the door's open."

"Thanks, Dad. You and Quarter be careful." Kristin was halfway up the drive when Mark heard her yell out the window, "Love ya, Dad!"

He watched until the cruiser came to a stop at the farmhouse, and then he spoke to his jogging companion. "Quarter, you may never win a beauty contest, but you sure are loyal." He took off running, but the head start would only last until Quarter sprinted into the lead. It would be an hour before the two would return and make their way up the long drive, but at a much slower pace.

Mark thought about Susan Clark as he showered following the workout. He wondered if she had simply decided to spend the evening with friends along the way. A severe storm had passed through the region that afternoon, so it was reasonable to assume that the young lady might have altered her travel plans. It was just speculation, and Mark had no way of knowing that the darkness accompanying yesterday's storm had also brought terror for Susan Clark.

———————◦◦◦———————

On that sinister night there would be no glow from the moon. Blasts of lightning ripped the sky and caused black clouds to bang together rumbling the earth. Evil came with the cold rain.

Two figures struggled to inch their way closer to the precipice of the mountain cliff. Their bodies pressed hard against each side of the vehicle as they pushed it ever closer to the edge. Even in neutral gear, the mass of steel and its contents made the car difficult to push. It was heavy, heavy as dead weight.

"Just a few more feet and over she goes," gruffed one of the men.

"Good. I'll be glad when it's over!" came a whispered response from the other side of the car. "This is nasty business!"

In another minute the vehicle went over the edge and hurtled three hundred feet until it splashed into deep water. The sound on impact echoed against the cliff walls and sent nocturnal wildlife scattering through timber. There would be no other witnesses. Chilling water rushed into the open windows. In minutes the vehicle became engulfed; then it tilted and plunged another sixty feet into the depths. Finally, it came to rest in the watery grave.

"Hmm, too bad. It was a nice car," remarked one of the men. "Maybe we should have kept it."

"Yeah, sure," the other replied. "And spend the rest of our lives in prison? I don't think so." He began to walk away, but paused for a moment, "Besides, she'll never need it again."

Chapter 3

Mark was dressed in jeans, a plaid shirt, and work boots. It was quite different attire from the business suits that he was accustomed to as a school administrator. He stepped out of the house as Quarter rose from a shady spot under the old apple tree. She ran toward Mark with her tail wagging and a pink tongue hanging out of her mouth.

"No, Quarter, you can't ride to town today. You stay!" Quarter came to a halt and perked her ears. She waited for a command from Mark to advance and gradually lowered her rear to the ground to acknowledge that this would not be her day to go for a joy ride.

Mark jumped into the vintage CJ-7 Jeep, stepped on the clutch, and switched on the key. The engine sputtered a few times until it began to click on all cylinders. Seconds later, the old relic was purring like a content kitten snoozing in front of a fireplace. Mark felt a sense of satisfaction as he shifted into first gear and headed down the drive: *Hmmm, not bad for something left over from the Korean War.*

The trip to Auburn would take twenty minutes. Mark enjoyed driving the county roads that took him past fields with acres of corn and soybeans growing closer to harvest with each passing day. The soybeans looked good this year. A dry spring had given farmers access to the fields for planting, and the ample rain that came weeks later produced tall green plants loaded with healthy vegetation. The pods would eventually turn brown and be pressed into various food products. He figured the beans looked good enough to yield at least fifty bushels per acre. More than half of the income would go toward expenses such as planting, harvesting, equipment, mortgage and taxes. In the end, a small farm might not generate enough revenue to support a family. Only a few people in the area had enough land to avoid working a second job, and most everyone in the county knew them. They were the farmers who traded for a newer truck every two years, and their barns housed modern tractors and combine machines. Those farmers also owned vintage equipment, but it was more for show and old-time tractor events rather than for working the land.

The country air felt fresh as it flowed through the open Jeep. It could have been a great day, but Mark's thoughts continued to drift back to his conversation with Kristin regarding the missing teacher: *Maybe she had car trouble and had to stop along the way. Why wouldn't she phone her parents to let them know there was a change in plans? It's strange; she couldn't have just vanished without a trace.*

The Jeep turned off the highway onto Auburn's main street. It was lined mostly with homes built a half-century earlier. They were two-story structures, but nothing that would appear on an historic register, just frame homes that provided a roof over the heads of one generation after another of Auburn families. Only one section of town contained newer homes, perhaps a dozen residences inhabited by people who held jobs in the city where the pay was better.

The main street was a straight shot of seven blocks. It started near the intersection of the state highway where a large, weathered sign proclaimed:

Welcome to Auburn
A Small Town with a Big Heart

An adjacent sign had been erected a few years ago. It was obvious that the sign was painted by one of the school district's less-talented art classes. Nevertheless, it sparked town pride:

Home of the Auburn Cardinals
2001 Conference Basketball Champions

Six seniors graduated from the boys' basketball team that year, so the townspeople thought it was fitting to hype the school district's first championship in two decades. The prospects for repeating the performance were slim because most of the underclassmen were lacking in size and talent.

A three-story brick structure built in 1847 sat in the middle of town. It served as the courthouse where various offices handled the functions of local government. The building had been sandblasted and tuck-pointed during a restoration project in 1985 thanks to a state-matching grant. The work had given the old courthouse a nicer exterior, but the interior of offices and meeting rooms retained a turn-of-the-century appearance.

Commerce wasn't thriving in Auburn, but the town continued to lure people to its quaint specialty shops. People could browse for antiques, crafts, hardware, and other items without having to hassle with the vehicle traffic and crowded aisles that came with the super discount stores. A small diner attracted early morning customers with biscuits and gravy. The daily luncheon specials consisted of tenderloin, fries, bean soup, and maybe even chicken-fried steak, providing there was enough gravy left over from the breakfast menu.

Mark drove past a small brick building that had the date 1858 etched in block lettering above its doorway. The Drovers and Merchants Bank was a fixture for the town. In recent years, some citizens had opted to invest their funds with larger financial institutions in the city. Interest rates were a little higher, and a few more "freebies" came with those accounts. However, many of the conservative people around Auburn still held some distrust for large banking institutions. They preferred to keep their money closer to home, so the Drovers and Merchants was the best option other than burying a tin can in the back yard.

The bank had the distinction of claiming an attempted hold-up by the Jesse James gang in the 1870's. Supposedly, enough gunfire from the bank employees and townsfolk sent Jesse, Frank, and the rest of the desperadoes high-tailing it back to their hideout in the caves of central Missouri. Old records at the Auburn County Historical Society never confirmed any such account. The records did document that some members of the gang may have passed through Auburn on their way to St. Joseph to meet with Jesse James. The old-timers in Auburn speculated the gang decided to pass on hitting the Auburn bank, instead opting to make their unauthorized cash withdrawal at the bank in Northfield, Minnesota. The citizens of Northfield were not very receptive to giving up their hard-earned money, and the James gang made a quick exit back to Missouri minus the bank cash, but filled with several bullet holes. Fact or fiction, it all made for a good story and helped the Auburn bank to lure new customers with a catchy marketing campaign: "Your money is always safe at Drovers and Merchants – even Jesse James couldn't steal it!"

Mark drove into the parking lot of the United Cooperative, a combination fuel and agriculture supply company. A half-dozen trucks and a few tractors hitched to anhydrous ammonia chemical tanks were parked in the lot. The Co-op provided diesel fuel, gasoline, and chemicals to most of the farmers in the county. Mark's only dealings with the Co-op prior to purchasing the orchard farm had been in contracting fuel for the school district's buses. State law required the superintendent to advertise for bids on diesel fuel. Each year, the Co-op won the contract because there were no other bidders. Mark thought it was a big waste of the district's dollars to advertise for bids in the county newspapers. There were no other suppliers within ten miles of Auburn, and the Co-op was just blocks from where the buses were maintained. Regardless, Mark complied and state funding continued to keep the school district solvent.

The Co-op was the unofficial meeting place for many of the county's more colorful characters. Nearly every day the salesroom, loading dock and parking lot contained a mix of farmers and others who discussed politics, crop prices, and local school athletics. Today, the conversations would likely focus on the recent burglaries and the whereabouts of the young teacher.

Mark entered the salesroom and was greeted with nods from several patrons that were seated on wooden crates. Most were clutching coffee cups and didn't seem in any hurry to conduct business at the sales counter. Elijah Carneal came out of his office when he saw Mark. Mr. Carneal had been the manager of the Co-op for so many years that people joked about him taking part in Pickett's Charge at the battle of Gettysburg during the Civil War. And, in fact, the respected gentleman's lineage actually did date back to the historic War Between the States.

"Hello, Mark. What can I do for you?" The greeting was straightforward, with the ring of a busy man surrounded by so many people with no place to go, and not in much of a hurry to get there. Mr. Carneal knew Mark was not a loiterer, so it was time to get on with business.

"I need some chemicals for the orchard," Mark said as he glanced at a piece of paper pulled from his shirt pocket. "Fifty pounds of insecticide and a thirty-pound sack of fungicide should do it." He thought for a second, and then added, "I'll need some of that sticker chemical to keep the spray on the trees in case it rains." Mark's comment brought a grin from the men who were seated close to him. Most of them had lived through years when drought eliminated any hope for decent yields. The Co-op "regulars" figured Mark was being overly optimistic, even though an unusual storm was passing through the region.

Mr. Carneal was elated that someone was finally doing business. "Mark, I'll have your order ready in a few minutes," the old gentleman said, shuffling into a rear storage room.

Mark decided to have a cup of coffee while he waited. A small table in the corner of the room held a half-full coffee pot, foam cups, sugar, and packets of creamer. The table was littered with several used stir sticks. An empty butter container on the table had been recycled to serve as a receptacle for contributions to the "coffee fund." The tub had collected less than a dollar in loose change. It was evident that the Co-op patrons thought coffee fell into the same category as the free advice one could get at the business.

Mark poured a cup of coffee, donated fifty cents to the "kitty," and then stepped outside onto the loading dock to survey the parking lot. An old, black pickup truck with rusting fenders was parked at the gasoline pumps. The truck's original paint had faded years ago and its dull gray engine hood apparently was borrowed from another vehicle. The truck belonged to Jubile Walker, one of Auburn's least popular characters. Jubile and his two buddies were troublemakers that people went out of their way to avoid. Mark had no desire for an encounter with the local thugs. They had indicated on numerous occasions that they held a grudge against Mark that dated back to their high school years.

"You get it done?" asked the fellow as he opened the fridge and grabbed two beers.

"We don't want anything to show she was here." He tossed one can across the room and it was snatched before hitting the floor.

"Yeah, but there wasn't much there," replied the other one as he kicked off his muddy boots and pulled the tab on the fizzing beer. "She must have twisted that ankle about a half-mile down the trail and hobbled until she got here." A wet spray exploded from the can and soaked his shirt. "I found the headband where she fell."

"That's good. It should be the last thing that connects her to us, and if the cops start

snooping around, someone else can take the rap." He chugged the rest of his beer and crushed the empty can in his hand. Then he lit a cigarette, took a few puffs, and blew a circle of smoke that drifted across the table. "We're back in business," he smirked and rested his boots on the table. "That is, as long as our friends took care of the girl's other stuff." The comment triggered agitation.

"Well, they darn well better have done their part. We're doing all the dirty work and they're clean as a whistle," he said slamming the beer can on the table and unleashing a loud belch. "You don't see them getting their hands dirty pushing a car over the cliff. They ain't volunteering to murder some young gal just because she sees us stashing that stuff!"

"Shut up, you idiot! Two more days and nobody will ever see us again. No one!" His face took on a nasty sneer.

"What are you smiling about?" the other man asked as he pulled another brew from the fridge.

"Oh, I just thought it was sort of funny. We're going to disappear...just like the girl."

Chapter 4

Jubile Walker, Spook Daniels and Aubrey Canterbury were the local rednecks of the county. The three had been enrolled in the Auburn School District when Mark served as an administrator. At a time when their classmates were setting academic and athletic records, Walker, Daniels and Canterbury seemed to compete for recording the most suspensions.

The three juvenile delinquents made the front page of the county newspaper in their junior year for a midnight break-in at the high school. It netted each of them a $250 fine and forty hours of community service. Unknown to the three young misfits, one of Mark's first actions as a school administrator was to install a security system in the district facilities. Sheriff deputies responded to a silent alarm and found the three hiding in the restroom stalls. Their pockets were stuffed with coins from the school vending machines. Judging from the empty candy wrappers on the floor of the toilet room, the overweight Canterbury had also seized the opportunity to add most of the candy bars to his share of the loot.

Walker, Daniels, and Canterbury were now in their late twenties. The disdain they held for their former school administrator came across on occasions when their paths had crossed. Forty hours of community service washing school buses and scraping dried food off lunch trays had made a lasting impression.

Jubile Walker's dislike for Mark went beyond the school burglary incident. His buddies always thought his name was really Jubule until Mark made it a point to give people the correct pronunciation. He had seen it on Walker's birth certificate on the day the lad enrolled in school. Evidently, poor spelling was a trait handed down from one generation of Walkers to the next.

"It's Ju*bile*, J-U-B-I-L-E, not Jubule," Mark would say whenever people mispronounced it. That's how it frequently came across on the school's public address system... "*Jubile* Walker... report to the principal's office."

Just about everyone in Auburn called James Earl Daniels, "Spook." He came by the nickname about nine months after his unwed mother spent a lot of time hanging around the town park with three fellows who had come to Auburn to paint the water tower. No one knew their last names. They were James, Earl, and

Daniel to the citizens of Auburn. The painters left behind two things in Auburn when the job was finished. The town had a shiny water tower, and little James Earl Daniels was resting comfortably in his mother's tummy awaiting an entrance into the world. When the little fellow finally arrived nine months later, the people of Auburn weren't sure if the father was James, Earl, or Daniel. The old-timers at the Co-op speculated it was "just plain spooky." Understandably, the paint crew was never invited back to Auburn, but the name Spook stuck forever.

The only real job that Spook ever held lasted only three days. He was employed by the U.S. Postal Service as a rural mail carrier on a trial basis. His first days on the job were impressive as he drove through the countryside hauling letters and advertising flyers in the bed of his pickup truck. In fact, he finished the route in record time on each day. However, his career came to an abrupt halt when several county residents reported receiving no deliveries for three consecutive days. An investigation by postal authorities revealed that several bags of mail had been tossed into ditches along the route. Evidently, Spook had decided that less mail meant faster service, but the postal officials weren't buying his theory. Spook's seventy-two hours of "service in rain, sleet, and snow" ended without an invitation to join the former postal employees association.

Spook's current source of income came once a month in the form of a government assistance check. Following the unceremonious dismissal, he informed his former employer that he had acquired a work-related injury. Rather than fight the bogus claim, the postal service agreed to forward the town bum a small stipend each month.

Aubrey Canterbury could have easily become the brunt of jokes about fat boys, but his association with Jubile and Spook afforded him some protection from being overly humiliated during his high school years. The relationship gave him a sense of power that he would never have found if left to fend for himself in the adult world. It was rumored that the daughter of a prominent citizen took pity on him during his senior year and afforded Aubrey a "one-night stand." It was just months after that lustful evening in the town park that Lucy missed her period. Shortly thereafter, the two were united in matrimony during a quiet ceremony in a neighboring town; no wedding invitations were sent out. The couple bore three children who enjoyed chomping super-sized combo meals just as much as their parents. By the fourth year of their marriage, the Canterbury's bathroom scales didn't get much use.

Aubrey might have dodged getting the nickname of "Toad" had it not been for a freak accident some years earlier. He and his two buddies had pulled into the Co-op just after eighteen-year-old Noah Wanatee arrived with a team of mules pulling a hay wagon. The Wanatees were reclusive people with a Native American heritage. They seldom came to town unless it was for necessary business. There had been years when people could not recall seeing the father, mother, or the boy in town. Their home was a small cabin in Hidden Valley near the top of Buffalo Mountain. The mountain wasn't mammoth, but its mass and elevation was sufficient enough to make the small print on a Missouri map. It featured two distinct peaks; one of which resembled the head and humped back of a bison. Timbered bluffs that spread for miles encircled the mountain. A spring-fed lake nestled below the bluffs provided recreation activities for the public. Very few people ever ventured into the higher elevations of Buffalo Mountain. It was rough terrain where a wrong turn on the narrow trails could easily bring out rescue parties.

The Wanatee boy had attended school in Auburn for his first year of formal education when he was twelve years old. His learning skills were behind other kids his age, so he was placed in a fourth-grade class. It was an awkward situation and the boy did not return to school the next year. Mark made one trip up Buffalo Mountain to visit with the parents about having their son return to school. After driving his vehicle as far as he could through the lower bluffs, he hiked another two miles to reach a plateau near the crest of the mountain. He found the Wanatee cabin nestled in a grove of trees next to a brook.

The one and only meeting with Noah Wanatee's father was not a very pleasant encounter. The father appeared to be in his late seventies with slumped shoulders that disclosed the onset of osteoporosis. However, it was obvious that in earlier years the man had been large and quite powerful. Mr. Wanatee made it clear that there was plenty of work to be done at home, and the boy would not be returning for any more schooling. Mark was exhausted from the hike up the mountain and in no mood to argue with the unreceptive parent, so he trekked back through the bluffs and chalked the matter up to just another experience in the life of a school administrator. Thus, the official account reported to the department of education indicated that Noah Wanatee had attended one year of public school education and was currently being home-schooled. The Wanatees were happy to be left alone and Mark never had to make another trip to the top of Buffalo Mountain.

On the day of the historic encounter at the Co-op, Noah Wanatee was giving his team of mules a bucket of water from an outdoor spigot. Walker, Daniels, and Canterbury started giving the young man a hard time with references to his Native American heritage. Noah Wanatee was tall and loaded with enough muscle to handle any of the three, but he had no desire to draw attention to himself. He ignored the taunting, but it only seemed to rile the rednecks more. Their vile insults culminated with Aubrey Canterbury boasting that he could ride a mule a lot better than any "injun" kid. Canterbury made a move toward the mules, prompting Noah to call out a warning.

"Not a good idea to bother the mules," Noah cautioned, stepping between Canterbury and the animals. The warning was useless. Aubrey Canterbury was determined to put on a show for the Co-op patrons. Besides, he knew that Jubile Walker and Spook Daniels were ready to jump into the fray if he needed help. By now, most of the fellows inside the Co-op salesroom had gathered on the loading dock, taking in the encounter.

"Well, well!" Canterbury shouted. "Looky here who's learned to talk English, and he doesn't want me to touch his girly friend with the long tail!"

Canterbury would live to regret his next move. He abruptly brushed past the young man and tried to hoist himself onto the backside of one of the mules. In the split second when Canterbury's large stomach touched its hide, the mule kicked up its rear legs and sent its haunches skyward. Canterbury's body resembled a rocket fired from the launch pad at Cape Canaveral, but the flight was short-lived. His body crashed twenty feet from the mule in a spew of parking lot gravel.

A dozen patrons at the Co-op stood in shocked silence thinking they had just seen the mortal ending of Aubrey Canterbury, due to his own stupidity. They were somewhat relieved when he uttered a groan and clutched his right leg.

"Oh craaaaap!" Canterbury yelled in pain. "That miserable piece of horsemeat broke my freakin' leg!" Most of the spectators nodded in agreement with the diagnosis.

The county paramedics arrived twelve minutes after they got Elijah Carneal's call reporting the accident. They loaded Aubrey into an ambulance and sped for the Auburn Medical Center, with him swearing all the way that he was going to get even with the Wanatee family. Three steel pins, a dozen bolts, and fourteen weeks later, Aubrey emerged from his full-leg cast to rejoin life in Auburn. His permanent gimpy limp and the way he flew off the mule gave birth to a nickname he detested ... "Toad."

Now, the three men leaned against the old pickup, muttering to themselves and glaring at their former school administrator. Mark continued to engage in friendly conversation with the Co-op patrons, who were using wooden pallets for seats on the loading dock. Eventually, one of the older fellows broached the subject of the missing teacher.

"Say, Mark, what do you make of that teacher not showing up?" The question drew the attention of everyone on the dock. "I figured you know her," the fellow asked as he tipped the stub of a cigarette into an empty coffee can that served as an ashtray.

"Well, I really don't know much about it," Mark responded. "I only met her last spring when she interviewed for the job and she seemed like a really nice young lady."

"The young ones don't seem to last long," an old farmer replied. He then spit a wad of chewing tobacco that flew off the loading dock and splattered onto the ground. "They teach a year or two and then go to the city where they can make more money."

Mark decided not to debate the issue since most of the other men sitting on the dock were nodding in agreement. Instead, he chose to address the subject to the entire audience.

"I'm meeting with Sheriff Larry Ray and the girl's parents today. Maybe we'll know more about what's happened to her after that." Mark's comments seemed to appease the group since they were all nodding once again.

One of the other men seated on the loading dock pointed a finger in the direction of the fuel pumps and joked, "Maybe she came to town, took one look at those three fellows and decided to keep right on driving to the next town." The reference to Jubile Walker and his buddies brought forth another nod of consensus.

Jubile finished pumping gasoline into his pickup truck and walked toward the Co-op building. Mark was sure there would be a nasty confrontation, but Elijah Carneal quickly stepped through the front door onto the dock. He purposely timed his entrance to block Jubile's path.

"Mark, I have your chemicals here. Anything else, my friend?" Mr. Carneal asked, winking his eye at Mark. The calm voice was reassurance that there wouldn't be any trouble at the Co-op, at least not on that particular day. "You know, Mark, there's an old saying that everyone is entitled to be a little stupid, but those fellas seem to be abusing the privilege." The old man flashed another wink, which didn't go unnoticed by others. Jubile directed a nasty sneer toward the Co-op manager who continued to politely smile. Elijah Carneal was old, but Jubile knew better than to take on one of Auburn's most respected citizens.

"Thanks. I believe that will take care of it for now," Mark said as he took the box of chemicals and a sales ticket from the Co-op manager. He gave Mr. Carneal a grateful look.

Mark loaded the chemicals into the Jeep and noticed that Jubile continued to flash a hateful stare. He couldn't help thinking about what he often shared with teachers in his school district: "All of the kids can't become rocket scientists, but surely they can all learn how to pump gas." Now, he had reason to question the accuracy of his statement as he observed Jubile's buddies leaning against the Co-op fuel pumps.

Mark cranked over the Jeep's engine and slowly drove out of the parking lot onto the main street. In the distance, dark clouds had once again shadowed the high peaks of Buffalo Mountain. They would hover over the mountain just long enough to hide more evil.

———————◦———————

Susan pressed her back against a wall and tried to stand, but the pain in her swollen ankle was too much to bear. She fell onto the floor. Her body ached from numerous bruises, but the physical pain was the least of her worries. She feared for her life:

Just a few hours earlier she had enjoyed a leisurely drive, taking in the beauty of the rural landscape. The final miles showcased the rolling hills covered in a blanket of beautiful maple trees. In the distance, Buffalo Mountain's cliffs formed a majestic backdrop in spite of the dark clouds warning of an impending storm. The landmark mountain had fascinated Susan ever since she first saw it displayed on a large screen in her hometown. She had been anxious to test the trails before moving into her new apartment. Twenty minutes later, she parked her car near a trail that appeared to wind into the mountain bluffs and donned a pair of running shoes with small metal spikes attached to the soles. The cleats would provide added traction on the uneven, rough terrain. She left her insulin pump in the car, opting instead to attach a smaller kit to the waistband of her running shorts. The sky turned much darker as ominous clouds moved across the mountain peaks just ahead of the powerful storm. She needed to hustle if she were to finish the run before the downpour. She locked the car and attached the keys to the band of her wristwatch, and then she headed up the trail at a moderate pace.

The first miles were an easy jaunt for the seasoned runner, but eventually the terrain became more primitive with steeper inclines that rose higher into the upper reaches of the mountain. Suddenly a patch of loose dirt gave way and vaulted Susan into an uncontrolled somersault. Her body banged against the hard earth and slammed into a large boulder. An ankle twisted in the fall and dark bruises began to appear over parts of her body. A gash on her knee trickled blood down her leg and changed her white sock to a scarlet color. She needed help.

Now, Susan sat on a damp floor staring at streaks of discoloration that spread across her ankle as she continued to ponder the events that had thrust her into a makeshift prison. The rough trail had taken her to such a high elevation that any attempt to descend on one good leg would be futile.

She had scanned the landscape and saw what appeared to be a clearing a half-mile from the trail. The open land might provide an easier access down the mountain, perhaps even some signs of civilization. She had fought the pain in her ankle as she rose off the ground and began to shuffle toward the clearing.

Chapter 5

The drive to the high school was only a few blocks, but it helped Mark to get his thoughts back on track with regard to the missing teacher. It was still a week before the start of school. He waved to several children riding bicycles and playing touch football; they were savoring what would be their last days of freedom until the Thanksgiving break.

Auburn's elementary, middle, and high school were all located on one campus. The consolidation was a cost-containment measure, which helped the school district's financial position. Most parents seemed to like it. They could transport all of their children to one central location even though they attended different grade levels. There were only ten vehicles in the school district parking lot. Seven belonged to custodians, secretaries, and administrative personnel who were busy getting the facilities ready for teacher meetings in just a few days. An SUV marked **Auburn County Sheriff** was parked next to a late model white truck that Mark didn't recognize as belonging to any of his former colleagues in the school district. The vehicle bore Nodaway County license plates, so Mark assumed the truck was transportation for Susan Clark's parents. The remaining vehicle was a late model maroon BMW in dire need of a carwash. The quantity of mud caked around the fenders seemed to indicate that the vehicle may have been driven on rough ground. Mark didn't dwell on the pricey vehicle's appearance because all of the cars in the parking lot had lost their luster due to the previous night's storm.

A small sign next to one parking space read *Reserved for Superintendent.* Mark recognized the vehicle that was parked in his former spot. It belonged to Dan Williams, the former high school principal who had been promoted to the superintendent position based on Mark's recommendation. The two men had maintained an excellent working relationship for several years, and Mark was confident that Dan would do a good job as the school district's chief administrator. Mark drove farther down the line and eased the Jeep into a parking space. He entered the building and immediately felt a sense of nostalgia as though he were walking through an historic time capsule.

The walls along the main corridor leading to the administrative offices were lined with dozens of framed placards. They displayed pictures of graduating classes dating as far back as the early 1900's. Many of the composites identified years when a senior class might number less than fifteen students. He paused for a moment in front of the years spanning 1940 through 1943. Those were among his favorites because they contained the pictures of the Rankin boys. All four brothers had entered branches of the military after their graduation from Auburn High School and served honorably during World War II.

A lot of people in Auburn were worried the young men would never make it back to their Midwestern roots. Those fears increased even more when five brothers from an Iowa family lost their lives on a ship that was torpedoed. Fortunately, Mr. and Mrs. Rankin's prayers each Sunday at the Auburn United Methodist Church were answered and the Rankin boys came home as men. Now, five decades later and a few pounds heavier, the Rankin brothers would don their military uniforms once a year and return to their old high school to celebrate Veterans' Day. On that special occasion, hundreds of wide-eyed children would learn what it was like to fight in "the second war to end all wars."

Ellen Downing greeted Mark with a big smile when he entered the administrative office. She had been a secretary in the school district for forty-five years. It was the only job she ever had. She was an Auburn graduate who often shared the fact that she served as an officer in the local chapter of Future Homemakers of America during her four years in high school. Ellen was slightly more modest in reminding new employees that she had outlasted a dozen administrators. The bright-eyed, skinny teenager with the engaging smile had become a silver-haired senior citizen who had to squint even when wearing her "granny" wire-frame glasses. It was fitting that everyone in Auburn, adults and children, referred to her as Granny Downing. Mark was one of her favorites. The two had a special bond that came from years of working together and attending most every activity at the elementary, middle school, and high school. Ellen prided herself in being able to tell the little ones entering kindergarten, "I knew your daddy when he attended this school." In recent years she had added, "And your grandpa."

"Ellen, when are you going to give up and start drawing your retirement?" Mark realized that it wouldn't take long for his former secretary to retaliate. Ellen cocked her head to one side and then squinted toward the ceiling.

"Hmmm, let's see," she paused for dramatic effect. "Oh, now I remember. I can't afford to quit because they're paying you so much in retirement there's nothing left for the rest of us. I may have to take a second job just to heat my house this winter."

Mark acted as though he was unmoved by the sad story, especially since Ellen had been threatening to take a different job for as long as he had known her. He reached into his pocket for a quarter and tossed it on her desk. "You're probably right," he responded with a coy smile. "Here's some of that retirement money to buy a cup of coffee on me." The secretary wasn't about to let Mark get the best of her and responded with sarcasm.

"Well, thank you, Mr. Donald Trump!" Ellen quipped. "Why don't I take this quarter and get two cups of coffee? One for me and one for Elvis Presley," she chuckled, and then rose from her desk to do a mock dance while waving her hands in the air as though she had just won a million-dollar lottery. "Mark, are we ever going to get you out of the 50's and 60's?" Twenty-two years of listening to Ricky Nelson and Buddy Holly songs drifting out of Mark's office had left a lasting impression on the congenial secretary.

The door to an adjoining office opened and Dan Williams stepped into the room. Before his most recent promotion to superintendent, Mr. Williams had been noted for being a no-nonsense principal whose strong voice echoed through the halls of the school.

Mark had respect for Mr. Williams because he knew it was no easy task being responsible for maintaining discipline in a high school.

"Hello, Mark," the new superintendent called out as he skirted the secretary's desk to stuff papers into a file cabinet. "How are things going for you?"

"Just fine, Dan. No students and no parents to deal with. How about you?"

"No problems yet, but it's always calm before the storm," he quipped. "You and Marnie are coming to the festival, aren't you? We're counting on having those yummy cheese turnovers at the potluck dinner."

"Absolutely!" Mark's response carried a bit of sarcasm. "What would the school festival be like without Marnie Sarkisian's famous Armenian cheese boeregs?" The annual community dinner was a huge tradition in Auburn. Students, parents, grandparents, and just about everyone that had anything to do with the district would show up to tour facilities, meet staff, and enjoy a free meal. Mark's wife would spend an entire day stuffing freshly kneaded dough with cheese and spices to create her specialty. Dan took Mark's joking as an acknowledgement that he and Marnie would indeed be attending the school event, but it was time to get on with business.

"The sheriff and the other people are waiting for you in the meeting room."

"Thanks, Dan. I better get in there before they assign me to after-school detention for being tardy." Mark laughed as he headed for a side door. It was the same room that he had used for years as he and a school board comprised of local citizens hammered out policies and haggled over school district budgets.

***

Susan slipped in and out of consciousness for hours. Her ankle throbbed and was swollen to twice the normal size. The shock to her system that came with the initial trauma had begun to wear off, but now she began to feel pain in other parts of her body. Bruises appeared on her shoulder and thigh, injuries that were not caused by the tumble on the trail. She gingerly touched the abrasion on her shoulder and her body jerked in reaction to the stabbing pain. She rolled over and stared at the dark ceiling, with tears flowing down her cheeks. She drifted into a semi-consciousness state as her mind replayed an earlier scene:

She had hobbled out of the timber thirty minutes after the fall on the trail. The trek had taken her higher up the mountain than she anticipated. Her injured ankle throbbed with nearly unbearable pain, but the prospect of receiving help appeared to improve. She had reached the clearing and saw wooden structures, possibly someone's homestead. After limping to an old building, she called for help. There was no sign of anyone to lend assistance, so she tried the front door but it was padlocked. Susan decided to go to the rear of the building to look for another entrance. It was a near-fatal mistake. She reached the back of the building and startled two men, who quickly threw tarps over the boxes they had been opening.

The next moments were terrifying. One of them grabbed her by the waist and raised her off the ground while another stuck a dirty hand over her mouth to muffle her screams. The struggle was brief as Susan was overpowered and carried into the building. Seconds later, she was dragged down some stairs and thrown onto a concrete floor in a dark room. Tremors of pain shot through her ankle as it twisted into an awkward position. She began to lose consciousness but realized it might be her only chance to escape. She mustered enough strength to kick one of the attackers in the groin. The fellow let out a painful howl and lunged at Susan, but the other man intervened and hustled the attacker out of the room.

The last thing she heard as the door slammed shut was one of them screaming, "Girl, you are dead!"

Chapter 6

Sheriff Garrett was seated at a long table with three other individuals. He rose and extended a handshake to Mark. The two men had been close friends during the entire time that Larry Ray had served as the Auburn County sheriff.

"Hello, Mark. Thanks for joining us." The sheriff began the introductions. "Folks, this is Dr. Mark Sarkisian. He was the superintendent for the school district when Susan was hired last spring." The three people rose from their chairs and shook Mark's hand as they were introduced. "This is Wilbur and Amelia Clark, the young lady's parents from Maryville. And this is Jeffrey Williams, a close friend of Susan's."

Susan Clark's parents appeared to be in their early fifties. Their demeanor reflected a humbleness that came from years of spending early morning and evening hours working their farm. The younger man who accompanied them was sharply dressed in tailored slacks and a cashmere sport coat. It was obvious that the high-dollar wingtip shoes on his feet had not been purchased at any local discount store. Mrs. Clark was the first to speak.

"We appreciate you trying to help us, Dr. Sarkisian. Susan spoke very highly of you and she was sorry to hear that you were retiring." The mother continued to affectionately hold Mark's hand.

"I assure you that the feeling is quite mutual, Mrs. Clark. Your daughter is going to be an asset to the children in Auburn, and I'm happy to do whatever I can to help." The response was intended to provide reassurance that the couple's daughter would be standing in front of students on the first day of school in spite of recent happenings. Mark shifted his attention to the young man standing next to the Clarks. "Jeffrey, are you a runner like Susan?"

"Well, not those twenty to thirty miles a week that Susan logged," he replied. "I haven't had the time since my company transferred me to this region about a year ago. Besides, Susan does enough running for both of us." Mr. and Mrs. Clark shook their heads in agreement as Jeffrey continued. "I tried to get her to come to work in our office, but she had this crazy desire to teach children and grade papers through half the night." The young executive's eyes rolled upward in an exaggerated show of disappointment. Mark sensed that Jeffrey wasn't very impressed with the teaching profession, but he brushed aside the comment rather than spend time debating the merits of a career in education.

"I suppose a lot of that is true, but I don't think I could enjoy glaring at a computer most of the day." The comment was an obvious reference to Jeffrey's work with a high-tech company involved in researching alternative energy sources.

"Touché, Dr. Sarkisian," he said, feigning a slight bow of his waist to concede that Mark had made his point.

Sheriff Garrett suggested that everyone be seated and asked the Clarks to go over details regarding the last time they had contact with their daughter. Mrs. Clark's eyes glistened as she glanced at her husband. "Wilbur, you go ahead, please."

Wilbur Clark gave a gentle touch to his wife's shoulder; his words were soft-spoken, reflecting a father's concern for his only daughter. He told the others that Susan had arisen early to help her father with the morning chores on the day she left for Auburn. "We finished milking the cows and fueling the equipment. Susan cleaned up and did some packing. It was about noon by the time we helped her load the car. She wanted to stop by Jeffrey's office before she left town."

"And that was the last time you saw your daughter?" Sheriff Garrett asked.

"Yes, she was supposed to call us that night after she was settled in, but we never got the call," Amelia Clark replied as she wiped a tear from her eye. Her voice feathered into the whisper of a mother fearing something tragic may have happened to her daughter. "Yes, that was the very last time we saw her."

The sheriff sensed that the mother was overcome with emotion and shifted the conversation to another person. "Jeffrey, what time did Susan come to your office?" The young executive crossed his arms and lowered his head in deep thought. He responded after several moments.

"Hmm, I suppose it was near the end of lunch time, maybe closer to one o'clock." The recollection came in a rather matter-of-fact fashion. "We went to the Bearcat Diner down the street from my office, but Susan wasn't very hungry. She was too excited about leaving for Auburn and getting prepared for the start of school."

"Did she mention anything about stopping to see someone along the way?" the sheriff inquired as he wrote on a small notepad.

"No, I don't recall Susan saying anything about making any stops. We talked about a lot of things," he added raising his palms in the air. "Susan always has a project to talk about." There was frustration in his voice.

"And she left you about 2:30 that afternoon?" the sheriff asked, continuing to jot down notes.

"That's about right. She wanted to get to Auburn early enough for a workout before it got dark." Jeffrey could have stopped at that point, but he continued and his voice rose with excitement. "My gosh, she couldn't miss even one day of her workout routine!" He realized the others were surprised by his outburst and were staring at him. He regained his composure and offered an explanation in an attempt to smooth over the display of irritation. "Well, I guess that wasn't so unusual because everyone in town is accustomed to seeing Susan jogging every day in the park or down some country road. She never liked just running around in circles on the university track."

"That's our Susan!" Mr. Clark chimed in. "She's always training for a race, but I think her schedule got a little messed up when she helped me with the morning chores."

Mark did a quick calculation in his head. "Well, it wouldn't take her more than two hours to reach Auburn even if she took a break somewhere along the way. There would still have been time to get in a good run before dark."

"That is, assuming she even got to Auburn and found a place to work out," the sheriff interjected. "We don't really have a town park that's laid out for joggers." He realized that the comment might cause undue alarm for the Clarks, so he followed with a question. "Is it possible that Susan might have stopped to visit friends along the way?"

"Susan has friends everywhere," Mrs. Clark responded. "We thought she might have decided to stay with one of her sorority sisters in St. Joseph, but none of the girls we called have seen her." Mrs. Clark's endearing smile was gone and her voice trembled. Wilbur Clark rustled in his pants pocket for something that would calm his wife. What emerged was a pack of chewing gum, which Mark immediately recognized by its distinct pink wrapper.

"That wouldn't be Teaberry, would it?" Mark hadn't seen Teaberry gum on grocery store shelves for years. Teaberry, Beeman's, Clove, and Blackjack gum were his favorites when he was a boy, but they were usually available only during certain times of the year. He always bought Blackjack gum during Halloween. It had a licorice flavor and was an icky gray color. If a kid strategically formed it in his mouth, it would appear as though he had a missing front tooth. Mark smiled, recalling that many of his elementary classmates would scream and run to tell the teacher that his tooth had been knocked out during recess. Blackjack was good for a laugh, but Teaberry was definitely Mark's favorite.

"Why yes, it is Teaberry." Mr. Clark smiled and handed Mark a stick of gum. "It seems to help settle the nerves whenever we get a little stressed."

Jeffrey had remained quiet, but the discussion about chewing gum brought him back into the conversation. "Susan got everyone hooked on chewing that pink gum when she joined a sorority on campus." The sheriff's confused look begged an explanation. "I believe it was a ritual that the pledges had to provide a piece of gum when it was requested, or they had to do kitchen duty at the sorority house." Jeffrey realized he had everyone's attention, so he decided to elaborate about the gum tradition. "Susan is always trying to be unique, so instead of selecting a common chewing gum, she ordered a whole case of that special flavor. The next thing you know, everyone's chewing Teaberry gum." The young man was becoming more inspired as he continued the story. What started as just an explanation about a piece of chewing gum had turned into a performance with exaggerated movements of his hands. "Sorority sisters, their boyfriends, Susan's parents, and later even me! It seemed like every time we went anywhere, someone would ask Susan for Teaberry gum." By now, the sheriff's jaw hung open as he watched the animated movements accompanying the story. "She always has to chew a piece when she's running. She calls her running stride the Teaberry shuffle." Suddenly, the narration halted as Jeffrey realized everyone in the room was showing surprise by the barrage of emotion about chewing gum. His embarrassment was obvious as he offered an apology. "Sorry, folks, I guess I got a little carried away with the Teaberry thing."

There was total silence until the sheriff broke the tension. "Who knows? It must have done some good because people have been reading for years about Susan winning races." He paused to gather his thoughts, and then continued. "Unfortunately, that's all in the past. What we need to focus on now is how we go about finding Susan." Sheriff Garrett told the group that the Missouri State Highway Patrol had begun an investigation along the route she would have taken to Auburn. Troopers were stopping at service stations and convenience stores asking clerks if they had seen Susan or her automobile. The sheriff and his deputies would be responsible for contacting businesses and citizens in the county. He was hesitant to label Susan as a missing person because it had been less than forty-eight hours since anyone had seen her. Sheriff Garrett decided to present a theory that he hoped would ease Mr. and Mrs. Clark's fears regarding the fate of their daughter. He speculated that she was a young person beginning a career in a new community. It was her first time to be away from family and her hometown for any extended period of time. She had a male friend who didn't appear very excited about her taking a job some distance from him. All of those factors seemed to indicate that Susan may have felt too much pressure and decided to take time to sort things out. After all, she would not have been the first young person who found her world moving too fast, so maybe she decided to slow things down.

The sheriff's explanation seemed logical, but secretly Larry Ray was concerned for the young woman's safety. As a long-time law enforcement officer, he had received numerous reports of women traveling on the state highways that were never heard from again. The nation's prisons were filled with felons who, when finally captured, confessed about how they had lured victims into their dark world. Susan had several characteristics that made for a perfect match. She was young, pretty, and very trusting. The sheriff's public persona was always optimistic, but deep inside he had a sick feeling that Susan had encountered something tragic.

Sheriff Garrett told the Clarks that his department would do everything possible to locate Susan. He reassured them that he would be in touch the next day after there had been more investigation in the area as to her whereabouts. Jeffrey assumed the meeting had ended and was headed for the door, but Mrs. Clark paused to share more information.

"There is something else you should know," Amelia said in a soft voice. "Susan has Type 1 diabetes. She requires insulin on a regular basis."

The news surprised the sheriff and triggered Mark's recollection that the aspiring teacher had mentioned her medical condition during the job interview. Now, the effort to locate the Clarks' daughter became even more urgent.

"That puts a little different spin on this situation," Sheriff Garrett said in a serious tone. "I'm not well-versed on the subject, but I understand there are different types of diabetes." Wilbur Clark placed an arm around his wife's shoulder as he followed up on the sheriff's comment.

"Many people have Type 2 diabetes. They often lead relatively normal lives as long as they regulate their diet and lifestyle." The explanation came from a father who had obviously done the research regarding his daughter's illness. "But Type 1 is more complicated because it makes a person dependent on insulin." The sheriff looked perplexed, so Mr. Clark got right to the point. "In other words, it can kill Susan if she doesn't stay on top of it every day." Mark had been satisfied just being a listener but now he addressed the parents.

"I realize that diabetes can be a serious condition," he said thoughtfully, "but Susan seemed to indicate that she was capable of dealing with it, and that it wouldn't be much of an issue regarding her teaching."

"Basically that's true, Dr. Sarkisian," Mr. Clark said as he pulled a handkerchief from his back pocket to wipe a tear from his eye. "For years, the injections were quite difficult for our little girl, but Susan never complained." Mrs. Clark gave her husband an endearing look as he continued to share information. "Medical science has progressed quite a bit since the early days of diabetes. Susan has an insulin pump that she wears under her clothes. It's a lot better than sticking yourself with a needle and most people don't even know that she has it on."

"I can understand why you want us to locate Susan as soon as possible," the sheriff said as he pressed for more information. "Mr. Clark, tell me what happens if she has a problem with the insulin pump device? Could it stop working at any time?" The question captured everyone's attention.

"Yes, that is a possibility," the father answered, but he was interrupted before he could continue.

"That's why Susan always has her emergency kit containing a syringe and two shots of insulin," Mrs. Clark quickly interjected. "She doesn't think it's really necessary, but she knows it helps to keep us from worrying." The mother smiled and softly added, "She's a good girl." Wilbur wiped a tear from his wife's cheek. She gave him a hug and tenderly kissed his cheek.

The meeting concluded and the sheriff left the room with Amelia Clark and Jeffrey Williams. Wilbur Clark delayed his exit to speak privately with Mark. He extended his hand and Mark felt a grip that had been molded by a lifetime of hard work on the farm. The father spoke barely above a whisper as he placed something in Mark's hand. "Thank you, Dr. Sarkisian, for being here for us... and Susan." It wasn't necessary for either man to speak again because both shared a common bond of love for their daughters. Mr. Clark lowered his head and walked away.

Sheriff Garrett returned to the room and joined Mark at a window facing the school parking lot. They watched as Wilbur and Amelia Clark got into the farm truck to begin their journey home. Jeffrey Williams was slow to enter the BMW, being careful not to get any dirt on his clothes. Mark wondered why he had chosen to drive his own vehicle rather than ride with Susan's parents. He figured it was either a matter of a more comfortable ride, or perhaps the young man intended to make another stop before returning to Maryville.

"Really sad, isn't it?" Larry Ray lamented. "Those folks having to worry about what happened to their daughter."

"It just rips at your heart," Mark said as he watched the white pickup leave the parking lot and cautiously turn onto Main Street. "Things like this shouldn't happen to anyone, let alone such nice people." Mark was curious about the effort to find Susan. "What's your next move, Larry Ray?"

The sheriff explained that his deputies were scouring the roads leading into the county for any sign of the missing woman. Several people had been interviewed, but so far there were no clues. "If she doesn't turn up today, my deputies will be searching the Pony Express Lake and Buffalo Mountain region tomorrow. We could use your help, Mark."

The decision to search the lake and mountain areas was a sign the lawman had not ruled out foul play, and Mark was a logical person to be involved. Several years earlier, he had helped the state conservation department create recreation areas at the lake and hiking trails that weaved along the mountain bluffs.

There was plenty of work to be done at the orchard, but he realized that locating the missing teacher was the highest priority so he agreed to meet the sheriff in the morning.

Mark left the meeting room and noticed that Ellen Downing and Dan Williams were still busy working in preparation for the beginning of the school year. "It was great to see both of you, but I'm sorry it had to be under these circumstances." Mark's former secretary was seated at a table assembling workbooks but still took time to pass on a compliment.

"I'll bet that when you and Larry Ray put your heads together, you'll get this thing figured out," Ellen said as she tapped the stapler and flung another workbook into a pile of already assembled materials that were close to spilling onto the floor. "You fellows have had challenges before and you always seem to make things come out right." The comment was a sign of her confidence in Mark's abilities. He had barely stepped into the hallway when he heard Ellen shout a reminder, "Don't forget; we're counting on you being at the festival!"

"I know, and we'll bring the cheese boeregs!" Mark shouted as he walked down the hallway, fully knowing that there would be more reminders forthcoming.

Mark got into the Jeep and realized he was still clutching the item that Wilbur Clark had placed in his hand. He smiled as he unwrapped the pink stick of gum and popped it into his mouth. The familiar flavor brought back memories of youthful days when parents didn't have to worry so much about the safety of their children. He thought about the Clarks having to deal with the trauma of a missing child. The image of Buffalo Mountain reflecting in the clear water of the lake had always formed a peaceful picture for Mark but, in spite of its beauty, Buffalo Mountain could be deadly.

———————————◗◦◖———————————

Susan slumped to the floor. She was exhausted from balancing on one leg as she leaned against a door trying to listen for any sign of life. She had heard sounds earlier, but her cries for help could not penetrate the wall of her prison. She was a captive in a room that appeared to serve multiple functions, such as a bathroom, dressing area, and place to lounge. The only fixtures were a crude shower pipe that was missing its head and a heavily stained porcelain toilet bowl. The lid to the toilet had been removed. Two old army cots were pushed against one wall of the room. Earlier she had felt along the walls of the darkened room until she discovered a light switch next to the locked door. She turned it on and a low-wattage, bare bulb that dangled from a wire connected to the ceiling gave a small glow of light to the room. It wasn't much, but it was better than lying in the pitch dark wondering what was lurking in the shadows. The small amount of light also revealed a six-inch air tube in the ceiling. The tube must have exited the building because when Susan stood beneath it, she could see a small glint of light. The tube would become her only source for distinguishing between night and day since her wristwatch and car keys had been stripped from her during the struggle with the two men. Fortunately, they had failed to see the small emergency kit that was safely tucked into a pocket of her running shorts.

Someone entered the room each day during times when Susan had either slipped into an exhausted sleep or drifted into unconsciousness. Each time, she awoke to find two sandwiches and bottled water. The meager food didn't provide much nourishment, but the fear for her life had ruined her appetite. The food seemed to be an indication that someone wanted to keep her alive, at least for now.

The muffled sounds coming from outside the building had ceased. Susan hobbled to the crude shower and placed her leg under the bare pipe. She turned on the single faucet and a weak stream of cold water flowed over her swollen ankle. Tears streamed down her cheeks. She prayed, "Lord, please let me see my family again."

Chapter 7

Marnie poured two cups of coffee and handed one to Mark as he stepped out the rear door onto the screened-in porch after his shower. Her favorite time of the day at the orchard was when the sun was just beginning to shine through the rows of fruit trees, causing the pasture grass to glisten with morning dew. She noticed that Mark was wearing his hiking shoes and not the steel-toed boots he usually wore when working around equipment at the orchard. He had given her an account of the meeting with Susan Clark's parents, and now he felt it was a good time to mention the encounter with Jubile Walker and his buddies at the Co-op.

"They're a bunch of lowlifes," Marnie said as she buttered two pieces of toast and handed one to Mark. "Maybe they know something about your missing teacher." Mark had already given the notion some thought.

"They're no-accounts for sure, but I don't think they would get involved in any nasty business with the teacher." Mark scanned the orchard and spied several chicken hawks circling the pasture adjacent to the orchard. "Then again, you never really know about people. You might think half the people out there are serial killers if you watch enough of those "cold case" shows on television. We've had a couple of cases like that in Missouri in the past few years." Mark noticed that one of the chicken hawks had altered its flight pattern and was now gliding in concentric circles much lower to the ground. The large predator had spyglass vision and was honed in on a slight movement on the ground.

"I hope Susan Clark doesn't become another one of those statistics." Marnie's voice was steeped with concern. The words came from a mother who had stayed awake many nights waiting for her daughter to walk safely into the house after being out with friends. But Marnie's concern wasn't only for the missing teacher. "I hope you'll stay around the lake area, Mark. You're not going on Buffalo Mountain, are you?" Her caution was understandable.

There had been stories circulating through the region for decades about strange happenings on Buffalo Mountain. Many of the tales may have been exaggerated, but people had become leery about going beyond the lower bluffs that encircled Pony Express Lake. The lake and lower bluffs were considered safe for people, but looming above those recreation places were the steep cliffs and dense forests that comprised the higher regions of Buffalo Mountain. It was in those hidden recesses that mysterious folklore originated. Many of the dark tales surrounded a family that lived in a primitive cabin and seldom left the mountain. The "old man" was a Native American Indian. It was rumored that he killed a fellow in a knife fight decades earlier when he worked at a beef slaughter plant at the stockyards in St. Joseph. He and his wife had made their way into the higher elevations of Buffalo Mountain shortly after he was found innocent of the charges. They had a child when the man was nearly sixty years old. As years passed, stories about a mountain boy who played with bears and cougars became a topic of conversations around the coffee pot at the Co-op.

There were other stories that kept people off the mountain. Many of the eerie tales involved animals that preferred the taste of human flesh rather than the berry and paw paw fruits, which were abundant in the timbers. Mark had generally disregarded the rumors of black bears and mountain lions lurking within the mountain's dark crevices. He considered them tall tales conjured up in the minds of old fellows sipping coffee with too much time on their hands. He knew the mountain lions were likely to be Missouri bobcats, critters larger than a housecat, but reclusive animals that preferred to be left alone. Mark figured the bears were no more than large, furry raccoons that puffed up when they sensed danger.

Marnie needed reassurance, so Mark told her the search for Susan Clark would likely focus around the lake area. He realized that what he was telling her was not completely true. While there was no evidence to believe that Susan had ventured into the mountain, Mark suspected that the hiking trails just might be an inviting challenge for the seasoned runner.

"Please be careful," Marnie cautioned. "I don't want you running into any strange people on that mountain, especially that Wanatee family."

"Honey, I don't think the Indians are scalping anyone in the 21st century," Mark said as he finished off the toast. "Even if he is still alive, the old fellow has got to be at least eighty and probably just wants to be left alone. There's no need to worry because I'll take Quarter with me." The attempt to calm Marnie's fears only brought sarcasm.

"That's just great. The only help you'll get from that big Labrador is if she licks someone to death while she's wagging that monster tail." Marnie wasn't sure she had Mark's complete attention because he was so engrossed in watching the chicken hawk skim across the ground just long enough to snatch a field mouse in its claws and carry it into the sky. Marnie decided to draw Mark back into the conversation, but not before she made fun of his fixation on the soaring bird. "For heaven's sake, Mark, it's not a California condor. It's just a chicken hawk!"

Marnie continued her assessment of the family pet once she regained her husband's attention. "You should know by now that Quarter never met a person she didn't try to slobber all over." Mark gave a nod to indicate that he agreed. His attempt to train Quarter as a watchdog had been futile. The gentle Lab had a pleasant disposition that made friends with everyone. "I used to see the Wanatee woman and the boy at the Co-op buying kerosene," Marnie said as she poured another cup of coffee. "I think it's been at least two years since I last saw her, but I haven't talked to anyone that's seen the husband in years."

"Maybe they finally got a generator and don't use kerosene lanterns anymore." Mark downed the final sip of coffee. "What I *do* know is that I'm not going to get anything done today if I don't get started." He put on a light jacket and grabbed his backpack. "I should be back around dinnertime." He gave Marnie a kiss on the cheek and whispered in her ear, "I love you, my *Anoosh*." The endearment was a throwback to the "old country." Mark would revert to his native language whenever he wanted to express his special feeling for his wife. She knew that a translation of the word was "sweetie", so the saying was special to her, just like Mark.

Quarter perked her ears the moment the front door swung open. She was airborne by the time Mark settled into the worn cushion of the driver's seat. Her leap sent ninety pounds of black fur into a flight pattern that was quite familiar to Mark. The Lab had enjoyed riding with him since she was a pup, although it was getting difficult to remember when Quarter had ever been small. Now she soared like a flying fortress that was fixed on a small landing pad. Unfortunately, the combination of the Lab's momentum and body mass carried her beyond the passenger seat of the Jeep. As usual, she landed with part of her body slumped on Mark's lap. The loveable pet seemed content to remain in that position, but she was obscuring the windshield.

"Quarter, sometimes you are a pain in the butt!" Mark yelled in mock disgust. He nudged the dog's rear onto the passenger seat and drove down the drive. Quarter didn't seem to mind the insult. Her large, brown eyes were tracking several geese flying in a V formation over the orchard. She gulped the cool air blowing in her face and remained focused on the flock until it disappeared into the distant sky.

———◦———

Susan didn't know if her ankle was broken, but the pain was excruciating and her body still ached from the other injuries. Her only relief came during those times that she slipped into semi-consciousness. It was not a good sign for anyone, let alone a person with Type 1 diabetes. She needed something to give her hope. Alone and in despair, a memory from her childhood gave her courage to survive:

She was eleven years old when the signs began to show. They weren't acute, but something felt different to the sixth grader. She was drinking an excess of liquids and was making more frequent trips to the bathroom. Her parents attributed the changes to early adolescence because she appeared to be going through a spurt in growth, but then there were bouts of drowsiness and a time when she lost considerable weight. There were too many warning signs for what should have been a healthy pre-teen. A series of long tests confirmed what the local physician had suspected. Susan had diabetes and it would be with her forever.

She recalled her first injection of insulin. The doctor was giving her instructions on how to self-medicate. He was gentle, trying not to frighten the child. "Don't be afraid, you will hardly feel anything," he said as he held a syringe. The needle might as well have been a harpoon as far as Susan was concerned. It looked long, sharp, and very scary.

Wilbur and Amelia Clark watched as the doctor gave a reassuring smile and pressed the needle against Susan's skin. She became frightened and pulled her arm away. The look of innocence turned to fear as Susan screamed, "Daddy!"

Wilbur Clark quickly raised his hand, gesturing for the doctor to delay the procedure. He leaned close to his daughter whose eyes were now filled with large tears and spoke to Susan in a soft tone. "Susan, Daddy has never lied to you and I won't start now," he said, pulling a handkerchief from his bib overalls and brushing Susan's tears away. "Yes, it might hurt at first, but it will soon go away and you'll feel better." He smiled and patted her knee. "Your mother and I will be right here with you the whole time, my little honey bun."

Mr. Clark continued to hold his daughter's hand and signaled for the doctor to proceed. The child never took her eyes away from her father's smile as the doctor pressed the syringe and delivered the life-sustaining insulin.

73

Minutes later, Susan and her parents sat at a table in the hospital dining area laughing and enjoying double-dips of butter pecan ice cream. She listened intently as the father spoke of how proud he was of her. He also chose to give her words of encouragement that would remain in her darkest hours.

...Susan sat in the silence of the murky room, listening to drips falling to the floor from the shower pipe. The memory of her father's words gave her hope: "Susan, I promise not to let anyone ever hurt you, but if something prevents me from being with you, have courage and be strong in your faith."

Chapter 8

It would take Mark and Quarter less than thirty minutes to reach Pony Express Lake. The first fifteen miles were good roadway until they reached a junction where the highway intersected a county road. The Jeep headed north from there on seven miles of worn asphalt that was in dire need of maintenance. Mark had a perfect view of Buffalo Mountain's twin peaks rising into a canvas of blue sky. The mountain and lake were thought to have been formed during a period known as the Great Ice Age. Mark could understand the scientific version but preferred to believe that the massive chunk of earth, forests, and pristine waters were inspired by Divine intervention. His explanation was simple: "Only God could paint such a beautiful picture."

The Jeep passed through a pine forest on a winding road that led to the lake campsites. Mark rounded a curve and suddenly hit the brakes hard enough to spill Quarter onto the floorboard. The Lab quickly got back on the seat in time to see the reason for the abrupt stop. A doe and two fawns had emerged from the pines and were crossing the road. The rumble of the old Jeep must not have been too disturbing because the deer would have been content to continue nipping on sprigs of grass had it not been for Quarter's incessant barking.

"Quarter, shush!" Mark's scolding came too late because the doe and her yearlings had heard enough. When he looked again, three whitetails were scampering along a trail on the other side of the road. Mark stared at the route the deer had taken. The trail was actually an old road that led to an abandoned quarry. Many of the mountain's craters had been made when the quarry was active, but the same streams that fed into Pony Express Lake now flooded most of them. He remembered one extremely difficult trail, which was formed when the recreation areas were developed. The narrow path snaked through the trees until it reached the quarry, and then it continued farther into the mountain where the terrain became more treacherous near the high bluffs. A bold hiker might trudge for miles along a stretch of land seldom frequented by anyone other than the Wanatee family. The area contained deep pools of water that prompted the conservation department to post signs discouraging people from going into that portion of the mountain. Even the local teenagers had found it more convenient to congregate in the parking lots of local businesses rather than risk damaging a vehicle while trying to find a secluded place to hang out on the mountain.

Mark gave Quarter a command to curb the Lab's desire to give chase to the deer. "Sit, Quarter!" His firm words were accompanied by the gentle stroking of his hand, but Quarter had already abandoned her enthusiasm for the chase. She was comfortably sprawled with her head resting on Mark's thigh. The arrangement made it difficult to reach the gearshift, but Mark didn't mind the inconvenience.

Minutes later, he pulled into an area designated for public parking at the lake. Several vehicles were at the campsites, which were scattered among the trees that bordered the shoreline. It was late in August and children would be heading back to school in another week. Judging by the number of wet swimsuits hanging from makeshift clotheslines, it was obvious that people were trying to squeeze in a few more days of family recreation before calling it quits for the summer.

Quarter jumped to the ground as soon as Mark brought the Jeep to a halt in one of the parking slots. She wandered toward two sheriff deputies who were engaged in conversation with people fishing at a nearby dock. Quarter loved the water, and it would not be long before people would toss sticks into the lake to be retrieved by the friendly Lab. The action would draw a crowd to watch her bound from the dock and paddle back with the "catch" clenched between her teeth. Fishing near the dock would not return to normal until Quarter tired of the activity. By then, the people closest to the Lab would be soaked as she shook water from her saturated coat.

"Hi, Mark! Thanks for coming." Sheriff Garrett approached the Jeep and gave his friend a pat on the back.

"Glad to help," Mark responded as he observed several deputies scattered throughout the campsites. "It looks like you have things under control. Is Kristin here today?"

"No, I sent her to St. Joseph again to meet with the troopers assigned to our area. We had another burglary. They made off with a cash box, computers, and some expensive tools. It looks very similar to the other thefts the state police are working on."

"Any suspects?" Marked questioned.

"Not really. None of the stuff is turning up around here. The area pawnshops haven't seen any of it. The loot is probably too hot to pass off in the county. Someone would likely snitch on them for reward money. They're either stashing it somewhere or filtering it into the Kansas City black market."

"You've probably got that right, Larry Ray. The economy is bad enough, so an extra thousand dollars in reward money would probably eliminate any honor among thieves."

"We're talking about some heavy-duty thievery," the sheriff said in an excited tone. "Computers and power equipment. Why, I wouldn't even be surprised if they tried to blow the safe at the Drovers and Merchants Bank!"

Mark thought the sheriff was exaggerating a bit, but he smiled and gave his friend a reassuring response. "The troopers working out of St. Joseph are sharp. They don't pin a badge on just anyone who wants to carry a pistol and wear the uniform. I imagine they'll nail the thieves before they can empty the bank in Auburn," he joked.

Sheriff Garrett was ready to get on with the business at hand and decided to switch the conversation. "We're interviewing the people along the shoreline to see if they saw anyone who resembled Susan Clark. We should finish here in a couple of hours. After that, we'll check the lower bluffs to see if anything looks strange."

Until now, Mark thought the sheriff had not actually considered Susan to be a missing person. Perhaps it was due to the years he spent in law enforcement looking for missing young people. Most of them were usually found hanging out with friends. Now, Mark wasn't so sure what to read into his friend's last comment. "Do you really think Susan might be somewhere on the mountain?"

The lawman stared at the mountain's highest peak. Neither man made a sound for several moments. Finally, the sheriff's response was barely a whisper. "I pray to God she's not up there."

The sound of splashing water came from the lake. Quarter was performing for anyone who cared to heave a stick into the water. Mark realized it was time to get on with the search. "I can cover some ground on the north bluff if it's okay with you. It might save your deputies some time." Larry Ray welcomed the assistance. Mark was one of the few people who knew just about every nook and cranny on the mountain.

"That's fine with me, but let's make sure we regroup back here by four o'clock in case we don't meet somewhere along the bluffs."

"Oh, you shouldn't have any trouble finding me." Mark grinned as he shouldered his backpack. "I'll be the guy that the rabbits are hiding behind thanks to Quarter." The sheriff laughed and waved goodbye to his friend, and then he rejoined the deputies who were still interviewing campers.

Mark had made his way along a path through the pine trees when he noticed Quarter lagging behind. He whistled to shift her attention away from sniffing the ground. "Here, Quarter, come on girl!" It didn't take long for the Lab to assume her usual position ahead of Mark.

The first mile was an easy stroll on wood chips that were still damp from last night's storm. The trail weaved around trees with limbs bearing lush foliage. The ground was carpeted with pine needles that had been warmed by morning sunlight. Mark gazed at the terrain. There was ample space between the pines to see a hundred yards on either side of the trail. There was nothing unusual, just trees, shrubs, chirping birds, and squirrels clattering that a human was nearby. In fact, Mark might have imagined that no human had ever passed this way if it hadn't been for a discarded soda pop can next to the trail. He was becoming frustrated. His only discovery thus far was a remnant from the *I'm a Pepper, You're a Pepper* generation.

Quarter was not about to be restricted to the confines of a trail and was taking pleasure in conducting her own investigation. Mark watched as the Lab's nose swept the ground. She was tracking faint scents, probably left by rabbits nipping on tender grasses sprinkled with morning dew. Her zigzag pattern became a futile exercise that had her running in circles. The bunnies of Buffalo Mountain were likely resting in deep burrows quite safe from the intruder with the wet nose and long, black tail. Mark enjoyed spending his time exploring the flora and fauna, but that wasn't his purpose for being there. It was time to press on.

Mark spent the next two hours searching the north bluff, which consisted of easy slopes and a few creeks that one could cross by stepping on partially submerged rocks. He wasn't even sure that it was worth the time and effort. There might not be obvious signs to the casual observer if something tragic had occurred on the mountain. If that were the case, it would take a lot more manpower than the Auburn County Sheriff's Department to do a thorough search. It was almost noon when he heard voices in the distance. He guessed that the deputies had finished interviewing people at the lake and were extending their search into the bluffs. That was okay with Mark because he had another two miles to cover that comprised that portion of the mountain. Besides, it was past lunchtime and Quarter's panting indicated she was ready for a break.

A small creek flowed at the bottom of a nearby slope. It would make for a pleasant, shaded place to rest. Mark was in decent shape, thanks to a steady regimen of exercise, but his legs were beginning to ache. He whistled for Quarter halfway down the slope but saw that she was already at the creek lapping water. He joined the Lab at the water's edge and hoisted his body onto a large rock. "Come here, Quarter!" he called, and then pulled a bag filled with goodies from his backpack.

The peaceful sound of rippling water and rustling leaves helped Mark take stock of his surroundings. He had traveled farther than he had realized. The quarry trail, or what remained of it, was winding up the mountain close to his present location. He could intersect that trail from the next ridge. It would be an easier route into the higher elevations even if the trail were overgrown with bushes and saplings. He hadn't been near the defunct quarry in years and no person would have any business being near it, other than Jubile Walker. The mountain's steep cliffs had suffered years of abuse from earth-digging machines and were too dangerous for casual hikers. The owners of the Central States Quarry Company had hired Jubile Walker as a watchman to discourage people from exploring at the site. Jubile's nasty disposition was a perfect match for the job.

"Quarter! Get out of there!" Mark's yell interrupted the Lab's latest adventure. She had poked her nose into the trunk of a fallen tree lodged on the creek bank. Now she was standing in water up to her belly, and she looked more like a saturated rug that needed to be hung on a clothesline to dry. Quarter continued to probe until she froze stiff with her long tail "on point." Something had captured her attention. Suddenly, a large toad launched from the tree trunk and splashed into the creek. After a few downward strokes, the toad was safely underwater burrowed in mud.

Mark had ample opportunity to relax and think as he watched Quarter's activity at the creek bank. It seemed unlikely that he would learn anything about Susan's disappearance by continuing up the mountain. He could reach the quarry in another thirty minutes if he got on the old trail. Then a quick search around the quarry would leave plenty of time for him to connect with the sheriff. He slung the backpack over his shoulder and eased off the boulder. "Come on, Quarter. We've got more ground to cover."

Twenty minutes later, the two emerged from the timber onto the old quarry trail. Heavy rains had eroded the compacted dirt that once supported truckloads of smashed rock being hauled down the mountain to be used for highway construction projects. Bushes and saplings were now recapturing the roadway, leaving only a narrow path with two grooves down the middle. Mark assumed those ruts were made by Jubile Walker's truck on those occasions when he left the quarry to meet with Spook Daniels and Toad Canterbury.

The pine forest that spread along the lower bluffs was now far behind. In its place was a canopy of maple and oak trees stretching for miles across the slopes of the mountain. In another six weeks, the green leaves would take on autumn's brilliant hues of red, orange, yellow, and bronze. The wildlife was more active in this part of the mountain with squirrels and rabbits scrambling for hiding places.

"Come on, girl. We're almost there!" Mark yelled to encourage Quarter to stay at his side. He turned to call her again but was startled when he nearly banged into a metal gate that stood partially open. A large sign near the gate issued a stern warning:

CENTRAL STATES QUARRY - NO TRESPASSING
VIOLATORS WILL BE PROSECUTED
...*OR WORSER!*

Most of the sign appeared to have been professionally painted, but the last words had obviously been added after the sign was erected. Mark gave Jubile Walker the credit based on his poor grammar.

A chain used to secure the heavy gate had been removed. It was loosely wrapped several times around an anchor post indicating someone had made his or her way to the other side of the gate prior to Mark's arrival. A building that had served as the quarry office stood a hundred yards in the distance. Parked on one side of the building was a black truck with rusted fenders and missing side mirrors. Mark contemplated going through the gate, but he didn't relish having a run-in with Jubile. He hesitated, but Quarter held no reservations and scampered past him.

"Darn it, Quarter. You have absolutely no respect for someone's property," Mark mumbled as he turned sideways to inch through the narrow opening between the gate and anchor post. He followed Quarter toward a cluster of buildings that formed the quarry's center of operations. There were several metal sheds that once sheltered trucks, dozers, and other heavy equipment used to mine and transport rock. An imposing piece of equipment was a huge "crusher" used to smash rock that was stripped from the mountain cliffs. A long conveyor sloped thirty feet into the air to a hopper at the top of the machine. Now the once-mighty equipment that had processed tons of rock each day stood abandoned and rusting.

Mark stopped at one building and took stock of the situation. Nothing seemed out of place, just parts of old trucks and machinery that had finally succumbed to years of use and abuse tearing at the mountain. There was lots of junk, but no sign that Susan Clark had ever been to the quarry. Quarter continued to busy herself snooping around piles of metal. Eventually, she began sniffing at a six-inch pipe rising about a foot above ground. Mark noticed the Lab digging in the earth surrounding the pipe and was about to call her when a nasty voice ripped the air.

"What the hell you doing?" Jubile Walker shouted as he headed straight for Mark. The rifle that usually was mounted in the rear window of the black pickup was clutched in his hands. Mark was quick to respond.

"Now hold on, Jubile. We're not doing any harm." It was the only thing Mark could think to say under the circumstances. He knew the man might just be unstable enough to shoot and then claim that he had mistaken Mark for an intruder. "I'm just helping Sheriff Garrett to look for someone." He hoped the explanation would get the irate fellow to settle down long enough to make an exit, but Jubile was in no mood to be accommodating.

"This here is private property and no one, not even you, got any business poking your nose around here!" he growled. His menacing voice was enough to make a person nervous, but the way he was waving the rifle was even more reason to believe that this was a volatile situation. "You don't see no damn woman around here! Now you and that mutt better get out of here, or I might just claim I caught you stealing at the quarry!" he snarled as he pointed the rifle barrel at Mark's chest.

Mark usually dismissed Jubile's ranting as somewhat humorous. This was not one of those occasions. It would be a stretch of the imagination to claim he shot a respected citizen who just happened to hike five miles to burglarize a defunct business of nothing but broken-down equipment. It was absurd thinking, but Jubile Walker could never be mistaken for Albert Einstein.

Mark took the last warning as an opportunity to leave. Jubile evidently didn't care if he was on official police business, so there was no sense in giving him the opportunity to brag that he was the one who finally put Dr. Mark Sarkisian in his place. It was time to make an exit.

"Come on, Quarter," he called. The Lab had continued to sniff and dig around the metal pipe, but a shrill whistle from Mark brought her back to his side. Mark held her by the collar.

"Now git!" Jubile yelled as he glared at the man and dog that were moving rapidly toward the gate. "If you come back, I'll get rid of you permanently!" He waved the rifle in the air to make his point.

Mark wondered if at any moment he would hear the sound of gunfire and then feel the sharp pain of bullets penetrating his body.

He resisted the urge to look back and didn't turn around until he led Quarter through the open gate. It was only when he was safely out of range that he reflected on the encounter. In spite of his nasty disposition, it was a rather extreme reaction for Jubile to threaten someone with a rifle. It occurred to Mark that he had only mentioned a missing person, but Jubile had referred to a woman. Could that have been a slip-up on his part, or did he just connect idle talk at the Co-op with Mark's trek up the mountain?

There was no need to waste any more time getting down the mountain. The quarry road might be an easier route, but it would take more than an hour on foot. Mark could make it to the lake sooner if he cut through the timber and intersected one of the hiking trails. It was getting late and the shortcut would be a better choice. "Come on, Quarter. Let's make some time," Mark called over his shoulder and sprinted toward the timber.

It had been two days since Susan left her hometown, headed for Auburn, Missouri. Two days of captivity. Two days in a smelly prison, barely staying alive on peanut butter and the small amount of insulin from her emergency kit. The peanut butter sandwiches didn't help much. She avoided eating the bread because the starch would be counter-active to keeping her blood sugar level regulated. Her body was starved for energy, and the only thing keeping her from falling into a diabetic coma was the shot of insulin she had injected a day earlier.

Her emergency kit held two vials of insulin; each contained seventy-six units of the lifesaving medicine. Normally, that would have been enough for only two days, but this was not a normal situation. Susan decided to use a half dose from one vial to give her body the strength to fight off the effects of her injuries. She would have to ration the remaining insulin, knowing that a reduced dosage could be a lethal decision.

On the first evening she had loaded medicine into the syringe and injected it into her thigh. She felt relief and tried to remain calm knowing that anxiety and stress had an adverse effect on a person with diabetes. Exercise had always been a way for Susan to help lower her blood sugar, but the swollen ankle didn't afford that opportunity. She was feeling tired and sluggish. Her trips to the crude toilet were more frequent as she continued to eliminate increased amounts of urine. She recognized those were signs that her body was once again starved for medicine.

Susan carefully placed the insulin that was left over in the first vial into the syringe and paused for a moment to ponder her decision. She looked at the remaining vial and hoped she would never have to use it. Then, she pressed the needle into her skin and waited for the medicine to give her another day of life.

Chapter 9

The quarry was a mile behind when Mark called for Quarter to slow down. The day's activity had taken its toll. His muscles ached and his body begged for a rest. A tall oak tree offered shade from the afternoon sun. He eased to the ground and slumped against the large trunk. Quarter selected a spot on bare dirt that would help cool her body. Her tongue hung from her mouth as she turned a complete circle and plopped on the ground, panting for air.

A slight breeze rustled the leaves overhead, but it failed to silence the squirrels perched in the branches of the huge oak. Mark was so drained of energy that he didn't even mind the constant rattle of branches swishing as the little critters jumped from one tree to another. The encounter with Jubile Walker had strained his emotions, and there were more miles left to travel than he had anticipated. It wasn't long until Mark's breathing became shallow. His heart rate slowed to normal and brought the rest his body craved. The cool breeze made it inviting to doze off, but the urgency to get off the mountain didn't allow time for a leisurely nap. His thoughts drifted to other times when he had hiked into the timber to share the joys of nature. Those pleasant memories helped him to feel very relaxed and his eyes slowly began to close.

KACHINNNNG!..KACHINNNG!

Suddenly, something ripped the air and tore through the canopy of leaves just above Mark's head. Next came the sound of a dull thud on the ground. Then, more noise and movement everywhere around him. There was no time to think- just react! Mark rolled several times to his left and tumbled down a small slope. He came to an abrupt stop when his body slammed into the trunk of a fallen tree. He shimmied through a haggle of branches and then burrowed into a crater of dirt that had formed around the uprooted tree. Mark hunkered down and became just a ball of humanity, shaking in fear.

Quarter was startled by all of the activity and perked her ears, sensing danger. Mark called to her in a raspy voice. "Quarter, get over here." The Lab hurried to the sound coming from behind the fallen tree. Mark snatched the dog's collar and pulled her against his body to keep her from making any noise. The blasts had come from a rifle cracking off one round after another, but now the only sound was Mark's heavy breathing. The woods had become still and quiet.

"If that nasty Jubile Walker is trying to kill me, he's a damn poor shot," Mark mumbled as he got a tighter grip on Quarter's collar. It was a bad situation. Jubile might still be out there waiting to cut him down. On the other hand, he didn't relish the idea of simply waiting to be executed. He pulled aside a clump of leaves just far enough to view the area that he had vacated moments earlier. There was no movement and no sound. He was perplexed: *Didn't Walker even want to check the body? Maybe he decided to hightail it to the quarry after missing with his shots.* Mark began to question himself: *How could I have been so stupid as to search this terrain without bringing a weapon? Did Walker murder Susan Clark and is he about to claim a second victim?* None of it made any sense. Jubile Walker was a nasty fellow, but none of his past escapades had been serious enough to be considered major crimes.

A snapping sound interrupted Mark's thoughts. Someone had stepped on a piece of rotten wood. His first instinct was to run, but he was compelled to identify the would-be assassin. He pulled aside the branches of his hiding place once again, being careful not to expose any more of his face than necessary. His eyes locked on movement near the tree he had been resting under. He tucked even lower behind the branches and tightened his grip on Quarter's collar to discourage her from bolting. The only option would be to make a run for it. Mark ran his fingers over the ground feeling for anything to use as a weapon. There was nothing, not even a large rock or a broken limb to use as a club. He was trapped. The fellow was now moving in Mark's direction. He was taking cautious steps and clutching the rifle as though he were stalking prey. Mark was overcome with fear as he pulled the Lab closer to his body. Thirty yards, twenty yards, and then the danger closed to within ten yards of the fallen tree. Mark had a clear view of his stalker. If it was Jubile Walker, then he had undergone a remarkable transformation in the past hour. This person was huge. He stood at least six-feet-nine inches tall and packed a solid 280 pounds of lean muscle. This was not Jubile Walker, but that was the least of Mark's worries as the rifle barrel swung in his direction. The man's finger tensed on the trigger. Quarter became anxious and started squirming, so Mark tried to calm her with light strokes to keep from giving away their position. He heard the sound of feet moving through the fallen leaves and coming even closer than before. It was time to take action: *I'll be murdered within seconds, and then someday a hiker will find my body lying where*

I was executed. I'm not going to give up without a fight and die in some dirt hole on Buffalo Mountain.

The man paused and crouched to the ground. Mark's eyes strained to see through the leafy camouflage. His body tensed as he prepared to spring forward, but Mark paused just before charging from the hiding place and was startled when he identified the shooter: *Noah Wanatee? I haven't seen that kid in four years; why is he trying to shoot me? Perhaps he didn't even see me lying under the tree, or maybe the Wanatees are just crazy enough to shoot anybody that comes near their place. It's suicide to try to jump him. He's thirty years younger with at least a hundred pounds over me... and he's got a rifle. I don't have a chance.*

The next moments helped change Mark's thinking. Noah Wanatee shifted his body as he focused on a spot a few yards past the old oak, and then he quickly moved away from the tree. Seconds later he stopped, just long enough to hoist the rifle and aim at something stirring on the ground.

KACHINNNG! The sound of the shot broke the silence in the woods. Instantly, a ball of brown fur popped into the air and dropped back to the ground. The shooter approached the animal and nudged it with the barrel of his rifle. It was a clean shot to the head, merciful from a hunter's viewpoint. He picked up the squirrel to examine it and then tucked the lifeless carcass into a pouch, which hung from his waist. Judging by the bulge of the pouch, the squirrel population on Buffalo Mountain had been reduced by several critters.

Mark debated whether or not to expose himself and confront Noah Wanatee. He tried to rationalize the whole incident, but things just didn't make sense: *I'm resting under a tree that happens to be home to a squirrel and Noah Wanatee doesn't see me? Hmmm, maybe he decided to shoot just to send a warning to me to stay off the mountain.* Mark had no answers and another look at Noah's grip on the rifle told him this was no time to ask for an explanation. He would sit tight and keep Quarter quiet.

Noah Wanatee stood motionless. His eyes searched the tree limbs for signs of any movement, like a sniper about to zap an unsuspecting victim. Mark could swear that his adversary was peering through the leaves looking right at him. However, if Mark was the target, Noah wasn't giving away his intentions. Mark remained motionless for fear that the slightest movement would bring an onslaught of bullets. The young man never flinched as his eyes did a final sweep of the landscape. Finally, he turned and began to saunter in the opposite direction.

Mark remained fixed on the figure as it moved away from his position. Fifty yards... one hundred yards... now cresting a small knoll at two hundred yards... and then, just a speck swallowed into the timber of Buffalo Mountain. He felt a sense of relief; his breathing became more normal. The time to make an escape was long overdue. Mark darted from the brush pile and charged for the lake. "Run, Quarter, run!" The command wasn't necessary because Quarter had already bolted from the hiding place.

The next thirty minutes were shear terror as Mark stumbled across a ravine and through thick timber. He frequently glanced over his shoulder to make sure he wasn't being pursued. There was no sign of anyone and he had no intention of slowing down. Quarter kept pace and only paused once when Mark tumbled to the ground after losing his footing. The fall caused red abrasions on his arms and legs, but those injuries were not going to keep him from reaching Sheriff Garrett at the lake campsite. His perseverance was rewarded when the forest became less dense and merged into a meadow filled with wild flowers. He had reached the lower bluffs. The terrain became gentle slopes with marked trails leading to the safety of civilization. A familiar voice called out.

"Where on earth have you been? I've been looking for you for thirty minutes," Larry Ray yelled as he hustled toward Mark.

Mark was still running downhill and stumbled out of control. Sheriff Garrett reached out to slow the momentum, but it only caused both men to tumble onto the ground. Mark's words came in explosive fragments. "I went to the upper bluffs... made it to the quarry... Jubile Walker... something really strange there!"

"Mark, slow down and catch your breath. I can't make head nor tail of what you're talking about." The sheriff grimaced as he shook dust and wood chips from his uniform.

Mark was sucking chunks of air into lungs that been taxed to their limit. The outbursts continued, but his words still didn't synchronize. "Someone took shots at us... or maybe at squirrels... I'm not sure... I don't know." Larry Ray looked confused, but he wasn't ready to deal with Mark's activity on the mountain. Something else held the lawman's attention. He clutched Mark's shoulders and spoke with a sense of urgency.

"Hold on, Mark. You need to listen to me right now!"

Mark was still trying to catch his breath, but as he glanced past the sheriff, he noticed two patrol vehicles driving out of the campsite area.

"Larry Ray, what's going on?"

"We're pulling out. I called off the search."

"What in the heck did you do that for? We might be on to something here," Mark blurted out in bewilderment.

"The state troopers found some items near the Missouri River that might belong to Susan Clark. If that's the case, the woman never made it more than thirty miles from her home."

Mark shook his head in confusion. The run-in at the quarry and the matter with Noah Wanatee had caused him to shift his focus away from the missing teacher. Now he was dealing with three issues that didn't seem connected- an irate local redneck, a trigger-happy mountain man, and a missing young woman. None of it was making any sense.

"Come on, Mark. We're heading out!"

"Larry Ray, what about that idiot Jubile Walker? Aren't you even going to check out the Wanatee kid taking potshots and scaring the heck out of me?" He couldn't tell if his questions were even registering because the sheriff was already headed down the trail.

"Mark, I don't have time for that right now," Sheriff Garrett yelled over his shoulder. "The state troopers are launching a full investigation into the girl's disappearance. I'm headed to meet with them now. Jubile Walker and the Wanatee kid will just have to wait!"

"But, Larry Ray?"

"Not now, Mark!" The sheriff cut off the protest. "I'll call you tonight." Within minutes, the red and blue emergency lights flashed as the sheriff's cruiser sped from the campsite, headed for the Missouri State Highway Patrol headquarters in St. Joseph.

Mark was exhausted by the time he reached the shoreline. He needed to wash the grime off his face and arms. The wind had increased, causing ripples of water to slap against the rocks along the shoreline. An ugly red abrasion sent stinging pain through Mark's forearm as he splashed water onto his body. He would be home in another hour pouring peroxide on the wound to prevent infection.

Quarter waded into the lake and slouched in water up to her chest. Her tongue lapped the water in an attempt to cool her body. "Come on, Quarter!" Mark called as he grabbed an old blanket from the back of the Jeep and spread it across the passenger seat. "It's time to go home." It had been a hectic day and there would be quite a story to tell Marnie. He thought about how alarmed Susan Clark's parents would be when they were notified about the findings near the river. His thoughts were still focused on the missing woman when he rounded a curve near the quarry trail.

A red pickup truck was coming off the trail at a high rate of speed, and the driver made no attempt to slow down. The pickup skidded onto the lake road and Mark stomped the Jeep brakes to avoid a collision. The CJ-7 swerved out of control and fishtailed to the side of the road. Dirt and gravel spewed in all directions. Mark's shoulders were thrust toward the steering wheel, but an instant later, he was whipped in the opposite direction until he slammed into the backrest.

The red pickup slid to the left and then the right, ricocheting off the dirt banks that shouldered the road. The truck nearly rolled as it precariously teetered on two wheels, but the driver regained control. He slowed only long enough to get repositioned on the lake road. Tires screeched and the smell of burning rubber filled the air. Seconds later, the pickup was doing seventy and headed for the main highway.

Mark's fingers choked the steering wheel as adrenaline pumped through his veins. "Damn fool! He could have killed both of us, Quarter." Mark glanced to see if Quarter was okay. The abrupt stop had thrust the big Lab onto the floorboard, but she quickly jumped back onto the seat.

The incident had lasted only seconds, but Mark had no problem identifying the driver of the pickup. Spook Daniels' stringy hair and scruffy beard always stood out in a crowd. He wondered why he hadn't seen Spook at the quarry during the altercation with Jubile Walker. Unfortunately, there would be no opportunity for questions. The gas pedal in Spook's pickup was being floored. In less than a minute, the two vehicles were separated by a mile stretch of roadway.

Mark pulled into the driveway at the orchard thirty minutes later. It was nearly sundown and Marnie was waiting at the door. He slowed the vehicle, giving Quarter a chance to leap to the ground and run to her water bowl. He then parked the Jeep under an apple tree and sheepishly approached his wife. He hoped the kiss that he planted on Marnie's cheek would help to cancel the worried look on her face. The show of affection concealed a man deep in thought.

The next twenty minutes were spent doctoring wounds and updating Marnie on the day's activities. Mark eased into an overstuffed recliner after a light supper, being careful not to jostle his bruised body. It was an early bedtime for someone who usually stayed awake into the late hours of the night. Marnie knew he needed a lot of rest, but any hope for a peaceful sleep ended when the telephone rang.

She rushed to answer before the second ring, but the damage was already done. Mark was startled awake.

"It's the sheriff." Marnie's whisper was nullified by Mark's painful groan from his bruises. He took the telephone with apprehension, knowing that a late night call from his friend would not be to just socialize.

"What's up, Larry Ray?"

"Mark, I'm sorry to bother you, but I have a favor to ask." The lawman's apology was sincere.

"What can I do for you, Larry Ray?"

"I'm going to Maryville tomorrow to meet with Mr. and Mrs. Clark. I think they would appreciate having you present."

"Hey, buddy. You know I'll help in any way I can," Mark said, and pressed the sheriff for an explanation. "Is there something I need to know? Is it serious?"

"Yes, serious. I'll pick you up about nine in the morning." The sheriff's tone was soft, but deliberate.

Mark decided not to ask Larry Ray for more information. The tone of his voice made it obvious that he didn't want to elaborate over the telephone. Any information he was willing to share would have to wait until morning. "I'll be ready at nine sharp," Mark responded. He was about to put down the phone when he heard a faint whisper.

"Thanks, Mark. You're a real pal."

Susan soaked a towel in cold water and wrapped it around her injured ankle to help ease her pain. She thought the swelling had gone down a bit. A yellowish color had begun to blend with the purple streaks on both sides of her foot. She knew it was a sign that the healing process had begun.

She had sustained a similar injury years earlier, but any relief she felt in her ankle did nothing to overcome the adverse conditions from the rest of her body. She was nauseous and could tell that her blood sugar was dropping. She had maintained an acceptable level by sucking on mints from her emergency kit. The remaining two shots of reduced insulin would be saved as a last resort. Susan closed her eyes and memories returned:

During her senior year in high school the cross-country team was vying for a conference championship. It was the most important race of the year, and it was promoted in the media as an historic event since it would be the one and only time that a female runner would be allowed to compete for a medal in the male division. All previous cross-country races required that the runners be separated by gender, but this race was *different. The coaches at the conference schools decided to make a one-time exception several weeks before the race. They theorized that by allowing a female runner who had won her division in every race since entering high school to compete with the male runners would make for great press coverage for what was still considered a minor sport at the high school level. Susan's recorded time for completing the race would be credited to her team in the female division and she had the opportunity to win a medal in the male division. It would be a difficult challenge since Susan would be competing against Earl Kirschner, the best distance runner in the region.*

The race would begin at historic Krug Park in St. Joseph, Missouri. The route weaved along a scenic boulevard system until it circled back to the park to end on dirt trails. Susan finished her stretching exercises and sat on the ground removing her sweats when a lanky boy approached her. She recognized the runner wearing the green and white colors of Lafayette High School.

"Hi! Are you Susan Clark?" the boy asked as he held out a hand to help Susan to her feet.

"Yes, I am," she answered with an embarrassed blush. Then she added, "And, I know who you are. I've read about your

races," she said and smiled at the handsome competitor. "You've posted low-eighteens in 5K races and placed in half-marathons. Those are very impressive stats."

"Don't worry, Susan. I think you're going to be tough competition for me," Earl Kirchner said as he gave her an affectionate wink. The compliment brought a laugh from Susan, which turned to embarrassment when she realized that she had giggled in front of an older boy. The race officials were calling for runners to gather at the starting line. Susan knew the friendly conversation had come to an end, but not before the boy gave her a pat on the shoulder for good luck. He took off, yelling over his shoulder, "See you at the finish line, Susan Clark."

...A cringe of pain surged through Susan's body and shocked her back to reality. Her good memories of the big race would have to be postponed until her racked body had more time to recover. She wasn't sure if she could hang on until the next shot of insulin.

Chapter 10

At six o'clock, bright rays of sunlight began to bathe the orchard fruit. Another week of warm days and cool nights would give the apples more intense color. The Jonathans, Red Delicious, and Winesaps would shine with different hues of red, but the Black Twig variety would take on a deep burgundy that the old-timers claimed made it a "keeper." Mark wished he had a dollar for every time he heard senior citizens claim, "You pick'er in October, put'er in the cellar all winter, and she's still a good eatin' apple in March!"

Mark was slow to rise and there would be no jogging with Quarter. The fruit trees would have to wait a few more days before being sprayed with chemicals that helped prevent damage from insects and diseases. His body was still drained from the previous day's activity at Buffalo Mountain. The spills along the trail had produced bruises that weren't apparent on the prior evening, so he would stay in bed a little longer to help regain his energy.

Marnie awoke earlier than usual because the recounting of the Susan Clark case had disturbed her sleep. The coffee pot was half empty by the time Mark joined her in the kitchen. She poured a cup of lukewarm brew for him and showed concern for his wounds.

"Why don't you take it easy today, honey?" she said, noticing several scratches on Mark's forearm.

"I'd like to, but the sheriff's counting on me to make the trip to Maryville. I think it's important not to let him down."

"That's perfectly understandable," she said, dropping two pieces of bread in the toaster. "I'd be crazy with worry if our daughter was missing, and I'm sure Larry Ray will appreciate your help." Then, she remembered something to tell Mark. "Shawn called this morning. He's bringing the twins today to try their hand at fishing in the farm pond. Is that okay, Grandpa?" Mark was still getting accustomed to the pleasing designation even though the twins would be in the third grade when classes resumed next week at the elementary school.

"That's fine with me," Mark said as he flashed a grin. "I'm just sorry I can't be here to see if Hope is brave enough to put a worm on a hook." Then he added, "Or to keep Chase from jumping into the water, trying to catch a fish with his bare hands!"

Marnie didn't think her husband's descriptions were an exaggeration since he often referred to their two grandchildren by endearing terms such as *the little princess* and *he's all boy.* "I'm sure the kids will understand, and you'll still have a chance to see them at the school festival tomorrow night." Mark had almost forgotten about the annual event because of all the excitement on Buffalo Mountain. It was a big deal for the school district and most everyone in Auburn would be there.

"I'm glad you reminded me," he responded and helped himself to a slice of buttered toast. "By the way, I guess you know what we're expected to take to the potluck supper?"

"How could I forget?" Marnie gave a look of exasperation. "The refrigerator's already crammed with cheese and dough that's about to become Armenian boeregs today; that is, if I ever get you out of the kitchen."

"Okay, I got the message." Mark raised his hands to signal a timeout and looked out the kitchen window to see a vehicle coming up the driveway. "I'm saved by the sheriff." He spread his arms and pretended to be an umpire making the call at home plate. Mark gave Marnie a wink of reassurance as he headed for the front door. "Yes, I'll be careful." She was standing in the doorway as the police cruiser

110

drove away from the house. She could read Mark's lips as he waved goodbye, *"I love you, Marnie."*

Mark was anxious to find out what the sheriff had learned from his trip to St. Joseph. He realized that Larry Ray might not want to give out too much information. However, in recent years, law enforcement agencies appeared to be more receptive to giving updates to the public regarding high profile cases. He came right to the point. "What's the news on Susan Clark?"

The sheriff knew that it was only a matter of time before the media would be releasing news on a daily basis regarding the missing woman. In fact, the reason the media people weren't already buzzing was because no critical information could be released until the Clark family had been notified.

"There's not much to report. Some teenagers fishing near the Missouri River came across some things that might belong to your teacher. There were a few articles of clothing scattered along the riverbank and some other female stuff. I need to see if her parents can verify if any of it belongs to her." He pointed over his shoulder to a duffle bag on the rear seat.

"That's just a few miles off the main highway," Mark said shaking his head in disbelief. "Did they find any sign of her car or

111

anything else to indicate why she would be at that location?"

"Not yet, but the state troopers already have a SCUBA team searching the river. They probably won't be able to see much underwater, so they'll just skim along the bottom feeling for anything unusual." The sheriff explained that the area in question was often used for more than fishing. "What we do know is that people think the river is a good spot to dump used tires, car batteries, and a lot of other junk. Right now there are three boats in the water with drag lines covering a five-mile stretch." The sheriff appeared reluctant to continue, but he knew that Mark expected to hear more. "There is one other thing you should know. The troopers found something else at the river scattered with those clothes and makeup items." Mark's curiosity peaked as he wondered what was making the sheriff so uncomfortable. "They found things that a person with diabetes would use," Larry Ray said begrudgingly. "It was one of those cases containing glucose tabs, insulin, syringes, and other things that help to keep a person with diabetes alive." He paused and then pressed his point. "If it is hers, then we've got a major case on our hands."

Mark's emotions were rattled, but he remained silent and gazed out the window of the cruiser. He had hoped there would be a pleasant ending to the mystery, that perhaps Susan would miraculously appear with a logical explanation of where she had been the past few days. He had even speculated that her vehicle might have blown a tire that caused her to crash into the underbrush along the highway. Maybe she was injured but alive and waiting to be rescued, thanks to some motorist who happened to see the partially-hidden vehicle. Earlier he had only felt concern for her safety, but now he sensed that something terribly bad had happened to Susan.

"Mark, you still with me, buddy?" The sheriff's question startled him.

"Oh, sorry. I was having one of those things Kristin calls a senior moment. You know, too much time on my hands, idle brain, that kind of stuff." Then, Mark quickly got back on track with a worried question. "Do you really think she's somewhere in the river?"

"It's very possible; I've seen cases where bodies have floated a long way from where they first went in. The river current by now could have carried her all the way to Atchison, Kansas." The scenario was making Mark squeamish. "Ten to fifteen miles a day. It's possible." The sheriff sounded as though he were being interviewed by a film crew from an unsolved mysteries television show. "Then again, we had that fellow a few years ago from Woodland, Missouri, who fell out of his boat while fishing. They didn't find him for months and figured he was probably three hundred miles downstream near St. Louis. He surfaced the next spring, not a hundred yards from where he first went under. Rocks and trees under the water kept him wedged all that time."

"Okay, I get the picture." Mark rolled down the window for some fresh air to fight off the nausea.

A quick look to his right convinced the sheriff that people like Mark weren't prepared to deal with such unsavory topics. "Sorry, I didn't mean to freak you out. It comes from being around this nasty business so much."

"It's okay, Larry Ray. I just feel so bad for the girl and her parents."

"Well, so do I, but she's still only considered a missing person. As a matter of fact, I'm not convinced that she is in the river." The comment surprised Mark.

"Really? What on earth leads you to believe that?"

"Well now, let's consider the crime scene." The sheriff paused and corrected himself. "That is, if it is a crime scene." He proceeded to put a different slant on the case. "I figure someone could have just dumped that stuff along the river bank. You know, to make it look like she went into the river."

"My gosh! What are you saying, Larry Ray?" Mark's attention was totally focused on where the sheriff was going with the story.

"It's just a hunch, but here's an idea for you." The sheriff's theory was quite the opposite of what the searchers at the river were thinking. "Let's speculate that Susan Clark was getting really nervous. She's a young woman with a lot of pressure on her. She has a new job away from her parents, no more peaceful family life, her boyfriend lives in another town, and lots of people are hounding her to keep training for the Olympic trials." Mark nodded in agreement as the sheriff continued to present the story in a conversational tone. "She wouldn't be the first person who ever decided to put a stop to all that pressure and just bail out."

The theory may have sounded a little far-fetched, but Mark had a lot of respect for Larry Ray's experience in law enforcement. Some years earlier, he was responsible for cracking a major case involving a renegade farmer who killed transients that he lured into a scam to buy cattle. The farmer evidently decided to add a few humans into the ground when he planted his crops. The sheriff's explanation may have seemed a little abstract, but the people of Auburn County knew that Larry Ray Garrett was no fool, and he was re-elected every time he ran for the office.

"So you think Susan Clark headed for a new job and panicked?" Mark asked in order to clarify the sheriff's theory. "Then she threw her belongings into the river and took off for nowhere?" His next question was rather sarcastic. "Are you kidding me, Larry Ray?"

The sheriff didn't take ridicule well. "I said it was only a theory, and you never rule out any possibilities, at least not this early in an investigation." Then he shifted the conversation. "By the way, I'm going to check out that situation on Buffalo Mountain tomorrow. Jubile Walker may be the watchman at the quarry, but he doesn't need to be threatening people." The sheriff sounded apologetic for ignoring Mark's pleas on the previous day. "As far as the Wanatees are concerned, the only critters they're shooting better be the four-legged kind."

Mark didn't want to blow the situation out of proportion, but he was glad that the sheriff wasn't taking the incidents lightly. "Thanks, Larry Ray. I know you've got more pressing business to deal with."

"About ready to start picking?" The sheriff's question caught Mark by surprise. One minute he was talking about a possible dead person in the river, and the next thing he asked about was the apple crop.

"We'll start picking a few hundred bushels of Gala next week, maybe even some

Braeburns and Fugis," Mark said with a smile. His mood usually perked when he could talk about the orchard. He enjoyed telling people that growing fruit was a part of his Armenian heritage.

"Gala, Fugi, and Braeburns?" The sheriff scoffed at the notion. "Why do you want to mess with those varieties of apples?" Mark was about to get the same lecture he had heard for years from the older people in the county. "Jonathon, my man! That's the best eating and cooking apple you can grow." Larry Ray Garrett fancied himself as a connoisseur of apples and shared that distinction with anyone who was willing to discuss the subject with him. "Why, I can remember sneaking into that orchard when I was a kid and stealing apples off that old tree right next to your house. They were tart Jonathons that made you squint when you took a bite, but the juice going down your throat was as sweet as candy." Larry Ray loved going down memory lane. Mark didn't mind since it provided temporary relief from worrying about the missing teacher. He had heard the apple story many times and each version became more exaggerated. Today was one of those occasions. "Yes sir, Mark, just stick with your Jonathon apple and you'll have a blue ribbon pie every year at the county fair." Larry Ray got a nod of agreement, but it was time to shift the conversation.

"I'd like to tag along tomorrow when you go to the mountain, that is, if you don't mind. I'm curious to hear Noah Wanatee's explanation of how he could mistake a six-foot tall man and a big dog for a squirrel." Larry Ray's cheesy grin acknowledged that his friend had made a good point.

"You're welcome to join me, but we'll need to be careful. I'm going to take a look around the quarry to see if there's anything that doesn't belong there." The sheriff was being coy, but it was obvious that he was referring to the rash of crime in the county.

"Do you think Jubile Walker may be involved in all of that theft business?"

"I'm really not sure, but I've got my suspicions and plan to check it out." Evidently the sheriff wasn't going to elaborate, even if he did know more about the robberies.

"If you suspect Jubile Walker, you might as well include Spook Daniels and Aubrey Canterbury." Mark decided it was time to share his frustration. "That weasel Spook was speeding down the quarry trail when I was coming home from the lake. He practically rammed me into an early grave."

The sheriff squinted an eye and clenched his teeth. "It wouldn't surprise me if those fellows have their sticky fingers on someone's tools, guns, and computers, but I don't think any of them are smart enough to plan these heists." He sounded bewildered. "Evidently, someone has enough brains to stay one step ahead of us."

Mark thought the sheriff was accurate in his assessment of the mental capabilities of Auburn's three goons. He knew their names would never have appeared on the honor roll, even if they had attended school on a regular basis.

The cruiser drew stares as it passed through the countryside on its way to Maryville. By now, most citizens in northwest Missouri had heard the news about the disappearance of the local beauty queen and track star. People living close to Susan's hometown had seen more than the usual number of law enforcement vehicles in recent days. A police car from another county would likely continue to fuel their anxieties.

"Do you know how to get to their farm?" Mark asked as the cruiser passed a road sign:

MARYVILLE, MISSOURI - 5 MILES
POPULATION: 11,972

Larry Ray glanced at the sign and made a casual observation. "Hmmm, I wonder if they're including the students at Northwest Missouri State University when they do their census. I'm not sure they would tally nine thousand citizens if the count were taken

119

during the summer break." Mark didn't reply because the sheriff had already shifted back to the original question. "I got directions yesterday at that meeting in St. Joseph. We'll turn off the highway in just a minute. The Clark farm is about two miles down the county road."

Susan had spent the last two hours on her knees bent over the crude toilet. Her body was rebelling and sending strange signals. She had the chills, but sweat profusely dripped from her body. The room was spinning, and she was purging nasty stuff even though there was very little food in her stomach. Yet, she refused to give up. If this was a challenge for life, she intended to make it across the finish line. Her thoughts drifted back to the big race:

Eighty-four runners began the race in St. Joseph. Susan kept pace with a large group to conserve her energy, but by the time they reached Corby Pond, she was ready to make her move. She eased to the front of the pack and led the runners up a gradual incline at Lilac Hill. At the halfway marker, she was among the top five racers.

Susan reached the dirt trails in the back section of Krug Park forty minutes later. The end of the race was near, but a mile of rough terrain and two runners separated her from the finish line. She was neck and neck with a runner at the final three-quarter mile mark when the two encountered a small brook. Both were forced to decide whether to go through the water or leap the span of six feet. They made their decision at the same moment. The boy took the first option and splashed to the middle of the brook before he slipped on a mud bottom and tumbled. Susan never broke stride as she pushed off with her left foot and barely skimmed the water before landing on firm dirt. She was thirty yards down the trail by the time her competition reached dry land, and she was closing in on the lead runner. He was running strong even after five miles, and he wore green and white colors.

Earl Kirschner crested the final hill with two hundred yards to go. He took a quick glance over his shoulder and saw Susan only five seconds behind him. She had started her final "kick." The last hundred yards was a flat-out sprint, and Kirschner wasn't about to let the sophomore get the best of him, no matter how cute she was.

Both runners were in a dash for the finish line. Spectators jockeyed for a better view of what appeared to be the makings of a photo-finish race. Wilbur and Amelia Clark were among those standing in the front row cheering. The cows on the farm had been milked earlier than usual on that day in order for the proud parents to make it to the race. Wilbur pumped his fist in the air to encourage his daughter to the finish line.

Susan pulled even with Kirschner with only fifty yards to go. Their bodies were pumping adrenalin. Earl Kirschner and Susan Clark knew there could be only one Midland Empire Conference champion; people seldom remembered the runner-up.

The finish line was forty yards away as both runners strained their ligaments and tendons to the limit trying to gain an advantage. Susan pressed her toes into the turf, trying to avoid having her heels touch the ground. Suddenly, her right foot hit a patch of wet grass and her ankle twisted, causing her to lurch forward. She was half-bent at the waist and still trying to maintain her stride, but she couldn't muster the strength to bring her body into an upright position. She fell to the ground and clutched her ankle.

Earl Kirschner needed only twenty yards for the victory, but a quick glance to his side let him know that Susan was no longer challenging for the lead. He slowed his pace and then stopped. Susan winced in pain as she slowly rose and balanced on one foot. She saw the indecisiveness on Earl's face as he took a step in her direction. Then she watched him turn and run the final yards to the finish line.

The headlines in the sports section of the St. Joseph Gazette read:

Earl Kirschner Takes 1st in MEC Championship
Susan Clark Limps to 2nd

...Susan pressed a damp towel onto her forehead and looked at her surroundings: just a smelly toilet, a makeshift shower, rotting cots, and a peanut butter sandwich. Ironically, she found a bit of sordid humor in her dilemma as she thought about life. The memory of the big race helped to bring some relief. She cracked a smile as she realized there had been other times when she had been disappointed and felt helpless, but she had always managed to cross the finish line. Now, she was determined to do it again.

Chapter 11

The sheriff sounded like a tour guide as he drove along the road leading to a ranch-style brick house. "I heard that Wilbur is the fourth generation of Clarks to farm this land. It's about two thousand acres mostly in row crops, dairy cattle, registered bulls, and breeding horses. That's a big farming operation in my opinion!"

Mark's experience with the orchard was all the farming he had ever done, but he knew that in the current economy, a farmer needed a lot of acreage and diversification if the business was to survive and pass to the next generation.

"They probably worked hard for a lot of years," Mark said as the cruiser passed two rusting tractors and an old combine machine parked next to a large barn on the approach to the modest home. "They certainly don't appear to be living like millionaires."

"It may not look like it, but there's probably a million dollars worth of equipment inside that other barn," the sheriff said as he nodded toward a large building sporting a fresh coat of red paint. "That old stuff sitting outside is just for the county assessor to see when he comes by once a year to determine personal property taxes." Sheriff Garrett pulled the car to a stop in front of the house. It appeared that Mr. and Mrs. Clark had other visitors, judging from the number of cars in the driveway. One of the four vehicles displayed a small sign in the rear window that read "clergy." The Clarks were apparently receiving moral and spiritual support.

Wilbur Clark answered the doorbell with a warm greeting. He was the same pleasant gentleman that Mark and Larry Ray had met just days earlier, but he was anxious for news about developments since the meeting in Auburn. Mr. Clark explained that several friends had stopped by to offer assistance, including the family's minister. Amelia Clark joined the men and suggested the four of them adjourn to the kitchen in order to have more privacy. Sheriff Garrett apologized for having to inconvenience the couple and accepted Mrs. Clark's offer of a cup of coffee. "Just three lumps of sugar and some cream, please." The sheriff cracked a slight grin and then explained. "I'm trying to cut back a little." Mrs. Clark and Mark exchanged eye contact and a mutual smile at Larry Ray's expense.

The sheriff explained that the search for Susan was still in the early stages and that law enforcement agencies were pursuing all leads. He emphasized that the discovery of items at the river did not necessarily indicate foul play. It seemed apparent to Mark that Larry Ray was trying hard to give encouragement to the Clarks. The conversation eventually came to a point where Sheriff Garrett reached for the duffle bag that he had intentionally set down behind him. He had indicated to Mark earlier that it might be best not to have an audience when the contents of the duffle bag were discussed with Susan's parents. Mark understood and excused himself to take advantage of Mr. Clark's invitation to take a tour of the house. He stepped into the living room and introduced himself to other guests. A quick look around the room convinced Mark that the Clarks lived a fairly simple lifestyle. There did not appear to be any expensive furnishings. The seat cushions on two recliners were showing a bit of wear, most likely from years of late night use in front of the 23-inch aged Zenith television. Mark guessed that if Amelia and Wilbur Clark were wealthy, they must be saving it for future generations. They didn't appear to be spending it on themselves.

Mark excused himself from the guests and glanced at other rooms as he slipped down a hallway leading to a bathroom. Everything was clean and neat, just what he expected from people that appreciated simple comforts after years of working the land. The bedrooms were located off the hallway near the rear of the house. The door to each room was open as if to signify that this rural family would not let recent events alter their trusting lifestyle. The first two bedrooms contained an array of impressive antique furnishings. Although Amelia and Wilbur believed in being frugal, it appeared the couple appreciated quality workmanship. Mark was about to step into the bathroom when his eyes were drawn to sunlight coming through the open door of the last bedroom. The room was located on the east side of the house to capture the morning rays. Streams of light flooded the entire room and spilled into the hallway.

Mark quietly stepped into the room. Unlike the other rooms, this one's motif was light-colored wood accented in pink- lots of pink. There was a pink bedspread, pillows, lampshade, carpet, and sheer curtains trimmed with pink valances. Displayed on a shelf in a corner of the room was a toy car about fourteen inches long. Mark didn't have to read the embossed lettering on the car because he had purchased one for his own daughter many years ago. That classic pink convertible was on the Christmas list of many pre-teen girls during the Barbie and Ken doll craze. Evidently, the pink stuck with Susan Clark throughout her childhood and remained her favorite as an adult. This was where she spent twenty-three happy, protected years.

Mark intentionally left the door fully open to signal a harmless intrusion into Susan's world. The wall to his left contained a mixed assortment of pictures, but the opposite wall displayed a collage of Susan's life. There were dozens of photos showing her at different ages celebrating victories at athletic events. A more recent photo featured Susan and her parents after she set a state record in a long-distance race. Wilbur Clark was holding a hand-painted sign that read "Future Olympic Champion!" Mark moved closer to a make-up table. Draped over the large mirror were a dozen or so victory ribbons of various colors. Hanging from each ribbon was a round medal imprinted with the figurine of a runner. His eyes caught sight of two smaller pictures on the dresser. They were quite different from the other photos of the talented athlete. It was a younger Susan holding a collie puppy. Mark thought it was unusual to see that picture among all the photos of her awards and leaned forward to study the pictures more carefully. The second snapshot appeared to have been taken in the same location and featured Susan hugging a mature collie. A note scribbled in the corner of that picture read "Molly and me, friends forever."

Oh, my God. Mark's eyes teared as he remained fixed on the photos of Susan and her pet, which had been snapped years apart. He was captured in a special moment of time: *She had everything going for her- popularity, success, status, and yet, in some ways, she never stopped being that little girl.*

"Dr. Sarkisian?" A voice coming from the doorway broke the silence. Mark was startled although the words weren't spoken in an accusatory tone. He was embarrassed as he turned to face Amelia Clark.

"I'm very sorry." Mark's apology came with the sincerity of a man who had just been discovered in a young woman's bedroom. "I didn't mean to intrude. I was just..." Mrs. Clark raised her hand in a gesture to hush the man who was standing in her daughter's bedroom stammering for words.

"Now, don't you give it another thought. Susan won't mind. People visit Susan's room all the time to enjoy the nice things she's accumulated over the years."

"Mrs. Clark, it really is a fascinating room." Mark's tone continued to sound apologetic. "There are awards here that span a decade, and pictures that just grab at your heart. and..."

"And pink. Lots of pink!" Amelia Clark interrupted and laughed.

"Well, yes. I did notice that she was rather partial to the color," Mark joked. He was feeling much better than a few moments earlier.

"She calls it her *Alice in Wonderland* room. You know, after the children's story." Mrs. Clark gestured around the room as though she held a magic wand.

"Of course, one of my favorites when I was a child," Mark responded cheerfully. "In fact, this entire room could have come right out of a child's storybook. And, there's the Teaberry gum connection. The pink wrappers sort of fit right into the whole magical picture."

Amelia Clark hesitated a moment and realized Mark was just poking fun. "Well, I suppose you're right, Dr. Sarkisian. I must remember to tell that girl what you said when she comes home." She smiled and gave Mark a pat on his shoulder. "Susan will be happy that you stopped in."

Mark's emotions were stirred as he lowered his head looking at the pink carpet. His hostess had taken an awkward situation in her daughter's bedroom and turned it into a pleasant conversation. Sheriff Garrett was in the family home trying to solve Susan's disappearance, and Mrs. Clark was capable of carrying on a casual conversation as though her daughter would walk through the front door at any moment. Mark was baffled, but he had never been involved in an investigation for a missing person. He wondered if it was the reaction of a parent in denial. Mrs. Clark was still smiling when he raised his head. The two gazed into each other's eyes, and Mark began to understand that the Christian woman had an abiding faith that her daughter would return home safe.

"Ready to head out, Mark?" a familiar voice came from the hallway. Sheriff Garrett and Mr. Clark had finished their conversation.

"I'll be right there, Larry Ray." Mark didn't feel comfortable leaving the room just yet. Amelia Clark never broke eye contact as she took hold of his hands. She had something important to say. Mark tilted his head to hear her whisper.

"Thank you for caring so much." She placed a frail hand on his shoulder and kissed his cheek.

"Mark, we better be going." The sheriff was getting anxious. "We still need to make a stop in Maryville before it gets too late."

Mrs. Clark gave Mark's hand a reassuring squeeze indicating that she would be just fine. Their brief exchange had been meaningful, and as Mark stood in the hallway, he saw Amelia take a picture from the cosmetic table and walk to the bed. She sat on

131

the pink spread staring at Susan and her pet dog…and she cried a mother's tears.

The sheriff had just backed out of the driveway when Mark asked if anything of value had come from the meeting with Susan's parents. "Some of the items we found could belong to Susan, but it was a little difficult to get positive confirmation because it's mostly generic stuff that anyone can buy in a lot of stores." The news wasn't very encouraging, but Mark could tell that the wheels were turning inside his friend's head. "The diabetic supplies, though, are just too much of a coincidence. My gut feeling is that they belong to the girl. Either way, it was important to make the trip."

"You mean to reassure the Clarks that you're doing everything possible to find their daughter?" Mark queried.

"That's all part of the process, Mark. I needed to verify some specifics now that the parents have had a few days for all of this to soak in." Mark was about to get another lecture on law enforcement investigations. "It's basic things like noticing unusual vehicles driving past the house or seeing any strangers near the farm. You've got to ask questions like that more than once." The sheriff spotted the questioning look on Mark's face and proceeded to explain his last statement. "If you quiz people immediately after a situation, there's too much anxiety and they can't thoroughly focus on the question."

"It's more complicated than people realize." Mark seemed perplexed. "Larry Ray, I'm not sure that I'm cut out to do investigations."

The sheriff brushed off the comment. "Today's meeting just confirmed what her parents told us earlier. No strange cars and no weirdoes as far as the Clarks are concerned." Mark could tell that his friend was having a difficult time with this case. "Buddy, it's not a good situation." Mark was growing weary of hearing about police procedures, but the sheriff's use of the word "situation" had struck a sensitive note. It seemed like such a casual, matter-of-fact way to sum up what was shaping up to be a tragedy. "I've got to make a stop in Maryville to update law enforcement there," Sheriff Garrett announced. "It should take only about half an hour, and then we can head for home. Is that okay with you?" Mark didn't really have a choice since the sheriff was in the driver's seat, but he had an idea that seemed better than drinking stale coffee that had simmered for hours in a police station.

"How about dropping me off at the boyfriend's office in Maryville? I wouldn't mind getting to know him a little better."

"It's fine with me," Larry Ray said, shrugging his shoulders. "He works at that satellite research company on Main Street. Do you think he can tell you anything we don't already know?"

"Probably not," Mark responded casually, "but maybe it will help for him to know that you're pursuing all leads." He paused to see if the sheriff had picked up on his use of police terminology. After several seconds of silence, Larry Ray cracked a smile as he pressed the accelerator and headed for the community of Maryville, Missouri.

Susan had been through three days of hell. By now, she knew the routine. Late at night the heavy door would creak open. Someone would step inside, but only if he saw no movement in his captive. Susan would feign being asleep or unconscious. Her captor might be old, judging by the slow shuffling of his feet, or perhaps he was worried that she was playing possum. He crouched next to the musky army cot and stared at the still form. His smell was a rancid mix of dirt and grime. Susan held her breath to keep from inhaling the foul odor, but eventually she had to sip a wisp of air through lips that were pressed together. She was vulnerable to this complete stranger as he glared at her motionless body. It was very creepy, but he never touched her.

Each visit was accompanied by meager helpings of food and bottles of water. It was barely enough to keep a healthy person alive, let alone someone whose life cells were beginning to show rejection. Susan had stopped enjoying the taste of peanut butter by the time she entered high school. Now, the sandwiches each day were helping to sustain her life.

Yes, Susan knew the routine, but she was growing weak and every passing hour brought her a little closer to death. Her prospects for being rescued were slim; too much time had elapsed. If she were to survive, it would have to come from her own will to live. She needed to formulate a plan of escape while her mind was still alert.

Susan injected the third shot of insulin and closed her eyes. Only one shot remained. Time was running out.

Chapter 12

Sheriff Garrett stopped the cruiser in front of an impressive building that bore a large sign identifying Satellite Research Associates. The Arizona-based company had received extensive media coverage when it expanded operations into the central part of the United States. SRA marketed a variety of energy alternatives to natural gas and electricity. Solar and wind-powered options were becoming more acceptable to people in the Bible belt region although the concept had caught on several years earlier in the southwestern states. Jeffrey Williams had joined SRA six years earlier with a degree in business administration. He was eventually made a junior executive and now served as the project manager for the company's energy-consulting services. He had not been excited about relocating; however, a visit with Mr. and Mrs. Clark to discuss converting their farming operation to natural resources had introduced him to their perky daughter. He cemented the relationship by helping Susan complete a university assignment that required designing an energy-efficient school facility. Her project featured igloo-shaped school buildings with solar panels, an idea that actually came from Jeffrey's prior experiences in Arizona.

Mark entered the front lobby of SRA and gazed at an impressive array of landscaping. An atrium featured tropical plants and small trees strategically arranged to capture sunlight cascading through numerous skylights. If Mark hadn't known better, he would have thought he was standing among the scenery in Hawaii rather than in a state known more for its cornfields. He began to walk toward a receptionist's desk, but before he made it across the lobby, a pretty blond flashing a bright smile approached him.

"Welcome to Satellite Research Associates. May I help you?" The young woman's sparkling-white teeth could have easily been used for one of those television ads promoting a brand of toothpaste or quality dental care. She was impeccably dressed in a gray skirt that complimented her lavender silk blouse. If the objective was to make a great first impression with visitors, the company had hit a home run with this young lady.

"Hello. I'm Mark Sarkisian from Auburn. I was hoping to speak with Mr. Williams if he's available. I'm sorry, but I don't have an appointment."

The woman appeared to make a connection with Mark's name and assumed that he was there to discuss Susan Clark. "It's a pleasure to meet you, Dr. Sarkisian. I'm Paige Morgan, the company's administrative assistant," she said continuing to display a friendly smile. "I'm sure he will take time to see you. I'll be happy to buzz him." She stepped to a nearby desk and pressed a button on an intercom.

"Yes, Paige. What is it?"

"Jeffrey, there's a Dr. Sarkisian here. He would like to speak with you if you're not too busy." There was hesitation and then a few moments of silence.

"Uh, sure. Just give me a minute to clear some things from my desk. I'll be happy to speak with Dr. Sarkisian." Mark had overheard the conversation, so there was no need to relay the message. Instead, the young lady invited Mark to have a seat and offered him coffee.

"Thanks, but I'll pass on the coffee, Paige." Mark didn't think he was being too familiar by using her first name. He took a seat on a plush sofa and was surprised when the perky administrative assistant sat next to him.

"If you don't mind, Dr. Sarkisian, I'll keep you company until Jeffrey joins you," she said and continued to flash a cheerful smile. "I could use the break."

Mark was delighted by the offer and proceeded to make small talk. "Maryville seems to be a nice town. Have you lived here very long?"

"I was born and raised here," she answered with a laugh, "all twenty-three years!"

"Then you know Susan Clark?" As soon as he said it, Mark realized the question must have sounded rather stupid. Of course she knew her. After all, Susan was dating the boss.

"Oh, everyone knows Susan." Paige hesitated and then decided to elaborate on the question. "But, I probably knew her better than most people because we were in the same high school graduating class. We even played on the same basketball team that won the Midland Empire Conference championship our senior year," she announced with pride.

"Good player?" Mark asked.

"Oh, yes! Susan is an all-around athlete, but track is really her sport. Not many people can keep up with her, at least not around these parts."

Mark smiled as he clarified the earlier question. "That's what I've heard about Susan, but actually I was asking about you."

"Oh, me?" Mark detected a slight blush. "Well, I enjoyed playing sports, but when practice was over, I hightailed it out of the gym." Paige tried to suppress a giggle, which quickly turned into a laugh. "You know, cruising with my friends and looking for boys." She blushed again and shifted the conversation back to her friend. "Now, Susan's a different story. She always stayed after practice to shoot baskets or run sprints in the gym." She gave Mark a coy look. "None of the other girls wanted to break a sweat, but Susan didn't seem to mind putting in the extra work. It seems to have paid off." She paused and gave Mark a wink of confidence. "Susan won all of those long-distance races and even got an invitation to the Olympic tryouts."

"Yes, I was very impressed that someone with so many opportunities elected to choose a career in education," Mark responded and then checked his watch wondering how much longer he would have to wait for Jeffrey Williams. Fortunately, he was enjoying the conversation with the young lady who dispelled the Hollywood stereotype of a well-endowed, short-on-brains blond. Paige wasn't just "window-dressing" for the company. She was SRA's unofficial public relations department.

"That's Susan. She may enjoy running, but she loves children!" The response came with another pretty smile. "She'll be a great teacher if she gets the chance." Next came the question that Mark had expected since walking through the front door. "Is there any news about Susan?"

Mark wasn't sure how to respond appropriately. "Well, there's probably not much more to tell than what you already know, but there are a lot of people trying to get this resolved." The explanation was terse, but it didn't seem to daunt the conversation.

"I certainly hope so because I can't wait to hear that greeting again." The young woman noticed an inquisitive look from Mark. "My middle name is Louise and whenever Susan saw me on campus, she would yell something really silly." She quickly looked around the reception area to make sure that no one else was close by. Her smile broadened as she gathered the courage to continue. Then, without warning, she fired off, "Well Hellooooo Paigey Lou!" Mark and his new friend broke into laughter, and by the time they regained their composure, tears of joy were flowing down their cheeks. Eventually, Paige put her finger against her lips to signal that it might be best to have the gaiety subside. It was one of the few times in recent days that Mark felt like laughing, and it helped to overshadow some of the stress that he felt regarding Susan Clark. The two were still chuckling when an office door opened and Jeffrey Williams stepped into the reception area dressed in a tailored three-piece suit.

"Dr. Sarkisian, it's nice to see you again," he said extending a handshake. "Please join me in the office. Would you care for coffee?"

"No, but thank you. Your administrative assistant was very accommodating and already offered refreshments."

"Yes, Paige does a great job." The compliment was loud enough for the young lady to hear it in the reception area. "Did she mention that she's a good friend of Susan's?"

"Yes, she did share that with me," Mark acknowledged. "As a matter of fact, Susan's the reason that the sheriff and I are in Maryville today. I'm sorry to bother you, but I thought it might give us an opportunity to get to know each other."

"It's no bother at all," Jeffrey said, gesturing for Mark to be seated in a posh leather chair. The next minutes were spent recounting what had transpired the previous day on Buffalo Mountain. Mark decided to share information about the findings near the river since Susan's parents had already been notified. The young man appeared to take the news hard.

"Oh, my gosh!" he uttered with a painful grimace. "Just a few days ago we were talking about our future together and now everything's all messed up!"

"I can understand how upsetting this is for you," Mark said, "but things aren't always as they seem. I think it's best to let the authorities do their job and pray that this will work out for the best." The trite rationalization didn't seem to help much, and Jeffrey took time to get control of his emotions.

Mark took a good look at the office arrangement for the first time since entering the room. It was spacious, and the furnishings conveyed the sense of a successful enterprise. He wondered if it was a bit too much since people residing in rural Missouri weren't noted for being extravagant. The objective may have been to suggest that it was possible to have a better lifestyle by becoming an SRA client. Streams of sunlight spilled into the room from large skylights that the company marketed as part of its solar energy package. The walls were tastefully decorated with paintings that captured Mark's attention. Instead of the usual office paintings containing splashes of color, these renderings featured rural scenes of barns, pastures, fences, country houses and farm machinery. Included was a tasteful mix of popular nostalgic works. Mark was no art connoisseur, but the nicely framed works of Thomas Hart Benton and Norman Rockwell stood out. A painting next to them put an immediate smile on Mark's face. The signature on the rendering was simply *J. Laurent*. The artist was a successful business executive who pursued a love for art after his retirement from the corporate world. Jacque Laurent never received international acclaim as an artist, but his talent for reflecting rural life in America endeared him to a niche of people who appreciated seeing it depicted on canvas. Mark assumed the impressive display of artwork reinforced SRA's attempt to create a public image that reflected corporate success while showing an appreciation for the simple things in life. The Jacque Laurent painting was a perfect fit for promoting the family values and traditions of a past era.

Mark's time spent surveying the artworks had given Jeffrey an opportunity to regain his composure. He now reconnected with Mark, whose attention now shifted to a large projection screen covering much of one wall. A different picture of land topography flashed onto the screen every few seconds as a bank of computer printers continued to pump data.

"That's an impressive theatre set-up," Mark said, pointing to the projection screen and several computers.

"Satellite Research Associates is on the cutting edge of the alternative energy market," Jeffrey responded with enthusiasm. He pushed a computer button and the pictures on the screen changed more rapidly. "Our satellite technology is state of the art. I can take you anywhere in the world from this room," the young exec boasted. "In fact, I can put you in any room in the world from this location."

Mark knew that SRA was an emerging leader in a growing industry that got its start servicing government contracts. The company's expansion now focused on the agricultural and domestic markets. Although only a junior executive, Jeffrey Williams thought his aggressive style and willingness to relocate got him the nod to head up the company's new venture.

"You've peaked my interest," Mark commented as he continued to watch the pictures change. "Did the prior year meet your expectations?"

"I don't think a company like SRA would make such a major investment if it didn't believe we could capture a major piece of the business," Jeffrey bragged. "I'd say within five years SRA will lock in at least ten percent of new households to utilize our services."

"Really? That sounds like it could turn into major profits." Judging from the young man's grin, Mark may not have fully grasped the company's potential.

"Millions?" Williams quipped. "More like billions! That is, if it all comes together, and I'm sure it will," he added confidently.

The information was interesting, but a new picture that flashed on the screen caught

Mark's attention. Jeffrey assumed that his visitor didn't have much interest in discussing SRA profits, so he shifted the conservation back to the technology. "We call those pictures MAGs; it's a lot sexier than saying Magnified Altitude Graphics," he explained. "Those pictures of land topography come into our computers through a satellite link. Then our software takes over and processes the solar, wind power, and other components for any region of the country. There's more than seventy years of climatic data in those computers dating back to when weather services started keeping accurate records." The lecture had been brief, but Mark got the message. It was apparent that Jeffrey Williams considered himself among that special breed of marketing executives who could "sell ice cubes to Eskimos."

"Very impressive, but what's the end product?" Mark primed himself for the closing.

"Ah-ha, yes! The end product." Jeffrey quickly latched onto the question. "The end product is an energy system that SRA custom designs for your home or business. It will take into account every factor that might adversely impact your financial picture." The man was on a roll with a smooth pitch that had been polished from dozens of prior presentations. Mark couldn't help but be impressed: *This fellow's got his spiel down so pat that he could be selling time shares for vacations in the Congo.* "The end product, Dr. Sarkisian, is a business plan that prevents loss and increases your revenue potential." Jeffrey pressed his case. "Here's an example for you." He moved closer to the screen and computer modules. "The satellite picture now on the screen is from a farm in the next county. It can produce two hundred acres of soybeans each season with an average of forty bushels per acre. Let's assume soybeans will bring a market price of twelve dollars a bushel." He started punching computer keys faster than an I.R.S. auditor manipulating a ten-key calculator. "That's eight thousand bushels of beans parlayed into $96,000 for the farmer." Jeffrey stopped long enough for a quick glance to see if Mark was paying attention. "Did I lose you somewhere along the way, Dr. Sarkisian?"

"I'm still with you," Mark replied. "It's very interesting, please continue."

"Now, here's the payoff." Jeffrey was a marketing tiger that had stalked his prey and was closing in on the kill. "SRA can put together a program that gives that farmer the potential to double his production. It's significant money for someone farming a small acreage, and major dollars for the larger operations." He paused to ask for confirmation. "Wouldn't you agree?"

"I definitely think that would grab someone's attention," Mark conceded.

"It usually does," Jeffrey said proudly as he moved closer to Mark for a more dramatic finish. "Now, apply the same formula to a thousand acres and you just made a million bucks! Case closed."

"Quite impressive," Mark said as another picture flashed on the screen. "Jeffrey, what's the satellite focused on now?"

"Well, give me a moment to check it out." He moved to a different computer and tapped the keys. "Hmmm, apparently the target area being scanned is northern Missouri." He pressed another key and the pictures changed more rapidly. "There's Brookfield, and here comes Chillicothe, next is Hamilton." He was calling out towns as though he were a traveler following a road map. "The next town should be Cameron, followed by Stewartsville." Mark felt like he was being treated to a three-ring circus, and Jeffrey Williams enjoyed the role of ringmaster. He abandoned the computer and walked to a spot below the screen. His index finger began tracking the satellite images as they moved across the screen. "Yes, there it is!" Jeffrey excitedly pumped his fist to make a point. "The satellite is doing its job taking shots along U.S. Highway 36." Both men continued to gaze at the satellite pictures until Jeffrey spread his arms in a sign of satisfaction.

"Well, Dr. Sarkisian, what do you think of that?"

"I'm not only fascinated by the technology, but the clarity of the pictures is amazing." Mark then posed a question related to his visit. "Can you bring up the Auburn area on the screen, specifically Buffalo Mountain?" Jeffrey hesitated for a moment, but the opportunity to showcase his expertise was too much to pass up.

"Sure, of course I can. It shouldn't take very long." He manipulated the computer keys and seconds later a series of new pictures appeared. "That should be Auburn." Mark waited for the picture to focus and gradually his community was on display. The images continued to enlarge until even the vehicles on Main Street were easy to identify. "Buffalo Mountain will be coming up next."

"Wow!" Mark exclaimed as a mass of earth, rock and a huge peak resembling a bison's hump came onto the screen.

"Heck, that's nothing. Watch this!" Jeffrey pressed more keys and the screen split into eight sections that featured different areas of the mountain. It was an impressive show. Buffalo Mountain had been divided into equal parts thanks to modern technology.

Mark carefully scanned each picture looking for anything that appeared unusual. He finished the first group but nothing looked out of the ordinary. The pictures slowly faded, leaving Mark staring at a blank screen and wondering: *Susan, where are you?*

A new series of pictures flashed onto the screen. Mark focused his attention to studying each one. He recognized many of the trails and slopes that posed a challenge for him during prior trips up the mountain, but there was no sign of human activity. Then something caught his attention just before the pictures began to disappear from the screen. "Hold those shots!" Mark yelled before the pictures completely vanished. Jeffrey pressed a computer key and the pictures were locked in. Mark stepped closer to the projection screen. The satellite had captured a secluded area near the top of the mountain. His eyes strained to locate something familiar, and then he found it. "It's Hidden Valley," Mark murmured to himself.

The valley was an anomaly. It was nestled between two high peaks and wasn't really hidden since many people knew of its existence. The green meadow and pristine stream could have come out of a movie set, but not many people had actually been to the valley. It was difficult to access and was private property. Israel Wanatee had purchased eight hundred acres on the mountain several years before it was sanctioned as a Missouri landmark. The state made a bid to purchase the land from Israel, but he declined the government's meager offer. Politicians at the state capitol got nasty and threatened to take over the land by condemning it under an obscure eminent domain law. It took only one shrewd attorney and sixty Native Americans marching on the capitol in Jefferson City to convince the politicians to back off and leave the Wanatee family alone. In a nasty display of revenge, the state officials neglected their responsibility to provide funds for maintaining the trail to Hidden Valley. Eventually, the trail became treacherous and state conservation agents posted signs to discourage hikers from going near the property. Rumors began to spread that the Indian family living in Hidden Valley posed a danger to society. One old codger at the Co-op claimed that his distant relative had entered the valley and was never heard from again, although there was never any verification that the story was true. In fact, there was no record of the Wanatees ever threatening or hurting anyone.

Mark was becoming frustrated as he continued to look for anything unusual in the picture. "Can you get any better resolution on this section?" He pointed at a specific spot on the screen. Jeffrey perked to the challenge and a more detailed image was on display. "Yes, there it is, just as I remember it!" Mark acted as though he had just won a lottery jackpot. "Do you recognize it, Jeffrey?"

"I can't say that I've ever seen it before," Jeffrey said somewhat puzzled. "It looks like a picture from an old pioneer journal." The response was loaded with sarcasm.

"It's the Wanatee cabin. I've been there once before," Mark said as he recalled his only meeting with Israel Wanatee, "and it wasn't a pleasant visit." His eyes panned the entire picture as he examined the log structure. Minutes passed with no conversation and Jeffrey became impatient.

"This is a waste of time," he said with disgust. "I haven't seen anything in that picture for the last three minutes except the same old cabin. I'm shutting the system down." Mark was surprised. He thought Susan's boyfriend would be more interested to find out if the reclusive Wanatees might have a connection to her disappearance, assuming she ever made it to the mountain. It appeared the visit to Satellite Research Associates was coming to an end. Mark's host reached for the "cancel" key on the computer just as the picture expanded to include more of the area surrounding the cabin. Mark flashed a quick glance at the picture, knowing that the satellite transmission would end any second. He focused on a spot about a hundred feet from the cabin. "Stop! Please don't shut down the system," Mark pleaded.

Jeffrey begrudgingly accommodated the request and removed his finger from the key, but interjected a bit of sarcasm. "Did you see a groundhog, Dr. Sarkisian?"

Mark ignored the comment and continued to focus on the picture. He was baffled by something that he couldn't quite make out. "What is that?" He pointed at a dark patch of earth in the picture.

"It just looks like dirt to me," Jeffrey said flippantly. "It's probably a garden they planted. Not a big deal unless you don't care for tomatoes and cucumbers."

"In late August? I don't think so." Mark continued to examine the configuration on the screen. "Perhaps it's something we're not supposed to see."

"Well, that's your theory, Dr. Sarkisian, but I'll have to respectfully disagree. I think you're barking up the wrong tree."

Mark didn't want to be rude, but he was beginning to wonder what Susan Clark found so special in the brash young man. The situation was awkward, but the sound of the intercom interrupted the silence.

"Jeffrey, I'm sorry to bother you, but the sheriff is waiting outside for Dr. Sarkisian." Paige's cheery voice broke the tension, and Mark seized the opportunity to say a cordial goodbye. He was about to exit the executive office when Jeffrey followed him.

"Dr. Sarkisian, please wait a moment," his voice quivered as he extended his hand to Mark. "I'm sorry if I seemed abrupt." The apology sounded genuine. "I just haven't been myself since Susan disappeared. Evidently, it's affecting my judgment," he said looking down at the floor. "Again, I'm sorry." Mark considered the change in attitude. Perhaps he had been hasty in his judgment of the man who now appeared rather humble.

"It's understandable; there seems to be a lot of people who are upset lately," Mark said as he shook Jeffrey's hand. "Let's just chalk it up to a bad day." Jeffrey nodded in agreement as Mark left his office.

———————◦———————

Susan opened her eyes but was too weak to pull herself into a sitting position on the cot. Her life depended on the last shot of insulin tucked into the tiny pouch just three feet away. She lowered her hand over the cot's wooden rail and stretched until her arm felt like it would be wrenched from its socket. She pressed her fingers onto the cold floor and forced them toward the pouch. Inch by agonizing inch, her fingers crawled like a spider creeping toward its prey. The pouch was out of reach, mere inches too far, so she took the only alternative and rolled her body off the cot.

Susan cried out in pain as her body slammed onto the floor. She was careful to avoid banging the swollen ankle, but it came at the expense of a badly bruised hip. She rolled onto her side and clutched the pouch. Her fingers trembled so much she could hardly separate the thin string that kept the small bag closed. In desperation, she clenched the string between her teeth and yanked to break the tread. She pried the pouch open and retrieved the syringe. Susan barely felt the needle penetrate her thigh to deliver the lifesaving fluid. Within minutes her body began to recover.

There was no sense in trying to get back onto the cot. Too much energy was spent just retrieving the insulin. Susan sat against a wall gripping the empty syringe, saddened that she had used her last drop of hope. She was alone, just sitting on a cold floor looking at a syringe, just looking at a... weapon.

Chapter 13

Mark stepped into the reception area and was greeted by Paige's sparkling smile. He approached her to convey his appreciation for the warm reception. The two were exchanging pleasantries when she casually posed a question that caught Mark by surprise.

"Weird isn't it, Dr. Sarkisian?" There was youthful innocence in her question.

"Weird? I'm afraid I don't understand, Paige."

"You know, Susan and Jeffrey were having a big argument while they were eating lunch before she left, and then she just disappears. Wouldn't you call that weird?" Mark was confused, but the look on Paige's face signaled that the young lady was prepared to share more of the story.

"I didn't know they had a spat," Mark commented with curiosity.

"Spat? I'd call it more like a full-blown battle," Paige responded with a quirky look. "It's so unlike Susan. I've never heard her raise her voice in anger or even seen her in a foul mood. Believe me, Dr. Sarkisian, she wasn't a happy person when she left Maryville." The descriptive vocabulary left no doubt that Susan's relationship with the boyfriend was on shaky ground. Mark assumed that her parents were not aware of the situation since they had made no mention of it during the meeting in Auburn.

"It's all news to me, Paige," he said, shaking his head in disbelief. "Thanks for telling me, but how did you find out about this?" Mark wasn't prepared for the bombshell he was about to hear. Paige's demeanor changed, and her words became more deliberate.

"Susan came back to the office after lunch to tell me goodbye. She was crying and said that her relationship with Jeffrey was over." She continued to share a story about how Susan had confided in her that she was ready to start her career, but Jeffrey was too controlling. "She said that Jeffrey had issues, and lately all he talked about was coming into a pile of money. What do you make of that, Dr Sarkisian?"

"That's heavy stuff," Mark responded, and then pressed for more information. "What was Jeffrey's slant on all of this?"

"Who knows?" Paige replied, hunching her shoulders. "He came back to the office really angry after Susan left. Then he stormed out and was gone for the day." She shook her head in confusion. "He didn't return to the office until the afternoon of the next day." Mark listened intently as the story continued to unfold. "You know, I think Jeffrey might have gone out of town. I had a question and tried to telephone his house until late that night, but I never reached him." She paused and gave Mark an odd look. "Now that I think about it, Jeffrey hasn't spoken much about Susan since the day she left town. I'd call that really strange. How about you, Dr. Sarkisian?"

"Paige, I'm just baffled. The sheriff and I spent an hour with the Clarks this morning and there was no mention of any problem between Susan and Jeffrey."

"That's because they don't know," she said, shaking her index finger. "Jeffrey threatened to fire me if I said anything about it to anyone, so I've kept quiet, hoping Susan would show up and everything would be okay. I didn't want to cause any more heartache for her parents." Tears flowing from her eyes streaked her makeup. Mark pulled a tissue from a container on the side of the desk and handed it to Paige. She lowered her head and dried her eyes. "I'm sorry. Maybe I should have said something sooner. I was confused, but I think it's something that you and the sheriff should know." She raised her head and looked into Mark's eyes. "Am I doing the right thing?"

"Yes, Paige, you've done exactly the right thing." Mark took the liberty of using another tissue to wipe a tear from her cheek. "I'll share this information with the sheriff and when we find Susan, we'll tell her how helpful you've been." Paige's eyes glistened, but her pretty smile had returned. The tender moment was interrupted by the honking of a horn outside the building. The sheriff was growing impatient.

"I know you have to leave, Dr. Sarkisian, but I'm really glad that you came today."

Mark said a goodbye and walked to the front door. It was apparent that the sheriff was fidgeting with papers inside the squad car. A few more seconds would not make much difference in Larry Ray's demeanor, so Mark decided to make his exit memorable for his new friend. He had a mischievous smile on his face as he stepped out the front door and yelled over his shoulder, "Goodbye, Paigey Lou!" He could hear laughter coming from inside the building as he walked to the police cruiser.

———◦———

Susan had lost track of time. It had been hours since her captors had checked on her.

The cold sweats and headaches grew more intense, but there was little she could do to prevent her blood sugar from dropping. Now she worried whether or not she even had the energy to escape. She needed to have some relief from constantly thinking about her current dilemma. It was causing depression, and that was something that could accelerate the deterioration of her body. She decided to focus on her loving parents, and eventually her thoughts came around to her last meeting with Jeffrey. Perhaps she had been hasty in ending the relationship, but their conversation at the diner had not gone well:

"I've told you before, Jeffrey, I'm not ready to make a commitment," Susan said in a sincere tone. "We've had some good times together, but I just don't think we're right for each other. I want to begin my career and experience new things, but you seem to be focused on how fast you can get rich."

"So, what's wrong with wanting to be rich and having nice things?" Jeffrey's voice was rising in anger.

"There's nothing wrong with that, Jeffrey, but it's just not a priority in my life. I'm more excited about teaching children than being the girlfriend of a company executive." The blunt comment didn't set well with the young man.

"News flash, Susan! News flash!" *Jeffrey blurted out in a voice loud enough to draw the attention of other patrons in the diner. "I'm not going to waste my life being a junior executive and making millions of dollars for the company. My plans are a lot bigger than that!"*

Susan was embarrassed by the number of people who were now staring at the couple because of the outburst. She attempted to tactfully defuse the situation. "Jeffrey, I admire your drive and ambition, but I think it's best that we remain just friends." She reached across the table to hold his hand, but he pulled it away. Her calm demeanor had upset him even more.

"I've heard enough!" He leaned forward with both hands on the table and lowered his voice so that only Susan could hear his veiled threat. "So, it's over between us," he said with a hateful glare. "Okay, but someday Susan, I hope you live to regret it."

...Now, as Susan prepared to fight for her life, she wondered if Jeffrey's premonition had come true.

Chapter 14

Mark could tell even before he reached the cruiser that Larry Ray was perturbed. Perhaps his friend would understand once Mark shared the information he gleaned from the visit to the SRA building.

"Well, it's about time," the exasperated sheriff grumbled.

"I'm sorry to keep you waiting, but I picked up some interesting information in there." Mark was convinced there was something suspicious that needed follow-up at the Wanatee cabin, and there was also the news that Paige had shared about the lovers' quarrel.

"You've got my undivided attention for the next ninety minutes," the sheriff said as he gunned the engine and headed out of town.

During the return trip, Mark told Sheriff Garrett about the discussion he had with Jeffrey Williams and interjected the tidbit about the spat at the restaurant. The sheriff agreed that it was strange that Jeffrey had given no indication of the couple's troubles during the prior meeting in Auburn.

"Yes, it's does seem odd. The guy probably just wanted to avoid embarrassment, or maybe it just slipped his mind since all of us were focused so much on finding the girl." The sheriff's theory seemed plausible, so Mark didn't make it an issue. He was more interested in focusing the sheriff's attention on the Wanatee family. Mark shifted the discussion to the cabin and the patch of disturbed ground that had appeared on the satellite screen.

"Now, that might just be an important piece of information," Larry Ray conceded. "I'd rather find out what happened to Susan Clark than pursue a lovers' quarrel." Mark thought the sheriff was treating the squabble too lightly, but Larry Ray had moved to a different topic. "And, I'm curious to find out if there's something the Wanatee family doesn't want anyone to know."

"That sounds great to me, Larry Ray." Mark was pleased with his friend's line of thinking. Until now, the sheriff had no reason to be suspicious of Israel Wanatee or his wife and son. They had kept to themselves since building their homestead on the mountain and having the child. The local authorities had no record of them breaking any laws or causing trouble for anyone. There had been only one police report to even mention the Wanatee name. It was filed after the incident at the Co-op involving Toad Canterbury and the mule.

Sheriff deputies were more sympathetic toward the mule when they filed a report that read: "An attack from behind upon an innocent animal, perpetrated by a 300-pound, human being." Sheriff Garrett had read the report and determined that the mule had a right to defend itself. The congenial sheriff commended his officers for doing a thorough investigation. As far as the Auburn County Sheriff's Department was concerned, Toad Canterbury got what he deserved.

"Tomorrow might be a good day to check out the Wanatee place," Larry Ray suggested. "While I'm at it, I might as well pay a visit to the quarry. Jubile Walker seems to be getting a little careless with that rifle." Mark was pleased that Jubile's threat wasn't being treated lightly, and a visit from the sheriff might just be what the obnoxious man needed. "I could use some company if you're not doing anything tomorrow." Larry Ray cracked a cheesy grin, knowing that Mark was chomping for an invitation. The prospect of finding out what might be buried near the Wanatee cabin made the mountain trek even more appealing.

"You can count me in, buddy." Mark slouched to a more comfortable position in the passenger seat. He smiled, quite satisfied that he was still involved with the investigation.

There was no further discussion during the rest of the ride back to Auburn. Larry Ray programmed the radio to a rock-and-roll station and passed the time humming tunes with the likes of Buddy Holly, Elvis Presley, and the Four Seasons. Mark tilted the backrest of his seat and peered out the side window. The early autumn scenery was beautiful along Highway 71 as the cruiser passed through the Missouri communities of Pumpkin Center and Savannah. It would have been easy to close his eyes and snooze if it hadn't been for a haunting question: *Where can she be?*

The man sat alone at a small table cleaning his weapon and listening to the wind howling a warning that another storm was coming. He poured some smelly liquid onto a small swatch of material attached to a long rod and then rammed it down the rifle barrel. He repeated the action several times. Finally, he withdrew the cleaning rod and pointed the rifle toward the light to examine the inside of the barrel. Once satisfied that the weapon was ready for action, he loaded a handful of shells and popped open another beer. He grabbed a pouch of tobacco and rolled a cigarette. The next half-hour was spent chugging beer and blowing rings of smoke. The sound of truck doors slamming shut signaled that he had company. Two men shuffled into the room to face their disgusted partner.

"Well, it's about time. You two have been gone for five hours!" he yelled, continuing to insert more shells into the rifle. "Did you get paid for the stuff?"

"Hey, settle down. There are 'cops' everywhere between here and Kansas City," the skinny one responded. "Yeah, we got paid, but it's only thirty cents on the dollar." He pitched a wad of cash onto the table. "They say it's too hard to fence the stuff because we're targeting so many spots in this area."

His chubby pal entered the conversation. "I told both of you that we needed to back off for awhile. Sheriff Garrett is no dummy. Sooner or later, he's going to put two and two together, and then all of us are going to land in prison." The mention of the Auburn sheriff brought an angry reaction from the man holding the rifle.

"Shut up, fat boy! I already told you that the job tomorrow night would be our last one. We'll settle up with our new pal, dump the girl's body, and drop out of sight."

"Speaking of the girl; how's she doing?" the skinny guy asked as he retrieved a beer from the fridge.

"She wasn't moving last time I checked on her. I think she's dying even without our help. Besides, what do you care what happens

166

to her?" He rose from the chair and aimed the rifle at an imaginary target across the room.

"I don't give a damn whether she lives or dies, but I wouldn't mind having some fun with her before it's all over." The suggestion seemed to irk the other two men.

"Man, you really are a sick S.O.B.!" the chubby guy screamed as he lunged forward. The other fellow used his rifle to block his path.

"Leave him alone, fat boy. I don't agree with his kinky ways either, but after tomorrow, she isn't going to be around anymore." He emphasized his point by cranking a bullet into the rifle chamber. "Besides, our new partner was the only one who wanted her kept alive and I don't think he's going to remain in the picture much longer." Then he aimed the rifle at an imaginary target on the far wall and pretended to take a shot. "Pow! Two birds down."

Chapter 15

Mark awoke early the next morning. He wanted to spend some time with Marnie before the sheriff arrived for the trip to Buffalo Mountain. He quickly showered, trying not to disturb his wife, but she was already busy in the kitchen.

"Umm, something smells really good in there," Mark called from the bedroom after getting dressed and pulling on his hiking boots.

"Armenian cheese boeregs and paklava for the school festival tonight. Did you forget about it?" Marnie asked as she pushed a rolling pin over freshly kneaded dough.

Mark had lost track of the days in all of the excitement surrounding Susan Clark. The Auburn School District hosted the festival prior to the beginning of each school year. It provided plenty of food, games, entertainment, and spirited conversation about the prospects for a good sports season. Although newly retired, Mark was expected to be at the event, but it was really Marnie that the community wanted to see. Her ethnic goodies were always popular at the community dinner served in the high school cafeteria.

"I'm sure Larry Ray and I will be back in time for the festival." Mark stepped into the kitchen and grabbed one of the boeregs cooling on sheets of waxed paper. He took a bite of the puffy turnover and a glob of warm cheese ran down his chin. "Wow, those are good!" Marnie used a dishtowel to wipe the trickle of cheese off his chin. A horn sounded, signaling that the sheriff had arrived. Mark was about to step outside when Marnie put her hands around his waist and leaned into him. She pulled his body close and gave him a soft kiss. He understood her message. His lips brushed her ear and he whispered, "Yes, I'll be careful."

Larry Ray blared the horn again. Mark tried to sneak two more cheese boeregs when Marnie wasn't looking, but she detected the theft before he got out the door.

"Mark Sarkisian, you keep your hands off those boeregs or there won't be any left for tonight's festival! I've still got to make two batches of paklava, and I don't want any of it disappearing when you get home." Marnie feigned anger, but she was pleased that he enjoyed her cooking.

"I promise that I'll only sample the paklava to make sure it's okay for public consumption," he joked. "By the way, make sure you put a note on the boeregs and paklava to indicate that it's authentic Armenian food. I wouldn't want anyone to mistake it for Greek baklava."

Marnie had heard the story numerous times from Mark's grandmother about how important it was to not confuse the ethnic cuisines. The kind-hearted woman had emigrated from the "old country" and spoke limited English, so her words always came out with a unique trill. People loved Grandma Sarkisian, and when she talked about her native country, it came forth with gusto. "It's Armenian paklava!" the usually soft-spoken, gracious lady would announce while waving both arms above her head for emphasis. "Those crazy Greeks call it baklava." Soon thereafter, she would make a concession. "Oh, paklava or baklava. Who cares as long as it tastes good!" That was perfectly okay with Marnie because she always thought the Greek and Armenian pastries tasted quite similar, but she kept that opinion to herself. It was a wise decision, and Marnie quickly endeared herself to Mark's family.

The loud horn sounded again and reminded Mark that the sheriff was anxious to get on the road. The lawman knew the window of opportunity for locating the missing teacher was rapidly closing. Mark shouted his signature goodbye as he headed out the door. "Love ya, honey!"

The room that held Susan hostage contained nothing resembling a rope or cord, so the laces of her running shoes would have to do. She bent the tongue of each shoe inward and began retrieving the laces. Clumps of dried mud made it difficult to pull the laces through each eyelet, particularly with bruises and swelling racking her body. The small glint of light coming from the air pipe wasn't much help. Finally, she held two twelve-inch strips of woven fiber. They might just be enough to form a primitive noose.

Susan clutched one of the running shoes and slapped the heel against the floor. It made a loud snapping sound. She knew the spongy innersole that provided extra cushioning during races would not be of any help, so she ripped out the innersole to strengthen the blow. A regular jogging shoe would have provided a weak defense, but the sharp metal spikes protruding through the leather soles provided a formidable weapon.

Susan sat on the cot massaging her bruised shoulder and wondered if her plan to escape was so bizarre that it could only happen in one of those Hollywood C.I.A. movies. The plan wasn't very sophisticated. It called for hitting her captor in the head with a worn running shoe and then choking him with twenty-four inches of shoelace. Somehow she would jab him with a used syringe deep enough to inflict major damage. Then she would run for her life.

The escape plan was a stretch of the imagination, but it was all she had. Susan prayed that it would work.

Chapter 16

"Are you ready for some serious hiking today, buddy?" came a spirited greeting as Mark stepped into the sheriff's SUV. "I brought the department's best all-terrain vehicle, but we can only go so far up the mountain with it," chimed Larry Ray. Mark tossed one of the warm cheese boeregs across the seat and listened to his friend's banter. "Well, all right! Good food, fresh air, and good company. It's going be a great day!" Mark wished he could be as optimistic as his friend.

Forty minutes later, the SUV was in four-wheel drive grinding along a trail that criss-crossed the mountain. The trail became impassable a half-mile from the quarry due to erosion and neglect which created huge ruts. The powerful vehicle was challenged to avoid getting mired in mud from previous rains.

"It looks like we're at the end of the line," the sheriff grumbled when he realized that gunning the engine anymore would result in calling for a tow truck. "We'll have to hoof it the rest of the way."

Mark exited the SUV and grabbed his backpack from the rear seat. He started up the trail and yelled back. "Come on, it's only a few hundred yards. Your tummy can use the exercise." He was fortunate that the distance between the two prevented him from hearing the sheriff's response to the reference that Larry Ray had packed on a few extra pounds.

It was an easy jaunt to the top of a knoll where the men could view the Central States Quarry center of operations. They descended toward the buildings and saw no obvious sign of life. Jubile Walker's truck was nowhere to be seen and the place seemed to be abandoned. The only sounds were the eerie scratchings of rusted equipment swaying in a slight breeze. It was Mark's second trip to the quarry in the past forty-eight hours and he hoped it would provide better results. He was determined to find out if Buffalo Mountain played a role in the disappearance of Susan Clark, and he suspected that the sheriff had something else on his mind. Apparently, Larry Ray was determined to make a point with the quarry's watchman.

"I just want two minutes with that Jubile Walker," the sheriff barked out as he moved his search from one quarry building to another. "When I get through with that idiot, he'll think twice before he threatens anyone again." Mark was thinking that he had underestimated the sheriff when he reported the earlier encounter with Jubile Walker. If Jubile was anywhere near the quarry, he sure wasn't showing his face to the lawman. The doors at each building were all padlocked, an obvious sign that Jubile wanted no one to have access to the facilities while he was away.

"Locked up tighter than a drum," the sheriff yelled from the rear of one building. "I don't think we're going find anything here today." Mark was checking the front door to the main office. He turned the knob even though he could see a padlock had been slipped through a latch to secure the door from entry. He was surprised when the door wobbled. The screws that anchored the door hinges were loose, most likely reamed from years of abusive slamming of the door. A firm tug might pull the entire door off the frame. Mark was tempted. He gripped the doorknob with both hands and braced himself to support the weight of the door when it broke free.

"Hold on there, Mark." Larry Ray had amused himself by watching his friend struggle with the door, but now it appeared Mark might actually be successful in gaining access. The sheriff decided it was time to intervene. "That's breaking and entering, and I'm not about to let you do it." Mark was startled. It was out of character for him to be intruding on a locked building, so he tried to rationalize the situation.

"Uh, sorry. I didn't want us to miss the opportunity to thoroughly check things here," Mark humbly apologized. Larry Ray was sympathetic, but uncompromising.

"I understand, but I'm playing it by the book," the sheriff said in an official tone. "I'll request a warrant from the county judge and my deputies will conduct a thorough search of this whole operation. Otherwise, anything suspicious that we might find inside today could be thrown out of court." Larry Ray's frustration was beginning to show. "My gosh, Mark, I had a hard enough time this morning convincing the judge to give me a search warrant for the Wanatee property just based on that pile of dirt you thought looked suspicious." The sheriff had made his point. The last thing Mark wanted to do was jeopardize a case against Jubile Walker.

"You're right, Larry Ray. I was just anxious to see if we could find anything that has to do with the disappearance," Mark said in a frustrated tone. "If Susan's still alive, her time is running out."

"I understand, Mark," the sheriff consoled, "but if she's on the mountain, then how do you account for her things being found thirty miles away at the river?" Mark didn't have the answer and couldn't explain why he believed so strongly that the young teacher was still alive. "We better get moving if we're going to check out that cabin. There's a few miles of hiking ahead of us," he said as he headed for a narrow path leading up the mountain. Mark knew that Larry Ray was right. The main purpose of the trip was to reach the Wanatee place and get a closer look at what he had seen on the screen in the SRA office.

"I'll be coming right behind you," Mark yelled, but the sheriff was already fifty yards up the slope. The wind died down and the annoying sound of creaking metal momentarily ceased long enough for Mark to catch a hint of something different in the air. He was surrounded by stillness except for a sound so faint that he wasn't sure it even existed. He stood motionless as a slight breeze wisped against his face. Then he heard the sound again, but it was softer than a whisper. The stillness was surreal. Mark felt uneasy as though he were being watched. He quickly spun around but faced only empty buildings and silence. The intensity of the wind increased and sent dust swirls through a graveyard of metal and machinery.

"Hey, are you coming or not?" Larry Ray called from the top of the slope. Mark hesitated and listened, but the haunting sound was gone. He gazed at a high peak and wondered if his imagination was getting the best of him.

———————⊃ο⊂———————

Susan heard the latch on the door grating against the locking mechanism. She was about to have a visitor. Earlier, she had shattered the bare bulb that provided the only light in the room except for what filtered in from the air tube. The room was cloaked with shadows, but her eyes gradually adjusted to the darkness. A person just entering the room would be at a disadvantage. She rolled onto her side on the floor, being careful to leave her back toward the door in order to conceal the shoe clutched in her right hand and the knotted shoestrings in the other hand. The syringe rested safely out of sight against her knee. She crunched her body into a fetal position with her eyes nearly closed to give the appearance of being asleep.

The sound of the door creaking open was frightening, but Susan remained still and tightened her grip on the running shoe. Someone stepped into the room and hesitated. "Damn, what did you do now, bitch?" he yelled, disgusted at the darkness in the room. Susan didn't flinch when she heard him shuffling toward her in the darkened room. He stopped and gawked at the lifeless form beneath him. *"I think I'm gonna enjoy this a whole bunch,"* he muttered. *Susan's lips barely touched as she drew in and exhaled tiny wisps of air to keep her breathing shallow and avoid letting her captor know that she was tracking his every move. A streak of panic shot through her body when she detected the sound of a zipper sliding open and clothes rustling. "Umm, that feels much better," the creep sighed as he pushed his pants to his ankles. "Now we can have some fun."*

Chapter 17

It didn't take long for Mark to catch up to the sheriff and pass him on the primitive trail leading to Hidden Valley. His daily jogging routine had prepared him with enough stamina to handle the incline of the treacherous path. The sheriff wasn't nearly as adept at hiking.

"Whoa, slow down a bit!" Larry Ray yelled. "I'm not in the best of shape in case you hadn't noticed. In fact, I'm bushed!" The distance between the two men had been steadily increasing, and Mark hadn't noticed that his friend was struggling to keep up. It became a moot point as Mark crested the bluff overlooking Hidden Valley.

"Sorry, buddy, I forgot you're not still playing ball for the Auburn Wildcats," Mark joked, recalling that years ago Larry Ray had been one of the school district's outstanding athletes. "There's the Wanatee place." He pointed toward a structure nestled among a grove of trees. "Come on, let's check it out."

The two men had to cross a small brook as they approached the homestead. Mark carefully stepped on rocks to cross the shallow water until he decided that one giant leap would get him to the opposite bank.

Larry Ray didn't have much confidence in Mark when it came to his abilities in track and field. "You weren't that good in high school track, so what makes you think you can do a standing long-jump across six feet of water?" Mark wasn't about to turn down the challenge, even though he was beginning to teeter on a loose stone in the middle of the brook. He regained his balance and crouched into a squat position with his arms cocked behind him, and then he sprang forward. It would have been a clean leap except the rock he was balanced on began to roll and reduced his thrust. The jump wouldn't set any records, but it was good enough to give him satisfaction as his boots slid onto green moss at the opposite shoreline. The feat was quickly overshadowed when he became entangled in rope. Mark had failed to see a makeshift clothesline that stretched between two pine trees. In the haste to prove his athletic prowess, he fell to the ground like a roped calf.

"What the hell!" Mark yelled as he worked to untangle himself. Larry Ray had opted to try leaping from one stone to another but had missed more than once. He stepped onto the opposite shore in waterlogged boots and wet socks.

"I'd say you just tumbled into the Indian family's laundry room," the sheriff said trying to contain his laughter. "You see those towels over there?" he added, pointing at a clump of folded cloth next to a pine tree. "They probably do their laundry here during nice weather." He sat on a dead log and began removing his boots as Mark attached the untangled rope to another tree. The next five minutes were spent with Larry Ray airing out his damp socks and chiding his friend about his lack of track and field talent. Mark gracefully accepted the playful ribbing because he was fascinated to learn more about the people who still did their laundry in a stream.

The two men cautiously approached the cabin ten minutes later. The pictures Mark had seen in the SRA office had not done it justice. The transmission from the satellite made the building look primitive, but the actual structure seemed to be a masterful feat of carpentry. The entire structure appeared to have been done by hand without the benefit of power tools. The foundation and chimney must have been created using large stones from the mountain, and the exterior walls were likely cut and shaped from timbers in the nearby forest. The two men circled the cabin and were surprised to discover a smaller wood structure. It was a crude building, possibly better suited for storage rather than habitation.

"I'll bet they used this little place for living quarters while they worked on the main building," the sheriff commented as he approached what remained of a padlocked front door. "There's no sense poking around this shack because it's probably just full of raccoons." He motioned for Mark to follow him back to the main cabin where they could get a better look at the impressive structure. "They must have done this whole thing with mules and axes judging by those heavy rocks and hack marks," Larry Ray remarked, shaking his head in amazement. "There was no electricity and no power equipment, and they built something that looks like it came from an architect's blueprint. It's very impressive."

"The Native Americans are known for their self-reliance and respect for natural resources," Mark commented as he continued to scan the building's exterior. Then something peaked his interest some distance away. "There it is, Larry Ray!" The yell came with a sense of urgency. "Come on, let's check it out." Mark broke into a hurried stride toward a plot of dirt that appeared to be freshly disturbed. In his haste, he failed to realize that the sheriff wasn't following. The lawman was stepping onto the porch of the cabin and was gingerly approaching the front door. Evidently the sheriff didn't want to be caught off guard investigating a pile of dirt if there was danger inside the cabin. He noticed that the latch wasn't secured with a padlock, so he knocked on the door. He kept a hand close to his holstered weapon.

"Hello? Is anyone home? This is Sheriff Larry Ray Garrett." There was no response and the second inquiry came with more gusto. "Hello in the cabin! Mr. Wanatee, are you in there?" There was only silence. The sheriff turned the doorknob and confirmed that the owners must not have expected visitors because the door opened slightly. He turned sideways and peered through the gap between the door and its frame. The only illumination inside appeared to come from what little sunlight filtered through the curtains shading the windows. The sheriff detected no movement, but he wasn't convinced that the place was empty. Law enforcement officers were trained to know that no movement could mean a possible ambush. Larry Ray wondered if having Mark tag along had been such a good idea. Now he was responsible for someone's safety besides his own. He unsnapped the leather strap that secured his weapon inside the holster and prepared to step into the cabin. It was an action he had often repeated during his career and the emotion always remained the same; the anxiety of being in a life-threatening situation followed by a silent prayer. The sheriff's hand gently nudged the front door to widen the opening, and then he took a deep breath before stepping inside.

"Hey, Sheriff. I thought breaking and entering was against the law." The shout from behind caught Larry Ray by surprise. Instinctively, he drew his weapon and spun around to confront the person who continued to banter. "You know, play it by the book and all that legal jargon." Mark had a silly smile on his face as he approached the front porch.

Larry Ray shoved his pistol into the holster and unleashed a flurry of expletives. It wasn't until he regained his composure that the language became more civil. "Mark, you son-of-a gun!" he said while shaking his fist in the air. "What are you doing sneaking up on a fellow like that? I might have shot you."

"I just didn't want to see you get in trouble for breaking the law," Mark calmly replied. "After all, you are the head law enforcement officer of the county."

Larry Ray was flustered, but he wasn't about to let Mark get the best of him. "For your information, wise guy, it's a gray area of the law whether or not it's a violation since the door was not locked." The sheriff made his point and then shifted the conversation. "Well, did you find anything over there?" he said pointing toward the pile of dirt.

"I'm afraid I did, and it's definitely not a tilled garden." Mark stammered for words that were appropriate. "It's has all the appearance of a grave, a very fresh grave."

The sheriff wasn't ignoring Mark, but his eyes were scoping the landscape. The mention of a gravesite put him on the alert that they might be in a dangerous situation. He placed an index finger on his lips signaling for Mark to hush just in case they weren't alone. Mark took a step toward the front porch, but the sheriff quickly motioned for him to stay put. He froze in mid-stride and kept his eyes fixed on the lawman crouched next to the door. The sheriff clutched the grip of his revolver and pushed the door open. From his vantage point, Mark could tell it was dark inside the cabin. The window curtains only allowed a small amount of light to funnel inside. The sunlight spilling through the doorway failed to illuminate the entire room. The sheriff pulled a small flashlight from a case clipped to his gun belt and turned it on. Mark's breathing became more intense as he watched his friend disappear into the cabin. Half a minute passed, then a minute, and then two minutes that seemed like an hour.

There was no sound from the cabin and Mark began to worry if something bad had happened inside. He wasn't sure if he should approach the cabin, but it seemed silly to just

186

stand outside unprotected. Finally, he couldn't take the suspense any longer; too much time had passed. He decided to find out what had happened to the sheriff. Mark searched the ground for something to use as a weapon, but the Wanatees seemed to have been meticulous in keeping the property in good order. The landscaping was neat and quaint, resembling a picture right out of a country-living magazine. Fortunately, it included a large cluster of wildflowers bordered by a row of round stones of various sizes. Mark pulled one of the rocks from the arrangement and tossed it in his hand to make sure it had sufficient weight to inflict damage. He mustered his courage and stepped onto the porch with the primitive weapon clutched above his head.

"It's all clear. You can come inside now," the sheriff said stepping into the doorway. He was amused to see Mark poised with the rock as though he were preparing to launch a shot put. "We better make it fast. There's no telling when those people are coming back, and I'd rather have deputies with me when I meet them face to face." Mark took a quick glance over his shoulder and hurried inside the cabin. The sunlight spilling through the doorway gave the dimly lit room an eerie feeling as tiny specks of dust floated in the air. The simple furnishings along the outer portions of the room remained in shadows.

"I'll have us some more light in a minute." The sheriff grabbed a kerosene lantern off a wooden table. "There's no electricity, but at least I found these," he said as he held up a used book of matches and raised the lantern's glass chimney. He struck a match and held it to the wick. Once the clear glass was lowered over the small flame, the room became illuminated in an orange glow. Sheriff Garrett handed Mark the lantern and retrieved his flashlight. Mark raised the lantern above his head in order to spread the light and it became obvious that the room had multiple functions. An unmade bed in one corner suggested that the two men were standing in someone's bedroom. The sheriff moved across the room to an area near the bed. Something had caught his attention and he aimed his flashlight toward a section of the floor. Larry Ray was on his knees with his head poked under the bed by the time Mark brought more light from the lantern.

"It's a trap door, about three-feet square," Larry Ray whispered as though he and Mark weren't the only people in the cabin.

Mark dropped to his knees and peeked under the bed. "Why would they have a trap door in the cabin? And, why is it padlocked?"

The sheriff had crawled under the bed for a closer examination and reminded Mark to keep his voice down. "It might be nothing,"

Larry Ray continued to whisper, "or there could be a tunnel." Mark scooted farther under the bed to hear an explanation. "Years ago people built underground rooms as hidden escape routes. You know, like the Underground Railroad that helped slaves escape to freedom during the Civil War." Mark's imagination was triggered: *If Susan Clark is just a few feet beneath us, then why can't we hear her calling for help? Are we too late?*

The sheriff yanked the padlock and Mark felt a rush of adrenalin. He could swear that he was hearing his own heart beating as the sheriff banged the floorboards with his fist, but the padlock held fast. He tried a second time and the lock refused to budge.

"Shoot it open, Larry Ray!" Mark gasped. "Susan may be down there! Go on, shoot the lock off!" He had ceased whispering and was now yelling. Larry Ray pushed himself out from under the bed and rose to his feet. Mark quickly followed, looking bewildered.

"Take it easy, Mark. I think you may have been watching too many cop shows on television," the lawman scoffed. "Just because there's a trapdoor with a padlock on it doesn't mean there's any foul play here. Maybe they're just storing supplies down there. It could be a potato cellar for all we know." The sheriff was making sense, but Mark wondered why anyone would padlock a potato cellar.

"I suppose you're right, but indulge me for just a moment." The sheriff didn't know where the conversation was headed until Mark bent down and beat his fist on the floor. "Susan!" Mark yelled. "Susan, are you down there?" Mark banged again and then paused to listen. There was nothing but silence.

"I promise you that we'll investigate the trapdoor when I return with my deputies to do a more thorough search," Larry Ray explained. "Come on; let's get on with searching the rest of this place. I'll take the main room and you can check out what's behind those three doors," he said, pointing the flashlight beam across the room.

Mark raised the lantern higher in order to see the doors that the sheriff had identified. He approached the first one and found it unlocked. He lost the advantage of the sheriff's flashlight when he stepped inside. The glow of the lantern revealed a large bed that occupied a major portion of the room. Mark supposed he was standing in the master bedroom, although it wasn't spacious by any means. A wooden chair and a small dresser completed the decor. The furnishings looked hand-made, most likely from the same timber that had been used to build the cabin. He had expected to find a dusty room, but instead he was impressed that everything looked clean. A framed picture on the dresser captured his attention. He picked up the 5x7 photo and studied it. It featured a young couple holding hands in front of a merry-go-round. Mark brought the lantern closer to read what was scribbled in one corner of the photo... *"Arixie and Israel Wanatee at Lake Contrary Amusement Park"*

Mark paused long enough to do a quick calculation: *My gosh! This photo is more than fifty years old. That amusement park doesn't even exist anymore. If these two are Noah's parents, they must have had the boy really late in life.* Mark continued to look at the picture of the smiling young couple. The longer he stared, the more he wondered what motivated them to put down roots in a desolate place at the top of a mountain. He carefully replaced the picture onto the dresser and exited the room.

The next door led to a bathroom. It wasn't elaborate- just a stool, sink, and tub. "Hey, at least they have indoor plumbing," Mark called toward the beam of light coming from the kitchen area. "I wonder how they get water into this place."

"Well, city boy, it's probably gravity-fed from a tank outside. It's likely to be freezing cold in the winter." Then the sheriff added a footnote, "It sure beats grabbing a corn cob and visiting an outdoor privy!"

Mark wasn't interested in hearing any more about Larry Ray's personal experiences with roughing it in the great outdoors, so he entered the final room. It had a simple design similar to the previous bedroom, with the exception of being smaller. There was only a single bed and small dresser. He looked around the room and realized that there was no closet. Instead, clothing hung from a row of pegs that were mounted on one wall. Mark gave the wall a closer examination and wondered why the pegs weren't lower to accommodate a person of average height. The clothes hooked over the pegs were meager; just two pairs of overalls, a plaid shirt, camouflaged ball cap, and a bath towel. Mark was humbled as he stood facing what represented Noah Wanatee's simple closet: *These people live such a simple lifestyle. They're completely isolated from the world, but perhaps they're content.*

He was about to leave the room when he noticed a small piece of paper on the floor. He held the lantern closer to get a better look at the object and his emotions stirred. Mark sat on the edge of the bed for several moments looking at one word on the pink slip of paper, *Teaberry.* He knew that it was a stretch of the imagination to think Noah Wanatee was fond of the same chewing gum as Susan Clark, especially since that brand wasn't generally found in the local stores. The obvious conclusion was that it belonged to Susan and the Wanatee family had some serious explaining to do. Mark was about to do a more thorough search when a shout came from the other room.

"Hey, Mark, come here. I found something you should see." The sheriff was evidently on to something, so Mark took a quick look around the bedroom for any other signs that the woman may have been at the cabin. He tucked the gum wrapper in his shirt pocket for safekeeping until he could show it to the sheriff.

Larry Ray was standing in the kitchen area with his flashlight pointing at a yellowed newspaper article attached to the cupboard door. "It's about the old Indian," he announced as he leaned closer to read the clipping from the *St. Joseph Gazette.* "This story must be a half-century old." Mark's interest peaked as he listened to the sheriff paraphrase the news story. "Well, son-of-a-gun," Larry Ray blurted out. "Mr. Wanatee is something of a hero according to this article."

"Okay, you've got my attention." Mark was rather frustrated that it was taking so long to get the story from the sheriff. "Just tell me what it's about."

"Well, it says that Israel Wanatee saved a lady from being assaulted outside of the Bucket Shop Restaurant in St. Joseph,

Missouri." The sheriff's recounting of the story sounded as though it were being delivered by a news broadcaster. "Evidently, the thug pulled a gun when Wanatee tried to help the woman." He paused to read more details before continuing. "That's when the Indian applied deadly force with his knife." The sheriff paused again but quickly continued when he noticed Mark getting agitated. "There was a trial and the jury found Israel Wanatee not guilty. It was definitely a clear case of self-defense."

"My goodness, I would not have imagined that such a quiet man would put himself in a dangerous situation like that," Mark exclaimed, shaking his head. "And no one else around Auburn seemed to know anything about it either. Is there any more to the article?"

"Just one sentence," the sheriff said as he finished reading the piece. "The people in St. Joseph wanted to give Mr. Wanatee a civic commendation for rescuing the lady, but he wasn't anywhere to be found. He just disappeared right after the trial."

"And sixty years later, Israel Wanatee is a recluse living on Buffalo Mountain, and we're wondering if he's somehow connected to Susan Clark?" Mark shook his head in disbelief, but didn't get an immediate response.

The sheriff was shining his flashlight around the room as though he sensed danger.

"We better get out of here, Mark." Larry Ray spoke with a sense of urgency. "I'll be back tomorrow with a lot more manpower." He motioned Mark toward the front door. "And yes, someone's going to explain about that pile of fresh dirt near the cabin."

"Hold on, Larry Ray. I found something in that bedroom that you need to see." Mark reached into his shirt pocket to retrieve the gum wrapper, but the sheriff quickly responded.

"Not now, Mark. I'll deal with the Wanatees later." He tried to hurry Mark out of the room, but it was too late. The sheriff got his wish sooner than expected. The front door suddenly banged open and both men were caught in a burst of intense sunlight. They shielded their eyes from the brightness and heard the sound of feet shuffling into the room. By the time they adjusted to the sunlight, two ominous figures were pointing rifles in their direction. The Wanatees were back, and they weren't happy to have visitors.

———◦———

The man who was about to molest Susan dropped to his knees and leaned forward until his cheek brushed against her neck. She resisted the urge to jerk away, knowing that she needed just a little more time to get him positioned for her retaliation attack. Feeling the stubble of a scraggly beard against her skin, she realized that the stench she smelled was coming from a dribble of chewing tobacco that had pooled on his chin. She felt nauseated, and for once since being captured, she was glad that there was not very much food in her stomach. He gripped her shoulder in an attempt to roll her onto her back. When he yanked her left shoulder, she knew it was time to strike. The abrupt movement sent Susan's right hand into the air still clutching the running shoe. She used the momentum to her advantage and hammered the weapon into his face.

Whap! The force of the blow ripped across one eye and slammed against his nose causing a gush of blood to spurt onto the floor. He released the hold on Susan's shoulder and fell onto the floor holding his nose and screaming in pain. Susan seized the opportunity to grab the ends of the knotted shoestrings in both hands and loop them around the disoriented man's neck, and then she pulled with every ounce of energy she had left. He reacted instantly, reaching for his neck and trying to free himself from the noose that was cutting off his airflow. Susan continued to pull the laces tighter and tighter until she *heard a sickening gurgle coming from his throat. She felt his struggle begin to subside and knew that the predator could not last much longer.*

For a moment, Susan wondered if she was actually capable of ending a life. She had been subjected to three days of uncivilized captivity, practically starved to death, humiliated, and degraded. Now she considered doing the honorable thing by saving the man who had tried to rape her. She made her decision and pulled the noose tighter. He let out a moan as his head was lifted off the floor until Susan thought his neck would snap any second. The shoestrings around his neck couldn't take the strain and finally split under the continuous pressure. Susan catapulted off the man's back. She rolled across the floor and saw the half-naked man gasping for air and trying to stand. She spied the syringe a few feet away and crawled to retrieve it. She grabbed the syringe and struggled to get to her feet, hoping to use it as a lethal weapon before he regained his composure. She disregarded the excruciating pain surging through her body and limped until she stood over him as he tried to get on his feet. Then Susan raised the needle above her head preparing to plunge it into the back of his neck, but he realized what was happening and knocked the syringe out of her hand. He was quickly recovering, but Susan's strength was nearly spent. She mustered the energy to drive her knee into the man's groin. He dropped to the floor screaming in pain. It was her only chance to escape, and she took it.

The door was only twelve feet away, but it might as well have been a mile. Susan took one agonizing step after another trying to reach it before the fellow writhing on the floor could recover. She stepped into a hallway and leaned against the door to inch it closer to the latch. A quick glance back into the darkened room confirmed the guy was still rolling on the floor in pain. "You bitch!" he screamed. "I will kill you!" The threat didn't have much impact after what Susan had just been through. She closed the door and slammed the latch into place to seal the prison.

Chapter 18

"What are you doing here?" Israel Wanatee said, pointing his weapon at the intruders. Noah took a strategic position by his father's side, clutching the same rifle that Mark had encountered two days earlier. It was a precarious situation, but the sheriff wasn't about to be intimidated.

"Now, just a minute, Mr. Wanatee. I'm Sheriff Larry Ray Garrett. I'll be the one asking the questions around here," the sheriff scolded. "You've got some explaining to do about what's buried outside." He stepped forward, but the sudden movement caused the two armed men to cock their rifles. The sheriff paused and raised his hands to show he was backing off. He cautioned Mark not to make any sudden moves. "I think that rifle the old man is holding is an 1874 Sharps buffalo gun." Larry Ray obviously knew more about weapons than the average citizen. "It fires a 44/90 caliber shot that will put a cannonball hole in a person from a distance of eight hundred yards." The sheriff had made his point, and now Mark stood frozen while gawking at the rifles aimed in his direction. He gave Larry Ray a nod to indicate that he understood the warning. Mark figured if the sheriff was willing to confront the two armed men, then he should be aware of the suspicious item found in the bedroom. He slowly reached into his shirt pocket and pulled out the gum wrapper.

"Sheriff, I found this on the floor in the small bedroom." Mark held up the wrapper without taking his eyes off the two men in the doorway. Larry Ray took a quick look at the distinctive sliver of paper and weighed his options. The revelation of the gum wrapper and the disturbed plot of dirt suggested that the old man and son might be associated with the missing teacher. If that were true, then he and Mark might never make it off the mountain. Larry Ray unsnapped the leather strap on his holster, never taking his eyes off the two men.

"What's the deal, chief?" the sheriff said, easing his hand onto the grip of the .44 Colt. "How did you come to have this in the cabin?" He pointed at the wrapper that Mark was still holding in mid-air. Israel Wanatee kept his finger on the trigger of the vintage rifle and looked at his son for the response. The younger man acknowledged his father and spoke for the first time since entering the cabin.

"I found the gum paper on the hiking trail two days ago," Noah Wanatee said in a calm tone. It seemed that the sheriff wasn't buying the story. "Yes, I know it's odd since very few people use the trail anymore." The young man sounded apologetic and posed a question to the sheriff. "Is it a crime to keep a chewing gum wrapper?"

"That's not the issue, kid," Sheriff Garrett said, pointing his finger at Noah's chest. "That little slip of paper may be connected to a missing person, and that fresh mound of dirt not a hundred yards away from your home doesn't help your case much!" Mark was afraid that a bad situation was about to get worse, particularly when he noticed the sheriff's right hand easing his pistol out of the holster. The older Indian was equally observant. Israel Wanatee shouted a warning in his native language and twitched his finger on the trigger of his rifle. Noah was caught off guard by his father's actions and quickly raised his rifle into a shooting position. Mark feared the cabin was about to erupt with gunfire. The sheriff drew his weapon and crouched into a firing stance as he pointed his gun at one man and then the other. He clenched his teeth and whispered to his friend. "You better take cover, Mark. It's *Custer's Last Stand*, and we're on the losing side."

Mark might have chuckled at the colorful choice of words if the gathering had been more congenial, but this was the real thing. He looked around the room but saw nothing that would afford adequate protection if the men decided to start blasting. No one flinched as each man waited for the other to make the first move. Mark wasn't sure what to do, but he wasn't willing to let a tragedy take place. Instead, he opted to do something reckless. He raised the palms of his hands as a gesture of peace and blurted out the only thing he could think to say.

"Whoa, hold on there, *Kemo sabe.*" The strange words startled everyone in the room. "We don't mean you any harm. We're just trying to find out what happened to someone." The explanation was sincere and captured the attention of the other three men. "Mr. Wanatee, that's the only reason Sheriff Garrett and I are here today," Mark continued. "If you say Noah found that *Teaberry* wrapper on the trail, that's good enough for me." He wasn't sure if his rambling plea did any good. The three men remained locked in a deadly stare that was accompanied by an occasional twitch of a nervous trigger finger. Mark lowered his head, dejected that he had failed to defuse the volatile situation.

Then something unexpected happened. Israel Wanatee's stoic face cracked a slight grin that gradually turned to a compromising smile. He eased off the hammer of the buffalo gun and signaled for his son to lower his rifle. The sheriff was perplexed, but he rose from the shooting position and reluctantly holstered his weapon. The near-tragic standoff had come to an end.

"You should leave now," Israel Wanatee said as he motioned toward the open door. Noah kept his rifle ready as a warning for the uninvited guests that they still remained on unfriendly ground.

Sheriff Garrett was willing to momentarily put the situation to rest, but not before he made his point. "Okay, we'll head out, but I want you to understand me loud and clear," he said, poking a finger at the older Indian's chest. "I'll be back with a search warrant and my deputies." Noah immediately raised his rifle, but his father motioned for him to remain calm. Israel Wanatee had fought other battles during his lifetime. Today he was satisfied with a truce that would maintain his dignity.

Mark just wanted to get out of the cabin in one piece and was relieved when the sheriff walked out the door. He started to leave but Noah blocked his path. The young man had something to say.

"Dr. Sarkisian, the dirt?" he choked with emotion.

"Yes, Noah. What about the dirt?" Mark detected sadness in the young man's eyes.

"It is my mother. She became so ill that we had to care for her in this room," Noah said motioning toward the bed in the corner of the living room. "She died two days ago," he continued after wiping a tear from his eye. "She loved the mountain, so her headstone will come from the mountain." Mark grasped Noah's hand to indicate that he understood his sorrow, but then Noah said something that confused Mark. "Please forgive my father, Dr. Sarkisian. He is suspicious that you men want our land just like the other man who came before you." Mark had no idea what he was referring to, but he didn't pursue it because Israel Wanatee swung the barrel of his rifle to signal that it was time to leave. He stopped Mark as he was walking past him on the way to the door.

"*Kemo sabe?* Good words, but wrong tribe." The proud man drew back his shoulders and set the record straight, "We are of the Meskwaki Nation!" The revelation threw Mark for a loop. He hadn't heard a reference to the ancient tribe of Native Americans since he studied American history during his college years. Centuries earlier, the name "Meskwaki" was often defined as the "red earth people" but Mark had no idea that there were any of them living in the region. Mark nodded to indicate that he understood and then eased through the doorway.

Sheriff Garrett was on the trail leading back to the vehicle when Mark finally caught up with him. He was steaming mad and assured Mark that a return visit accompanied by deputies would bring results at the Wanatee place.

"That's your business," Mark said, not wanting to further anger the sheriff. "But it's too much of a coincidence for that *Teaberry* wrapper to just show up." Then Mark remembered to tell the sheriff what he had learned while exiting the cabin. "Listen, Larry Ray, I sure don't have all the answers, but when Noah Wanatee tells me his mother is buried in that primitive grave and some guy has caused them to be on their guard, well then things just don't add up." Mark gave the sheriff a stern look and announced, "I'm convinced Susan Clark was on this mountain."

"It doesn't make sense," the sheriff said shaking his head in disbelief. "We find some of her stuff at the river thirty miles from here, and then the gum wrapper shows up not a mile from where we're standing right now. Mark, it just doesn't add up."

"I'm as baffled as you are, Larry Ray, but the clock is ticking and there's only so much time left to find her." The sheriff didn't voice his opinion, although he feared that

Susan's time might have already expired. He looked toward the sun and realized it was getting to be late in the afternoon. "It will be dark in a few hours and the mountain is too dangerous at night," he declared. "I'll come back with my men at first daylight. If she's on the mountain, we'll find her," he paused, "one way or the other."

The two men followed the trail for twenty minutes before taking a break. Larry Ray sat on a boulder, removing his boot. "Sometimes I don't know about you, Mark. One minute I can understand you and the next minute you switch to another language." He shook a pebble from his boot and rubbed his toes. The comment brought back childhood memories for Mark when his parents spoke only the ethnic language when discussing topics that were not intended for young ears.

"Well, it wasn't Armenian, and evidently it's not Meskwaki," Mark chuckled. "I thought it meant 'trusted friend' in their language, but I must have picked the wrong tribe." He hunched his shoulders like a man in doubt. Larry Ray pulled on his boot and scratched his head.

"Well, I don't really care if it was Native American, Armenian, or Swahili for that matter. I'm just glad it calmed things down back there," the sheriff said, stepping into his boot. Mark accepted the compliment with a smile and started back on the trail. It wasn't long before Larry Ray yelled another question as he hustled to catch up. "By the way, Mr. Smarty-pants. Where the heck did you learn to speak an Indian language?"

"I wondered when you would get around to asking," Mark responded without turning around. "Evidently you didn't watch many television reruns of *The Lone Ranger and Tonto* during your law enforcement training." Larry Ray couldn't see the satisfied look on Mark's face.

It was nearly dusk when the sheriff dropped Mark off at his house. Both men were exhausted, but they still had obligations that evening. The school festival would be getting underway soon. Mark stood outside the farmhouse watching the taillights of the police vehicle disappear in the distance. Quarter was excited to see him, but then she plopped down and inquisitively gazed into a large tree that was home to a noisy locust. The moon was partially shadowed by clouds that would deliver another round of moisture later in the evening. Mark yawned and stretched his weary body. The evening seemed to be quite pleasant other than the annoying buzz of the locust. There was nothing to indicate that in a few hours he and his wife would find their lives in peril.

Susan could still hear the molester screaming in pain as she paused to gather her strength outside of the room where she had spent three torturous days. Her thoughts shifted to getting out of the building and she worried if the man's partner was nearby. She quietly moved along the hallway until she reached the stairs that she had been dragged down just days earlier. She listened for any sound coming from above. Hearing nothing, she took one painful step after another until she reached a closed door at the top of the stairs. She paused to listen again and then turned the doorknob. She was surprised when she stepped into the room and saw sunlight for the first time in three days. She went to a window and scanned the grounds. There was no sign of the other fellow or a vehicle, but she needed to get as far away as possible before he showed up. She opened the front door and savored a breath of fresh air. Then she began to limp toward the path that led down the mountain.

After fifteen minutes of struggling on the rough terrain, Susan's body finally gave out and she fell to the ground. Her blood sugar level was already dangerously low before the fight for her life at the building. Now her cells were losing the battle against hypoglycemia.

Death could come at any time from kidney failure, stroke, heart attack, or any number of maladies. She remained semi-conscious on the trail for several minutes until she detected someone coming in her direction. Her vision was blurred and she couldn't tell if it was a man or woman.

"Help me. Please, help me!" Her plea was weak, but it caught the person's attention. The man was startled to see a young woman lying in the middle of the trail. He cautiously approached and knelt by her side as she struggled to explain her predicament. "Please, I need help...need liquids...insulin...there's danger." Susan pointed a weak finger in the direction of the building that had held her captive. The man appeared to be somewhat bewildered but offered assistance.

"Take it easy, lady," he said in an excited voice. "I'll get you some help, but you better take in some water first." He helped Susan into a sitting position and gave her a drink from a water bottle that had been attached to his belt.

"Thank God you came along when you did," she muttered as she continued to gulp the water. "I had almost given up hope that anyone would find me. It's not safe here." She clutched the man's shirt and tried to get up but was too weak and fell to the ground.

"Easy, lady, you're not in any condition to travel," the man cautioned as he sprinkled drops of cool water on Susan's forehead. "Just close your eyes and rest a few minutes until you get your strength back." She knew it was good advice. Trying to make it off the mountain could be fatal in her present condition. He continued to help lower her body temperature by dabbing water on her head and arms. For the first time in days, Susan began to relax and feel there was still hope to make it off the mountain alive.

Chapter 19

It was almost 7:00 p.m. when the Sarkisians arrived at the festival and entered the high school gymnasium. Judging by the large crowd of adults and children, most of the people in Auburn and their relatives from nearby communities had decided it was a good opportunity for some entertainment and fellowship. Decorations with banners, streamers, and balloons bearing the school colors were displayed throughout the building. Numerous gaming booths encircled the perimeter of the gymnasium and offered chances to win prizes in return for a nominal donation to the school district's education fund. The proceeds would be discretely distributed to families that lacked the financial resources to purchase school supplies. The adults who weren't participating in games with their children were either visiting the classrooms and teachers or enjoying a free potluck dinner in the school cafeteria.

"I'll take the cheese boeregs and paklava to the lunchroom and meet you back here,"

Marnie said, knowing that Mark was anxious to visit with people in the gymnasium.

"That will be mighty fine," Mark responded. "Shawn and the grandkids should already be here. I'll see if I can locate them."

Several parents greeted Marnie as she walked through the hallway leading to the school cafeteria. She was popular in the community and people appreciated the little extras she did to support the school district. It was obvious that she volunteered due to a love for children and not because it was something expected of the superintendent's wife. In addition, the patrons had grown to love the "goodies" that Marnie provided at special events. Many of the Auburn locals had never tasted the Armenian foods before she and Mark arrived in the community, but now they were hooked on them. Marnie continued to add a bit more sugar, nuts and honey to her paklava over the years, which helped to gain more support for the superintendent and the school district.

By the time she reached the cafeteria, several people were following her hoping to be first in line to taste the delectable foods. Many of the visitors had already gone through the serving line and were seated at lunchroom tables enjoying the food and conversation. One table stood out from the rest. It was occupied by the Canterbury family, leaving very little seating for other diners. Marnie noticed two empty chili bowls in front of Aubrey Canterbury. A mess of crumbled crackers and brown stains on the tablecloth indicated the contents of the bowls were probably now percolating inside Toad's belly. She continued to watch as a volunteer server approached Toad with an offer of second helpings. The obese Canterbury didn't utter a word. He simply motioned for the kindly senior citizen to refill his empty chili bowls and dump a handful of crackers on the table. The scene with Canterbury disgusted Marnie, but she continued distributing her cheese boeregs and paklava onto the dessert table.

"Not a very pretty sight is it, Mrs. Sarkisian?" expressed a dapper gentleman as he pointed toward the Canterbury's table.

"Dr. Wayne, I'm sorry I didn't see you there." Marnie's attention shifted to a man wearing an apron and wiping off a vacated table. "Yes, it's obvious that Aubrey never read an Emily Post book about etiquette."

People were fond of Dr. Andrew Wayne. He had provided medical care to Auburn families for forty-five years. Many, many years earlier, there was speculation that the young doctor would stay in the area only a short time. The Co-op gang even took wagers on whether or not the talented physician could make a decent living in the rural area. However, the doctor with the gentle disposition fooled everyone when he declined several lucrative offers to practice medicine in the city hospitals. Dr. Wayne continued to serve each generation of Auburn families, and none of the old-timers ever collected on the bet. Some years later, the question at the Co-op shifted to, "How much longer do you think 'old Doc' Wayne will continue to practice medicine?"

Marnie was enjoying her conversation with the popular physician. "Dr. Wayne, I want to thank you for all you've done. It's been a blessing for our area."

"It's very nice of you to say that, but I'm not sure everyone in Auburn County would agree with you," he responded, while revealing a slight blush. "Some think I could have benefited the area much more with regard to treating a few patients."

The comment surprised Marnie. "Why, I can't imagine anyone suggesting something like that." She had never heard a negative comment about Dr. Wayne.

The doctor nodded in Toad's direction. He was finishing off his third bowl of chili. "Do you see Aubrey Canterbury over there?"

"Yes, of course," she responded with raised eyebrows. "It would be hard to miss him."

"Well, some folks have intimated that I should have done a lobotomy on Aubrey instead of just setting his broken leg the day he got bucked off that mule at the Co-op." The doctor broadened his smile and gave Marnie a wink.

The comment caused her to burst into laughter loud enough to draw the attention of several patrons. Her face took on an embarrassed color of rose. She quickly regained her composure and whispered, "Dr. Wayne, I know you're just joking, but I completely agree."

Aubrey Canterbury remained oblivious to much of the activity in the lunchroom. He sauntered to the dessert table and sampled several treats before loading a plate with cheese boeregs and squares of paklava. By now, many of the early arrivals had finished their meals and had left the cafeteria to participate in the other activities. Dr. Wayne posed a question as he continued to briskly wipe a table.

"I understand that Mark has been helping the sheriff with the search for the missing teacher," he said, lowering his head to the table to eyeball his handiwork. "Have there been any new developments?"

"That's a good question," Marnie replied and grabbed a dishtowel to help with the cleaning. "They're going to continue searching for her tomorrow on the mountain. Mark's worried that with her medical condition there isn't much time left."

"Perfect!" The doctor stepped back to admire the table he finished cleaning.

"Perfect?" Marnie was confused by his choice of words.

The doctor ran his hands across the shiny table. "I'm referring to the table. It's perfectly sanitized for the next group of diners."

Suddenly Marnie realized that Andrew Wayne remained a doctor even when cleaning a table. "Dr. Wayne, I thought for a moment you were referring to Susan Clark." The doctor realized that he had confused his message.

"Please accept my apology, Marnie. I must have gotten a little carried away with my cleaning chores," he joked. "It probably comes from having too much time on my hands now that I'm semi-retired." His eyes revealed a mischievous glint. "Perhaps it's time for me to start frequenting the Co-op." The two shared a laugh, but it wasn't long until Dr. Wayne pursued the original conversation.

"Now, back to the Clark woman," he announced in a professional tone. "It's true her illness is serious, but not necessarily life-threatening unless she ceases to take her medication or suffers an episode." Marnie flashed a confused look. "Yes, an episode," Dr. Wayne continued. "The absence of medication can trigger the onset of an incident that is commonly referred to as an episode in our stuffy medical jargon." Marnie couldn't help but be amused that, in spite of the respected physician's expertise, he could still poke fun at the medical profession. The country doctor was on a roll, continuing to speak as though he were giving a lecture to first-year medical students. His demeanor had shifted from a volunteer kitchen helper to professor of medicine. The white apron he wore would have to double as a physician's smock. Marnie was enjoying the show and listening intently. "You may be wondering about those other factors," the doctor said in anticipation of his friend's question. "Intense anxiety would be one," he stated while raising his index finger to emphasize the number. "The human body is a wonderful work of art *and* science. The good Lord knew what He was doing when He created us!" Dr. Wayne was beginning to sound more like a country preacher. Several people had postponed their meal to hear the doctor as he became more animated by waving his hands and speaking with gusto. "But, all of those organs and systems that contain millions of cells that are supposed to work in harmony can get out of whack during times of trauma. And folks, trauma can cause death!" He emphasized a final point by banging his fist on the table.

The crowd was mesmerized. It may not have been an award-winning speech, but Dr.

Wayne's performance had impressed the impromptu audience. Marnie appreciated the information regarding Susan Clark's medical condition; however, she suspected that "out of whack" was not a term referenced from the *New England Journal of Medicine.*

"I suppose I should be leaving," Dr. Wayne said, tossing the used dishtowel into a pile of discarded cloths. "I have the dubious honor of manning the hospital emergency department in order for the younger staff to attend the festival with their children." The old physician always delighted in telling people that he retired to fish and flirt, but he actually enjoyed continuing to provide care for patients and occasionally filling in at the Auburn County Medical Center. He gave Marnie a hug and started for the door, then turned around to give her another piece of information. "By the way, Mrs. Sarkisian, please tell your husband that he should carry some insulin with him if he intends to continue looking for that woman. She'll most likely be in dire need of it." Dr. Wayne shook his head in a solemn manner, and then added, "That is, if it's not already too late."

"Thanks, I'll be sure to mention that to Mark." She gave a goodbye wave and then joked, "Don't work too hard tonight."

"You needn't worry about that," the doctor called out as he left the cafeteria.

"There's usually not much excitement in the emergency room after midnight."

However, this night would prove to be traumatic for the beloved doctor.

———————◗○◖———————

Earlier that day, Susan had rested for several minutes while the stranger who found her on the trail continued to provide comfort and water to her. She felt more relieved, but her vital signs were still dangerously low. She needed professional help and it wasn't to be found anywhere on the mountain. "I think we should try to move on now," she told the stranger who had remained silent while she rested.

"Okay, lady, but you better take it slow because you still look shaky to me," the man said as he helped Susan to her feet. "I think there might be a shortcut we can take."

Susan wasn't in any condition to disagree, but she wondered if leaving the regular trail was such a good idea. The concern became a moot point when voices were heard coming from the next bend in the trail. She worried that her earlier captors had caught up to her, so she asked the stranger to help her get off the trail. He didn't hesitate to accommodate Susan and carried her to a thick cluster of paw paw shrubs where they could conceal themselves. There was no sense in risking an encounter until they knew if the approaching people were friendly. As they drew closer, Susan could see two men carrying rifles. One man was considerably older than the other. She hoped they could provide assistance and was about to call out when the man huddled next to her grabbed her arm.

"No, stay put," he whispered. "It's not safe." There was a look of fear in his eyes as he watched the men shuffle past the overgrowth and continue along the trail. "They're dangerous men," he whispered to Susan. "They live in Hidden Valley and won't be any help to us." The stranger continued to watch the men until they disappeared from sight and then told Susan it was time to leave. "Come on, we better get going in case they double back," he said while keeping his voice barely above a whisper as though the danger was still present. He helped Susan get up, but her legs gave out and he caught her before she collapsed. "It's okay, I've got you." He was quick to react for a man of his size and Susan fell into his arms. "You're in no condition to walk anywhere. I better carry you, lady." Susan didn't object because she was about to pass out. He struggled to pick her up and Susan wondered how such an obese person could possibly carry her down the mountain.

"Thank you for helping, sir," Susan murmured as her eyes closed. "I'm sorry; I don't even know your name." The man continued to carry Susan's limp body as he walked in the direction of the quarry.

"It's Aubrey. Aubrey Canterbury, but my friends just call me Toad."

Chapter 20

Mark continued to circulate through the gymnasium while he waited for his wife to return from the cafeteria. He watched the children competing in games, and many people stopped to talk with him. Most of them asked whether or not he was enjoying retirement, but eventually the discussion came around to Susan Clark. Although he couldn't share much information, Mark thought that people in Auburn were getting nervous about the adverse impact the disappearance could have on the community. Just about everyone knew that there was a deadline regarding Susan's chances for survival without medication. The national media was likely to pursue the story if she didn't surface within the next twenty-four hours, and the quaintness of Auburn would change overnight.

Mark decided to take a break from the gymnasium activities and wandered through a hallway where amateur entertainment was provided. One room featured three sisters who had performed at the festival for the past forty-eight years. Mary Rose, Carolyn, and Roxy Wilson's first singing engagement at the festival came when they were members of the choir at Auburn High School. The community enjoyed their performance and welcomed the girls back long after they had received their AARP membership cards. They were billed as the Singing Shamrocks, but no one knew how the name originated. The ladies certainly didn't look Irish, and *Oh, Danny Boy* wasn't a song on their program. Some citizens joked that the name may have come because of an occasional nip of Irish whiskey between performances. Now, as senior citizens, the sisters still loved to put on a show. Tonight's audience was bursting into laughter as the three ladies donned Afro wigs and harmonized to *Stop, In the Name of Love*. Mark was also enjoying the performance, but it didn't take his mind off Susan Clark. The sight of so many families sharing happy moments only increased his desire to find her alive. The mixed emotions overshadowed the music in the room, but the audience applause brought him back to reality. The sisters finished their act and were replaced on the stage by an elderly Elvis impersonator attired in a purple jump suit and white silk scarf. Mark decided it was a good time to return to the gymnasium.

"Oh, there you are! I've been looking for you," Marnie said in a cheerful voice when she saw Mark enter the gym.

"Hi, honey. I decided to get away from all the commotion for a few minutes," he said pointing toward the hallway that featured more amateur entertainment. "The three sisters are still belting out tunes, although they're a little off-key this year."

"I can understand," Marnie said in a sympathetic tone. "All three of those ladies have had hip, knee, or other joint replacements. It's a miracle they're not singing from walkers and wheelchairs." The two shared a moment of laughter until Mark felt a tug on the back of his trousers.

"Hi Grandpa! Hi Grandma!" There was no mistaking the sound of the twins greeting their grandparents. Hope and Chase Sarkisian had been enjoying games at the festival, but now they were anxious to share a fishing experience with their grandparents.

Shawn Sarkisian appeared to be worn out from trying to keep up with the twins' energy. He was happy to see his parents, especially since they usually jumped at the opportunity to be with their grandkids. His desire to get some relief by unloading the little ones was squelched when he saw that Mark was obviously very tired. "Its okay, Dad. I imagine it's exhausting to be retired and trying to find something to occupy your time."

Mark ignored the ribbing, knelt on one knee and wrapped his arms around the twins. He pulled the two little ones close to his body and gave them a loving bear hug. "Hey, you two. Did you catch any fish today?"

"I did Grandpa!" Hope beamed as she put her arms around her grandfather's neck. "I caught a blue eel!"

Mark gave a confused look to his son. The pond at the farm had never been stocked with any fish that resembled an eel. Shawn quickly interjected a correction. "She means a bluegill, Dad."

"Blue eel or bluegill; either one is okay with your Grandpa." Mark's wink was rewarded with a huge smile from his granddaughter. Then he turned his attention to the grandson. "Now, Chase, tell me what you caught."

The little boy wasn't going to let his twin sister get the best of him. He crossed his arms and proudly announced, "I caught a lot of worms and some grasshoppers." He paused a few moments as his eyes filled with wonderment. "And, Grandpa, I caught a big toad!" Then he proceeded to stick out his tongue at his sister.

"Chase Sarkisian! Put your tongue back in your mouth," his father reprimanded. Mark and Marnie didn't even attempt to contain their smiles.

"Its okay, Chase," Marnie said, planting a kiss on his cheek. "Evidently your father has forgotten how many times he was told to stop playing with frogs and worms when he was your age." Shawn nodded, conceding that his mother had made her point.

The grandson wiggled his finger and beckoned Marnie to bend closer to him. He hugged her and whispered in her ear, "Thanks, Grandma; next time I'll get some worms for you." Marnie eyes filled with tears of joy.

"I guess I've got my second wind," Shawn said, looking at the two little ones who were eager to play more games. "We can visit a few more booths and then go to the cafeteria for some dinner." Shawn's goodbye to his parents was cut short because the twins were already pulling him in the direction of a ring-toss game.

The missing teacher continued to be the focus of conversations as Mark and Marnie circulated through the gymnasium. Several rumors were being fueled by wild imaginations. Some people speculated that the items discovered near the Missouri River were evidence of a homicide or perhaps even suicide. Others theories were fueled by folklore with claims that Susan had been attacked by a mountain lion or some mysterious creature that had roamed the mountain for hundreds of years. Mark had heard enough. He was anxious for the evening to end.

Marnie's attention shifted as she watched two officers in uniform enter the gym. "There's Kristin and Corporal Nichols." She smiled as the deputy sheriff and state patrolman approached.

Kristin Sarkisian and Collin Nichols had been close friends since attending the law enforcement academy at Missouri Western State University. They both had joined the Auburn County Sheriff's Department following graduation. The young man transferred to the Missouri State Highway Patrol two years later. It was a good career move that did not require relocation, and it gave the trooper an opportunity to continue interacting with local people he was familiar with, including Deputy Kristin Sarkisian.

"Good evening." The trooper acknowledged Marnie and shook Mark's hand. "It's nice to see you again." Mark wasn't surprised by the formal greeting. Collin Nichols had always addressed Kristin's parents with respect. Many people in Auburn County were aware of the trooper's fondness for the Sarkisian's daughter, although he always maintained a high level of professional decorum.

"Hi honey." Marnie gave Kristin a hug. "I'm so glad to see you and Collin at the festival. There are a lot of people here tonight."

"Maybe too much of a crowd," Kristin cautioned. "It helps to have some law enforcement presence when you have characters like that hanging around." She pointed to a corner of the gymnasium. Mark noticed that Corporal Nichols was keeping his eyes on two men leaning against a wall. Most of the people in attendance were socializing and shuffling to different booths, but the two men kept to themselves.

"Hmmm, I wonder what Jubile Walker and Spook Daniels are doing here." Mark had good reason to be suspicious. The two rowdies rarely made it to school when they were students, and they didn't appear to be very engaging on this evening.

"It's hard to tell, but we're keeping an eye on them just in case they do something stupid." The trooper crossed his arms and stayed focused on the two rowdies.

Kristin came right to the point. "Do you see how they're scanning the crowd? We saw them in the cafeteria earlier and they were doing the same thing. You can bet that they're up to no good." Her partner nodded in agreement and wondered how Spook acquired the large bandage covering his left cheek.

"Judging from that wound on his face, it appears that Spook already tangled with the wrong person," the trooper observed. "He looks like he fell into a meat grinder." The levity directed at the thug produced a snicker from Kristin.

Marnie wasn't ignoring the conversation, but she was more interested in discussing other things with Kristin. "Honey, it's nice to see you, but I thought you were off duty."

"I would be, but this is an unusual evening," Kristin answered. "There are a lot of people away from their homes and businesses. It's a perfect opportunity for the wrong people." The others caught Kristin's reference to the burglaries in the county. "Collin and I will be leaving in a few minutes to go on stakeout." Kristin noticed a concerned look from her father. "You don't need to worry, Dad. I'll be fine with Collin as my backup," she said with an affectionate look at the trooper.

Jubile and Spook slipped out of the room and went to the cafeteria to get Aubrey Canterbury. The hallway outside the lunchroom was packed with people talking about how Toad had made quite a mess of himself and the cafeteria. The excessive indulgence on chili and cheese boeregs had not agreed with Toad's digestive system and the result was an ugly sight. Cafeteria workers grimaced as they hurriedly mopped blotches of vomit that had been deposited on the floor as Toad dashed to the nearest restroom. As if the scene weren't nasty enough, a putrid stench indicated that a case of diarrhea accompanied Toad's upset stomach.

"That fat idiot!" Spook yelled in disgust. "We needed him tonight, so he feeds his face and drops his bowels. I swear that I'll murder him if I ever get my hands around his neck!" Spook's ranting was drawing too much attention and prompted Jubile to push him away from the crowd.

"Shut up, Spook," Jubile rasped. "You've got everyone looking at us. Pretty soon they'll start asking questions." His fist pressed into Spook's chin. "We'll swing by Toad's house and pick him up. Now get moving and keep your mouth shut!" Walker snarled as he shoved his buddy toward an exit door.

The Sarkisians finished visiting several booths and decided to leave for home. Mark needed sleep. He planned to call the sheriff early in the morning to request being included on the return trip to Buffalo Mountain. Marnie was happy the evening was coming to an end. She clutched Mark's arm as they walked down a hallway toward an exit door. A few more goodbyes to friendly patrons and the evening would come to a close for the Sarkisians. They could not have picked a worse time to leave.

———◦◦———

Earlier that evening, Jubile and Spook were about to search the mountain trail for Susan following her escape. They were relieved when they saw their buddy coming toward them. Susan was unconscious by the time Toad reached the quarry. His buddies helped to carry her into the chamber she had escaped from just an hour earlier. Her breathing was shallow.

"I've got to hand it to you, Toad," a sneering Jubile Walker said as he pressed a wet towel against Spook Daniels bloodied face. The earlier battle with Susan Clark had taken a toll on Spook's body. "It was a stroke of luck when you came upon the girl on the trail. If she had gotten off the mountain, it would have been all over for us."

"It's a good thing that I took the main trail instead of that washed-out quarry road," Toad replied chomping on a stale donut. "It was a close call when the two Indians almost caught me with the girl. I wouldn't want to tangle with either one of them."

"Oh, shut up, Toad," Spook yelled holding up a mirror to check a nasty gash across his cheek. "The only thing you ever

tangled with was a large plate of food." The two men were about to go at each other when Jubile intervened.

"Both of you settle down!" Neither man was brave enough to challenge Jubile, so they backed away from each other and took a seat. "We need to make plans for tonight. Now, listen to me."

For the next ten minutes, Jubile laid out his plan for robbing the Drovers and Merchants Bank in Auburn. The bank cashed a lot of checks when payday came around at a major employer in the county. That meant a substantial amount of cash was held overnight in a financial institution that had a safe with a faulty lock and an outdated security system. Aubrey Canterbury had worked at the bank for a short stint until he was caught helping himself to the pennies, nickels, and dimes that he was supposed to count and then place into paper tubes. While he didn't get a severance, he did gain enough information to know about a glitch with the safe's locking mechanism and when the best time was to pull a heist.

After six months of prior burglaries, Jubile and Spook were ready to make a big strike and skip out of the country. Toad had been a somewhat reticent co-conspirator by serving as the lookout during the earlier thefts, and now he was too involved to back out. As for Susan Clark, Jubile said that it was too bad that she happened to show up at the wrong time.

"All three of us need to be at that school event tonight," Jubile had said as the other two listened intently. "It's important that people see us in public." Toad started to object but was quickly silenced. "It's an alibi, you idiot!" Jubile screamed. "If everything goes okay, the cops will figure that the heist took place while everyone, including us, was at the festival." He leaned back in the chair and crossed his arms, quite confident that he had everything planned. "When they discover the stuff we hid near the cabin, they'll arrest the Indians. We'll be long gone, and a certain someone else will be clear to take over Hidden Valley. That is, if he's still alive."

"What about the girl?" Toad asked. Jubile's patience was wearing thin with the reluctant thief, but he had already planned on the two parting company when the night was over. His response to the question was terse.

"Let's just say that after tonight, she's expendable."

Chapter 21

Mark put his arm around Marnie's shoulder and pulled her close to shield her from the cool mist sprinkling tiny beads of moisture onto their clothes. The light posts in the school parking lot failed to provide much illumination. A haze encircled the bulbs causing them to glow like small moons suspended twenty feet in the air. A light fog drifted over the grounds and prompted Marnie to joke that it resembled the final airport scene in the movie *Casablanca*. A third evening of rain would likely produce soaked fields and ruin any plans the farmers might have for soon getting back into the fields.

The two were sidestepping puddles on the asphalt when they heard the shrill of tires spinning on the wet pavement. They turned toward the sound and were caught in a blinding glare of headlights bearing down on them.

The rusty pickup was about to pull out of the parking lot when Jubile and Spook spotted the Sarkisians walking to their vehicle. Jubile's distain for Mark had reached a peak and he saw the opportunity to exact vengeance. "Hang on, Spook!" Jubile stomped the accelerator and burned twenty feet of rubber into the asphalt. "We're going to scare the hell out of that son-of-a bitch!" His fingers choked the steering wheel as the pickup bore down on the defenseless couple.

"Look out, Marnie!" Mark yelled and instinctively shoved her behind a parked car. A second later the pickup sped past the spot where they had been standing. Jubile slammed his foot on the brake pedal and caused the pickup to fishtail back and forth until it finally skidded to a stop. "That fool tried to kill us," Mark shouted as he rushed to help Marnie to her feet. "Honey, are you okay?"

"A little shaken, but I'm still in one piece." Marnie brushed bits of dirt and pea gravel from her clothes. "That was too close to be considered an accident," she sighed, not realizing the danger wasn't over. The doors of the pickup clanked open and angry voices were heard. "Mark, watch out!" Marnie's warning came just in time.

Mark turned as Jubile Walker tried to land a haymaker to the back of his head. He ducked to avoid the fist, and the off-balance Walker fell to the ground. In a few seconds he was up and back on the attack. Mark would have to take the offensive in order to protect himself and Marnie.

The last time Mark threw a punch was decades earlier when he was a kid growing up in the Delray section of Detroit, Michigan. The Delray community consisted of only a few city blocks. The residents were mostly immigrant families that had settled close to the major industrial city. At age fifteen, Mark and his buddies enjoyed participating in an after-school boxing program at St. John Armenian Church. The activity was intended to promote fitness and self-defense; it also kept the youths out of mischief while their parents were at work.

If he weren't facing such a precarious situation, Mark might have found humor in remembering how the Armenian boys altered their names when they competed with other boxing clubs. The lads weren't ashamed of their heritage, but they didn't want to appear to be very different from other kids. The printed programs for the fights gave Mark and his Armenian buddies fictitious names. Varge Kachigian, Noray Manoogian, Krikor Simonian, Zaven Tarpinian, and Asadaur Sarkisian were simply listed as Johnny, Michael, Bobby, Tommy and Mark. Their coach was a fun-loving Polish man they called "Uncle" Bockel. He mentored the boys about life with colorful phrases like, "Always fight fair, but when your opponent leaves himself open, fake to midsection and nail the palooka with a right cross!" Now, Mark nervously repeated the coach's words under his breath as Jubile stumbled to his feet, determined to continue the assault. Mark nervously chanted: "Fake to the midsection and shoot the right cross; fake to the midsection and shoot the right cross." Jubile yelled a profanity and charged. Marnie's scream carried across the parking lot as she covered her eyes, not wanting to see her husband get thrashed by the younger man. Jubile was three feet from Mark when he cocked a fist and prepared to unload a vicious blow. The slight hesitation exposed his stomach just long enough for Coach Bockel's sage advice to pay off. Mark faked a quick left jab at Jubile's stomach causing the hooligan to flinch and expose his chin. The jab was followed with a solid right cross to the jaw that sent Jubile's eyes rolling in his head. The force of the blow staggered him backwards a few feet, and then he dropped like a sack of potatoes.

"It's over, Jubile," Mark yelled, rubbing the knuckles on his right hand. The thug thrashed in pain on the wet asphalt as a gush of blood streamed from his mouth. "Now, get up and get out of here, and take your friend with you!"

Marnie peered between the fingers that shielded her face during the brief fight. She was startled to see Mark standing victorious over the town ruffian, but her feeling of relief didn't last long. Spook had been a "no show" in the fight; instead, he had spent the time edging to a position behind Mark. His gangly arms encircled Mark in a bear hug just long enough for Jubile to get to his knees.

"Don't let him go, Spook!" Jubile yelled, spitting blood from an ugly gash on his lip. "We're going to teach him a lesson tonight!" He staggered to his feet and ran to the truck to grab a section of pipe. Mark struggled to break free, but Spook was a parasite clinging to his back. They tumbled to the ground as Jubile rushed forward wielding the steel weapon. Mark had become easy prey for a slaughter. Marnie stepped in front of Jubile before he reached the two men wrestling on the ground, but she was no match for his strength. "Stay out of the way, bitch," Jubile growled, pinning Marnie against a parked vehicle and threatening her with the pipe, "or you'll get some of the same medicine that I'm gonna give your husband!" A thrust from Mark's elbow caught Spook in the ribs causing him to release his hold. Mark tried to go to Marnie's aid, but Spook recovered and was back in the fray. He tackled Mark and forced him to the ground. "Hold him really tight, Spook!" Jubile yelled as he pushed Marnie aside. "This blow's gonna cause some major damage." He swung the pipe over his head and prepared to strike. Mark closed his eyes and hoped the beating would not render him unconscious.

"I wouldn't do that if I were you!" a voice of authority shouted at Jubile. "It would be extremely hazardous to your health." Jubile turned to face the barrel of a pistol.

"Collin, thank God you're here," Marnie sighed.

"Not a problem, Mrs. Sarkisian," the trooper said politely as he stayed focused on the two hoodlums. "Spook, I would suggest you take your hands off that man, or I may invite Dr. Sarkisian to demonstrate his boxing skills on you, too." Spook was visibly shaken and jumped away from Mark. "Now move over there next to your buddy, Spook. I'd prefer to have you standing in front of me." The trooper used his weapon to point the way. Spook didn't need any further encouragement and hustled to Jubile's side.

"Thanks, Collin, we're lucky you came along." Mark extended a handshake, but realized the lawman preferred to keep his gun trained on the two men. "A few more seconds and this could have been really bad," Mark stammered as he tried to regain his composure.

"It was just good timing, Dr. Sarkisian. I saw Jubile's pickup sitting in the middle of the parking lot with the motor running and both doors wide open. I figured these fellows were up to something shady." Jubile and Spook were staring at the ground, worried that they were headed to jail.

"We're very grateful, Collin," Marnie said as she resisted the urge to hug the officer in front of two men he was holding at gunpoint. She had been partial to the young man ever since Kristin expressed affection for him during one of those special conversations reserved just for mothers and daughters. A tear betrayed Marnie's inner thoughts as she gazed at the handsome trooper.

"Are you and Mrs. Sarkisian okay?" The trooper spoke without taking his eyes off Jubile and Spook.

"I think we'll be fine, Collin." Mark shifted his attention to the other men. "What happens to these two?" Jubile spit a mouthful of blood onto the ground and gave Mark a nasty stare.

"We can charge them with assault and lock them in the county jail for tonight," the trooper responded regarding the legal procedure. "Tomorrow they'll be standing in front of a judge. All you have to do is sign a complaint, Dr. Sarkisian."

"Assault!" Jubile shouted in anger. "Look at my bloody face! If you're going to charge anyone with assault, then you better put handcuffs on the guy who busted my lip!" Jubile spit a grotesque swirl of blood containing a broken tooth to the ground.

Corporal Nichols had a coy smile on his face as he addressed Jubile's complaint, "Hmmm, I must have missed that part of the fight."

Mark requested some time to speak with his wife in private. The conversation was brief. "Marnie and I have decided not to file charges," Mark reported and then turned to address the two assailants, who had expected to do jail time. "Tonight puts an end to it once and for all, Jubile." A severe threat accompanied the tone in Mark's voice. "You'll regret it if you ever come near my family again."

Corporal Nichols decided to express his disappointment with the decision to not prosecute. "I intend to honor your wishes, but I'd just as soon let them rot in jail. They're like wild dogs, not good for anyone." The comment evoked a defiant look from Jubile. He considered retaliating, but the handgun pointing at his chest put an end to any thoughts of rushing the lawman. Marnie squeezed Mark's hand to reassure him that she supported their mutual decision. She had always professed that there was worth in every human being, and now that belief was being put to the test. If the Sarkisians were going to err, it would be on the side of compassion. "I'll turn them loose tonight, but not before I give them a piece of advice." The trooper stepped forward until he was face to face with the two rogues. "This is your one and only warning," he said in a slow, sinister tone that only Jubile and Spook could hear. "If you ever go near these people again, I will personally come after you and see to it that you never cause another person a problem."

Spook was visibly shaken, but his partner remained defiant. "Are you threatening me?" Jubile was blubbering through a blood-soaked handkerchief.

"You got that right," the trooper said, and then pointed to the pickup truck. "Now get out of here before I convince these folks to change their minds about prosecuting you." Spook took off running like a scared rabbit, but Jubile sauntered toward the truck mumbling that he was going to get even with the Sarkisians and the state trooper. Corporal Nichols waited until the pickup pulled out of the parking lot before he turned his attention back to the Sarkisians. "I have to leave now. Kristin's probably wondering what happened to me." It was a subtle reminder that the Sarkisian's daughter was involved in a police stakeout that evening.

"You go on, Collin. We'll be just fine," Mark assured him.

The young lawman gave a respectful goodbye and started for his cruiser, but Marnie suddenly ran to him. She grasped his hand and spoke softly, "Collin, thank you for keeping Kristin safe." The officer smiled and gave Marnie a reassuring wink.

"You know I'll do my best, Marnie." It was the first time he had ever called Kristin's mother by her first name. She hoped it wouldn't be the last.

Susan remained on the floor where she had been dumped after being returned to the small building on the quarry property. It housed a crude shower, metal lockers, and a few army cots that once provided relief for harried workers who mined the mountain. Now, the structure had become a prison to one individual.

There was silence, except for an occasional rumble of thunder telling her that a storm lingered over the mountain. She surmised that her captors had left the premises, and now she regretted not having called out to the two men that had passed close to her on the trail. She knew there would be no chance for another escape. Her body had reached its limit and was shutting down.

Susan's thoughts were of her family. She worried about how they would cope with the news of her death. Her sadness was mixed with anger. It just wasn't fair for two loving people to lose their only daughter in the autumn of their lives. She thought about Molly, the loyal pet that had been her constant companion for thirteen years. Susan had intended to have Molly with her at Auburn, but those plans changed a week before the two were scheduled to leave...

Molly was sleeping on the carpet next to Susan's bed as she got ready for their morning jog through the countryside. "Come on, Molly, get up, lazy-bones. You're not that old," she called cheerfully. But, in fact, Molly was old. The congenial pet had difficulty getting on her feet, and Susan realized that Molly's days of running had come to an end. Molly struggled to rise again, but her body didn't cooperate and she slumped to the carpet. "Take it easy, my sweet girl." Susan's eyes filled with tears as she ran a gentle hand over Molly's soft coat. "You just rest."

The veterinarian confirmed that Molly's days were almost over and suggested that the Clarks make her as comfortable as possible. Molly seemed content to stay next to Susan's bed on the day that Wilbur and Amelia Clark spoke with their daughter. "Susan, we want you to know that Molly will be buried on the hill overlooking the pastures where the two of you used to run. She'll be at peace there." Susan hugged her parents and spent the night lying on the floor next to Molly.

Now all alone and desperate, Susan continued to reminisce: "Be at peace, close to the Lord." It was what her parents always said when she was a child just before she said her nightly prayer. On this stormy night, she closed her eyes, folded her hands, and whispered,
"Now I lay me down to sleep,
I pray the Lord my soul to keep.
If I should die..."

Chapter 22

It took Jubile and Spook fifteen minutes to get to the Canterbury house after leaving the school parking lot. The house was located on a country road where the only lighting came from an occasional farmhouse with an outdoor floodlight mounted on a pole. Jubile killed the headlights and shut off the only working windshield wiper as the pickup sloshed into the Canterbury's muddy driveway. He and Spook trudged through the mud and banged on the front door. Mrs. Canterbury came to the door clad in a flannel nightgown and in her bare feet.

"Tell your husband we're here to get him, and make it quick. We're heading out right now," Walker yelled impatiently.

Mrs. Canterbury had never been fond of her husband's two friends. "Aubrey's sick and can't go with you tonight," she yelled and started to close the door. Jubile quickly stuck his foot inside to prevent the door from shutting.

"Don't give me any crap, lady. He wasn't sick an hour ago at the school when he was shoveling chili into his gut," he said with disgust.

Mrs. Canterbury wasn't about to tolerate someone that had been whisking her husband away at all hours of the night for the past six months. "Now see here, Jubile Walker, you had better watch yourself around me or I might decide to have a conversation with Sheriff Garrett." Jubile knew that the woman wouldn't hesitate to squeal to the authorities about his illegal activities, even if it meant indicting her own husband.

"Lady, you go talking to Larry Ray Garrett and it will be your last conversation with anyone," Jubile threatened as he gripped her arm. "Now for the last time, where's Toad?"

"Aubrey's been sitting on the pot since we got home," Mrs. Canterbury said, squealing in pain. "All of that chili and cheese stuff gave him the 'runs'. He can't even get his trousers up before he's back flushing the stool, so why don't you just leave him alone?"

Spook had been shuffling his feet in the shadows of the front porch during the encounter. He stepped through the doorway and pointed a finger in Mrs. Canterbury's face.

"You tell that lazy bastard of a husband that he can poop his pants all he wants! We don't need him tonight or any night!" The woman backed away as Spook moved toward her in a rage. "You tell him he ain't getting paid anything. No way, lady, not one penny!" He raised his fist at Mrs. Canterbury, but Jubile intervened and pulled him toward the front door.

"Come on, Spook, leave her alone," Jubile said, recalling the woman's earlier threat to contact the sheriff. "She's just crazy enough to rat on us and spoil what's been a good thing for all of us, including her." The comment caught Mrs. Canterbury's attention. She had grown accustomed to some luxuries that were afforded by her husband's late-night activities. She considered the recent purchase of a newer automobile and jewelry as fringe benefits that accompanied Aubrey's association with the town hoodlums. Initially, she wasn't keen on the idea of her husband serving as a lookout during the thefts, but greed had a way of swaying her morals. It also helped to soothe her feeling of being cheated in life, due to her shotgun wedding to the town buffoon. Mrs. Canterbury was now reconsidering having that conversation with Sheriff Garrett.

Toad listened from the bathroom throughout the altercation. The toilet flushed several times during the brief encounter between his wife and the men. Jubile figured the stench that Toad was struggling to endure in the bathroom was punishment for being too much of a coward to show his face. As the two intruders exited the house, Jubile yelled a threat loud enough to be heard throughout the house, "I ain't done with you yet, Toad! You'll be looking over your shoulder for the rest of your short life!"

———————◦———————

Three months earlier, Jeffrey Williams sat alone in his office playing solitaire while images of land topography flashed across the computer screen. The SRA satellite equipment was doing its job, but the bored executive was loafing. He was transferred to the Missouri office a year earlier in what he thought was an opportunity to move into a management slot. However, the rumor at SRA headquarters was that the "promotion" was awarded when the corporate chiefs saw it as a preferable option, rather than dealing with possible litigation for firing the brash geological engineer who demonstrated questionable ethics. Thus, the new assignment resulted in Jeffrey supervising only one person, a pleasant administrative assistant named Paige. She regularly out-performed him.

Jeffrey initially spent most days trying to persuade farmers to invest their hard-earned capital in SRA, but the services weren't cheap and all of the dollars were considered at risk. Sales were meager as most of Jeffrey's prospects chose to keep their nest egg in the local bank. In fact, most clients who did commit to the company were actually recruited by his female co-worker, a hometown girl and recent graduate from Northwest Missouri State University.

It was a typical ho-hum day for Jeffrey when he put down the playing cards and leaned back in the cushy chair to stretch his arms. His long yawn was interrupted by something he saw on the computer screen. The satellite picture was locked onto a strange parcel of land located in Auburn County. The configuration and shading indicated that the soil might contain mineral deposits, which were not typical to the region. He pressed the computer keys to access more data. Within minutes, the SRA equipment validated that the unusual land consisted of eight hundred acres on Buffalo Mountain. The following morning Paige found a note on her desk that indicated that Jeffrey would be gone for the day doing field research.

Jeffrey made the ninety-minute trip to Buffalo Mountain and trekked another two hours to the area that was identified by the satellite. Jeffrey made it a point to avoid any recreational hikers he might have seen on the trails. He gathered samples of soil and made it

250

off the mountain without being detected. Later that evening, he examined the samples in the small lab at the SRA facility, just as he had done on numerous occasions for potential clients in testing the qualities in their soil. He studied the first battery of tests and questioned the results. A retest using fresh samples produced the same analysis match. The third test left him with a lump in his throat.

Jeffrey had little experience with the mineral niobium, but he knew it was rare and valuable. Its heat-resistant qualities made it highly desirable for hardening steel and other industrial uses. It was so rare that the United States imported most of the niobium used in the country. Whoever owned the mountain property had wealth beyond their wildest dreams, and Jeffrey wanted to be that person.

A check with the Auburn County Assessor's office revealed only one couple listed as owners on Buffalo Mountain. Arixie and Israel Wanatee had purchased the eight hundred acre tract sixty years earlier. The remainder of the mountain region came under government control a few years later. One way or another, Jeffrey was determined to get his hands on the Wanatee land.

Chapter 23

Two law enforcement vehicles were parked side by side partially hidden in the darkness across the road from the Drovers and Merchants Bank. The officers carried on a casual conversation as they kept watch on the facility from their respective vehicles.

"Well, I'm glad you finally showed up," Kristin Sarkisian said to the state trooper who had arrived moments earlier. "I was beginning to wonder if I needed to run this operation on my own," she joked.

"Sorry, Kristin, I was delayed at the school festival and couldn't break away any sooner," Corporal Nichols explained.

"Anything serious?"

The trooper hesitated before responding, not wanting to upset his partner with news about her parents' incident in the school parking lot. "Nothing I couldn't handle, but thanks for asking." Collin smiled as he joined Kristin in her vehicle. He offered her coffee from a thermos he had brought with him. The two officers filled the next hour with police talk related to the investigation into Susan Clark's disappearance. Nothing had turned up from the search along the riverbanks since the original discovery of items that were believed to belong to Susan. Two days of dragging the river had snagged a lot of debris floating beneath the water. Searchers were growing frustrated, knowing that the woman's medical condition limited the timeline for finding her alive. The stakeout assignment would have been boring for the trooper if he hadn't been paired with his favorite deputy. He seized the opportunity to shift to lighter conversation.

"Kristin, do you ever think about giving up police work and doing something else?" he asked in a matter-of-fact tone.

"Not really," Kristin answered, somewhat surprised by the question. "What else would I do that's as challenging as helping people and trying to catch the bad guys?"

The trooper wasn't sure how far to pursue the topic, but he decided to take a chance. "Oh, I don't know, maybe settle down?" He tried to appear calm but his heart was beating faster.

"Well, of course, I think about settling down," Kristin said, as though it was a foregone conclusion. "What woman doesn't dream about marrying a handsome man, buying a home surrounded by a white picket fence, and having children...lots of children?"

Collin Nichols almost spilled the coffee he was pouring from a thermos onto his uniform. For several months, he had resisted the urge to ask the petite deputy to go on a date, thinking that her main interest was pursuing a career. Now he wasn't so sure. "Don't you have similar feelings, Collin?" Kristin was fishing for an answer as to why the handsome fellow she had been fond of since meeting him hadn't shown more of a romantic interest in her. A response would have to wait because a sudden flash of light coming from inside the bank building across the road startled both officers. Any further social talk would have to wait as both officers reacted to what they had just seen.

"Yes, I saw it," Collin said as he scanned the bank with his binoculars. "It must have been the reflection of a flashlight," the trooper said, without lowering the binoculars. "Someone's inside and doesn't want it known. You better call it in and ask for back-up." Kristin felt nervous as she used her two-way radio to contact the sheriff's department. "Unit 3 to Central Dispatch." She paused a few seconds and then repeated the call. "Unit 3 to Central Dispatch; come in, Central Dispatch."

"Central Dispatch to Unit 3," a familiar voice transmitted from the sheriff's department. "Sorry for the delay, Kristin." The police dispatcher's apology was sincere. "I was handling a priority call from the sheriff. He's working a bad accident twelve miles south of Auburn and needs additional emergency responders," the dispatcher reported. "Oh, hold on. It's the sheriff calling in again." The radio went silent. Collin had exited the vehicle during the conversation with the dispatcher and was now taking a position that afforded a better view of the building. The shotgun that was normally bracketed inside his cruiser was now in the trooper's hands.

The police radio squawked and the dispatcher came back on. "Sorry again, Unit 3. It's a real mess at that accident, but no fatalities."

Kristin interrupted before the dispatcher could continue. "Trooper Nichols and I are at the Drovers and Merchants Bank and request additional assistance." There was no immediate reply because the dispatcher was relaying the message to the sheriff. The rain had increased, making it more difficult to see through the darkness, but Kristin caught a glimpse of her partner motioning for her to join him. She was still waiting for a response from Central Dispatch when she made the decision to vacate her cruiser.

"I don't think we can wait much longer," the trooper said when Kristin crouched by his side behind a drainage culvert along the side of the road. "They could be making their getaway any minute now. Do we have help coming?"

She conveyed that the request for back-up assistance had not been confirmed. "Then it looks like we're on our own for now." Corporal Nichols was concerned but didn't want to make the situation worse by frightening the deputy. "Don't worry, Kristin. We've got each other," he said with an encouraging smile.

The two-way radio in the deputy sheriff's vehicle crackled, but the two officers who were advancing on the building never got the message. A few seconds later, they were standing at the front door of the bank building. "Central Dispatch to Unit 3, Central Dispatch to Unit 3. Come in Kristin." The dispatcher continued to transmit, hoping the deputy was still close to her vehicle. "Kristin, back-up units will be on their way as soon as possible, but the sheriff estimates it will be at least twenty minutes." The dispatcher's voice took on a sense of urgency. "Unit 3, do you copy? Come in Unit 3!"

"I'll take the front and you cover the back of the building," Collin explained as he handed a walkie-talkie to Kristin and switched on the field microphone that he was wearing. "Take this and stay in touch, but keep the volume low in case they're nearby," he cautioned. "Don't take any unnecessary risks and maybe we can wait them out until more units arrive." Corporal Nichols wasn't worried about Kristin's courage, but he knew that her previous experience had not involved any potential shooting situations. She gave him a nervous smile and headed around the corner of the building.

The area behind the building was unusually dark. The two floodlights intended for security purposes had been disabled. Evidently, the intruders had managed to also bypass the antiquated alarm system. Kristin ran a hand across her face to wipe the rain from her eyes and used her flashlight to survey the area. The rear door to the building was closed. She strained to see through the darkness and saw a vehicle had been parked near shrubs at the back of the lot. The longer she looked, the easier it was to recognize the old pickup truck. When she looked back at the building, the rear door was standing partially open. She ducked behind a trash dumpster and rested the walkie-talkie on the container's lid. A dim light shone through the gap in the door and it was growing brighter by the second. Someone with a flashlight was about to exit the building. There wasn't time to retrieve the walkie-talkie as she unholstered her revolver and took aim at the door. A man emerged, carrying a rifle in one hand and a large bag in the other. Kristin aimed the beam of her flashlight at the man's face and called out. "This is the Sheriff's Department! Drop the rifle and raise your hands!" The startled man jerked backward and threw the rifle to the ground. He raised a hand to shield his eyes from the light shining in his face. The large bandage across his cheek was a dead giveaway to his identity. "Keep your hands up and don't make another move, Spook Daniels!" the deputy commanded while keeping her weapon trained on the man.

"Don't shoot me; I've got my hands up. I surrender; don't shoot!" Spook had always been a spastic thug. Now his nervous chatter was a veiled attempt to signal his pal who had left the building earlier to get the pickup truck. The early exit had positioned the man to see the deputy sheriff when she approached the rear of the building.

Kristin was about to use the walkie-talkie to contact Corporal Nichols, but she was concerned her prisoner might do something stupid and go for his rifle. She grabbed the handcuffs attached to her gun belt and stepped forward as she followed the procedures she had learned at the police academy. "Turn around and put your hands behind your back!" A rush of adrenalin was playing havoc with her nerves. A few more seconds and she would feel relieved to have the cuffs on Spook. She gave a final command. "Hold still, and don't make any sudden..."

Bam! Bam! Two shots tore through the back of Kristin's uniform and slammed her to the ground. Jubile Walker approached the fallen officer who was lying in a pool of water.

"Damn, Jubile, you nailed her good," Spook yelled as he looked down at the deputy's limp body.

"Yeah, she never knew what hit her. Maybe I'll put another one in her just because of her father," he sneered and then put the rifle barrel close to Kristin's head.

"Forget it, somebody's coming!" Spook said, pulling at Jubile's arm. Corporal Nichols heard the gunfire from the other side of the building. He notified Central Dispatch with an urgent call for assistance. Now he was running toward the rear of the building. The saturated ground made it difficult for the trooper to maintain his balance as he sloshed through the muddy sod. A shot rang out as he turned the corner of the building. A bullet just missed his head and ricocheted off the wall. Spook was revving the truck's motor as Jubile leaned out the passenger window cracking off shots at the trooper. Corporal Nichols dropped to one knee and returned fire.

Bam! Bam! Bam! Three blasts from the trooper's shotgun peppered the truck's tailgate and shattered the rear window, spraying glass into the cab. Spook momentarily lost control and the pickup slammed against one tree and then another. The truck was full of shotgun pellets and badly dented, but not disabled.

Spook stomped on the accelerator and sent a spray of mud spewing behind the truck. In a few more seconds the truck would be bogged in mud up to its axle. Spook rammed the gearshift and spun the truck onto more solid ground. The trooper discarded the shotgun and pulled his handgun. He fired four rounds in rapid succession, but the truck was already sliding across a field and headed for a side road. In seconds it disappeared into the darkness.

Corporal Nichols retrieved his flashlight from where it fell during the gun battle and rubbed it against his jacket to remove dirt from the lens. He beamed the light toward the rear of the building expecting to see his partner, perhaps shaken, but otherwise okay.

"Kristin, where are you?" he called out and slowly walked toward the dumpster. There was an eerie stillness and the only sounds came from big drops of rain plunking onto the trash dumpster. "Kristin, answer me," the trooper spoke in a whisper, being cautious just in case the fleeing men had left one of their own behind. One hand held the flashlight, but the other had a firm grip on his pistol. Suddenly, the beam of light captured something unusual. His first steps were taken with caution, but then he broke into a run when he recognized the uniformed figure lying on the ground. "Oh no!" Collin cried out. "Not you, Kristin." Tears filled the trooper's eyes. He dropped to his knees and encircled her face and body with his arms, as if to protect her from any further injury.

The silence of the night was shattered by a lone trooper cradling a fallen comrade and screaming into a walkie-talkie, "Officer down! Officer down!"

Shortly after his initial visit to Buffalo Mountain, Jeffrey's Williams hiked there again. The second trip would be more adventurous for the man who now envisioned a lifestyle of the rich and famous. He made his way back to the knoll overlooking the ancient valley. His geological training reasoned that the niobium mineral was deposited in North America when glaciers carved the valley many centuries ago. He approached an elderly woman sitting on the porch of a rustic cabin. She identified herself as Mrs. Wanatee and remained cautious about the man, who introduced himself as a speculator wanting to purchase property on Buffalo Mountain. Jeffrey didn't waste any time as he presented an offer that was many times higher than the original cost of the property. Mrs. Wanatee was old, but she was forthright. "This land is not for sale," she replied in a soft voice. "Not for any price." She turned to go inside the building, which caused Jeffrey to become visibly upset.

"Are you kidding me, lady?" His voice was abrasive. "I'm offering you and your old man more money than you've seen in a lifetime, and you're turning your back on it? Are you nuts?" Mrs. Wanatee raised her head toward the sky as though she were in deep thought.

When she spoke again, her words were filled with emotion. "We are the caretakers of this wonderful land that the Keeper of the Mountain led us to many years ago. It belongs to every living creature; we will respect and protect it for other generations." She paused a few seconds before closing the discussion. "You must leave. My husband and son will not want you here."

Anger boiled within Jeffrey. He needed a plan. "Okay, you old hag," his hurtful words burned like venom. "I wouldn't want to mysteriously disappear on Buffalo Mountain and become part of your silly folklore." The nasty sarcasm was a waste of energy. The woman had retreated to the safe confines of the cabin. Jeffrey muttered to himself as he made his way along the rugged trail that led to his car. He wasn't going to give up until he got his hands on the priceless land.

He was halfway down the mountain when two men appeared out of the timber with their rifles aimed at him. His life changed forever at that moment.

Chapter 24

Sheriff Garrett and other officers who were responding to the earlier call for assistance picked up bits of the action at the bank on their scanners. The storm was playing havoc with their communication equipment. The static added to the confusing sounds of intermittent gunfire crackling through the police radios. Sheriff Garrett heard enough to know that the situation was not good. He pressed the accelerator and sped down the highway at eighty-five miles per hour. "Unit 1 responding," the sheriff called into his radio. "Three minutes away...all units respond... emergency, code 1."

The cruiser crested a hill with its emergency lights flashing, and the sheriff caught a glimpse of a truck coming right at him. The occupants had no intention of slowing down. "Floor it, Spook!" Jubile yelled as he leaned out the window and aimed his rifle. The two vehicles were separated by only a hundred yards of dark highway when Sheriff Garrett saw flashes of gunfire coming from the truck. Jubile was cranking off rounds as fast as he could squeeze the rifle trigger. The tire that Corporal Nichols had shot out at the botched robbery was flat as a pancake and challenging Spook to keep the truck on the road. Two of Jubile's shots shattered the windshield of the police cruiser and another took off the side mirror. The sheriff had a good idea who he was dealing with, and he was determined to not let them get away. There was no time to call for assistance. The two vehicles narrowed the gap to within seconds of each other.

"Damn fools don't care who they kill," Sheriff Garrett growled as the pickup sped directly toward him. "Well, this time they picked the wrong lawman to play chicken with."

He tightened his grip on the steering wheel and braced for the collision.

"He ain't stopping, Jubile!" Spook screamed. "The damn lawman's gonna hit us dead on!"

Jubile disregarded his buddy's ranting and continued to fire more shots. "Shut up and keep it on the road!" He stuck his head inside the truck and gave his pal a nasty look. "Ain't no cop gonna stop me tonight, Spook! Didn't I already prove that to you back at the bank?" There was no time for a response. Spook lowered his head and prepared for the impact of the crash. His action jerked the steering wheel sharply to one side and the truck skidded across the roadway. The police cruiser banked off the rear fender of the truck and spun out of control onto the shoulder of the road. Sheriff Garrett braced himself as the vehicle rolled once and slid into a muddy ditch on the side of the road. Seconds later, he unbuckled his seatbelt and kicked open the passenger door. He tumbled to the ground and crawled behind the mangled cruiser. It temporarily shielded him from the bullets that were penetrating the seat he had just vacated.

Spook had managed to keep the truck upright in spite of the hard hit from the cruiser. He slammed on the brakes and screeched to a stop across the road from the disabled police vehicle. Then Spook grabbed his rifle and joined his partner in trying to rid themselves of the lawman once and for all, but this wasn't Larry Ray Garrett's first gun battle. The sheriff crouched behind his disabled vehicle, pinpointing the flashes of gunfire from across the road. He fired three shots that shattered the window glass of the pickup and brought a painful scream from his assailants.

"Aaahhh, I'm hit!" Jubile yelled and slumped to the ground, holding his shoulder. Spook screamed hysterically as blood gushed from cuts on his face caused by shards of glass. "Damn sheriff got both of us when he blew out the window," Jubile groaned and pressed a dirty rag against his bleeding shoulder. He could hear sirens in the distance and realized that the sheriff would have help arriving soon. "You ain't gonna die from those cuts, Spook. Now, get in the truck and get us out of here." Another shot from the sheriff plunked into the frame of the black pickup as Spook ducked into the driver's seat. He stomped on the gas pedal and sent the truck slogging through a muddy soybean field. Sheriff Garrett took his last shot as the truck fishtailed in an attempt to get on solid ground. "Ease off, Spook." Jubile winced in pain. "We're out of range now and you're killing me every time you hit a bump."

"I can't help it." We've got a blown tire and a bullet hole in our radiator." Spoke wiped a stream of blood coming from a jagged cut on his forehead. "She's leaking like a sieve. I don't know if we can make it back to the quarry."

"You damn well better get us back, or else you'll wish the lawman had finished you off back there." Jubile spit a wad of blood out the window and a sinister look crossed his face. "I've got some unfinished business to take care of at the quarry." He slumped in the seat, holding his wounded shoulder and stared out the window. Revenge was the only thing on Jubile Walker's mind.

A deputy sheriff's vehicle spun to a stop and the officer rushed to the overturned cruiser. Half of the car was blocking the roadway, but the remaining portion resembled a pile of crunched metal, partially buried in mud on the shoulder of the road. "Sheriff, you look like you've been in a battle," the deputy said as Sheriff Garrett tried to stand. "I'll call for an ambulance."

"Never mind that," the sheriff said, while holstering his weapon. "Just fill me in on what happened at the bank." He leaned against the cruiser and grimaced as he felt a large bump on his head.

"It's not good, Sheriff Garrett." The deputy gave his report as he handed the sheriff patches of gauze and a roll of adhesive tape from an emergency kit. "Kristin and the trooper interrupted a robbery at the bank. There was a shootout." The deputy's voice became shallow when Sheriff Garrett made eye contact with him. "There's one officer down." The deputy lowered his head and spoke softly. "It's Kristin."

The sheriff took a deep breath before speaking. He regained his composure and asked the question. "And, is she okay?"

"I don't know, Sheriff." The deputy gave a bewildered look. "The radio transmission was garbled and all I picked up was that the EMTs were transporting her to the Auburn Medical Center."

Larry Ray Garrett threw the emergency kit into the trunk of the deputy's cruiser and issued an order. "Get me to the medical center and make it fast! His eyes filled with tears. "We're not going to lose that girl. No sir, not on my watch."

———◦○◦———

Amelia Clark busied herself dusting Susan's room as she waited for a telephone call regarding her daughter. She had prayed that the news would bring relief; that perhaps Susan had incurred an episode with her diabetes during the trip and now had it under control. It had been four days since the disappearance, and Amelia wasn't sure she wanted the phone to ring. Susan's room didn't need cleaning, but the activity helped Amelia to feel close to her daughter. Wilbur had gone to town to meet with local authorities and mentioned that he intended to stop by the SRA office to see Jeffrey Williams. Amelia was dusting pictures on a dresser when she noticed for the first time that a photo of Susan and Jeffrey had been turned face down. It seemed odd that Susan had neglected to take the picture with her to Auburn.

"Amelia, I'm home," Wilbur called out as he walked down the hallway to the pink bedroom. He hugged his wife and continued

holding her in his arms, "I'm sorry, dear." The sheriff didn't have anything new to report." Tears welled in his eyes. "Maybe tomorrow we'll get some good news." Amelia shared her concern regarding the picture with her husband.

"Wilbur, it's not like Susan to forget something like this unless she meant to leave it. Don't you think it's strange?" He pondered the question.

"I'm not sure what to make of it, but I did find out something when I went to the SRA office." He was about to share information that would surprise his wife. "Jeffrey wasn't there, but Paige was in the office and I spoke with her." Wilbur noticed a smile appear on his wife's face. "That young lady is really sharp. I think she should be running that business instead of Jeffrey."

Amelia was pleased that her husband was impressed with Susan's friend, but she was more concerned with what he had gleaned from the conversation with the young lady. "That's nice, Wilbur, but tell me what Paige had to say. Was it about Susan?"

"Well, she was really perturbed at Jeffrey because he had taken off for wherever and told her he might not be back for a day or two. Now, that's what I call strange." Wilbur related that Paige had been reluctant to reveal that Susan and Jeffrey had problems with their relationship. "Paige finally just blurted out that Susan said she was finished with Jeffrey. Now, what do you think of that?"

"I guess it's true what they say about the parents being the last ones to know," Amelia said, shaking her head in disappointment. "I agree with you, Wilbur. It's really strange that everyone is searching for Susan, and Jeffrey just takes off without telling anyone where he's going." She clutched her daughter's picture close to her heart and spoke softly, "Lord, please keep her safe."

Chapter 25

The Sarkisians had retired to bed shortly after arriving home from the school festival. Mark quickly fell asleep, exhausted from a full day of activities. The ring of a telephone in the middle of the night was seldom good news.

"Hello," Mark answered groggily. "Yes, this is Dr. Sarkisian. What is it?" Marnie heard only bits of the conversation, but she could tell that something was terribly wrong. "Yes, of course," Mark confirmed to the caller. "We'll come as soon as we're dressed." He ended the call and his voice quivered. "We need to get to the hospital right away."

Ten minutes later the Sarkisians were halfway to Auburn Medical Center when a Missouri State Highway Patrol vehicle intercepted them and took the lead position to provide a speedy escort. The blaring siren and flashing emergency lights cleared the road of slow-moving night travelers. Mark concentrated on staying close to the trooper but periodically glanced at his wife. Marnie's head was bowed as she prayed. "Me too, honey," Mark whispered. "I'm praying for her, too."

The two vehicles turned onto a roadway leading to the Auburn Medical Center and sped past an illuminated sign that pointed the way to the emergency department. An ambulance and several police vehicles were parked near the entrance with their red and blue flashers still activated. The trooper escorting the Sarkisians pulled his cruiser to the side of the road and waved Mark toward a vacant parking slot next to the emergency entrance. As soon as Mark and Marnie walked into the medical center, they caught sight of several state patrolmen and deputy sheriffs milling in the waiting area. Dr. Andrew Wayne was coming down a hallway and quickened his pace to meet the anxious parents.

"Dr. Wayne!" Marnie called out and ran to him. "Dr. Wayne, we got the call about Kristin and--" Marnie didn't finish the sentence because the doctor raised his hand to interrupt.

"She's going to be just fine," Dr. Wayne said. "The Lord and I brought her into this world, and we're not quite ready to let her out of it just yet." Mark was surprised by the doctor's calm demeanor in light of the fact that a host of emergency personnel, police officers and the parents of a shooting victim had invaded his quiet emergency room. "Now, take it easy and let me explain what happened to your daughter." Dr. Wayne pulled an examination report from the pocket of his lab coat. "Kristin took two shots to the back at close range from a small caliber weapon." Marnie gasped, but the doctor quickly continued in order to calm her nerves. "Fortunately her bullet-proof vest took the brunt of the damage." He observed a look of relief and continued with the explanation. "However, the force of the impact rendered her unconscious for a period of time." He scanned the examination sheet for more information. "Evidently, a trooper on the scene initiated first aid until the paramedics arrived." Dr. Wayne gave a concerned look. "She's very lucky the state trooper was there. It could have been much worse."

Mark was overjoyed at hearing the report, but he asked the doctor for more information. "Andrew, just how badly hurt is she?"

"She'll have some severe bruising and pain for a few weeks, but the x-rays showed no broken ribs," the doctor said referring again to the examination sheet. "The prognosis for a complete recovery is good," he summed up with a smile. "We've already transferred her to a room down the hall. Now, how would you like to see your daughter?"

Marnie threw her arms around Dr. Wayne and squeezed him. "Andrew, how can we ever thank you?"

The doctor had remained a humble man throughout his career. The events on this evening would not change his demeanor. "No need to thank me. I'm just happy I was here to help."

The Sarkisians and Dr. Wayne stepped into the room that Kristin had been moved to following her trip to the emergency room. The lighting had been dimmed and a nurse that the Sarkisians recognized was busy dealing with equipment that monitored a patient's vital signs. Jean Raines, R.N., was a close friend, and her children had attended school in Auburn during the years Mark had worked in the school district. She finished with the bedside equipment and approached Kristin's mother.

"Now don't you fret, Marnie; your daughter is doing great," the nurse said as she gave Marnie a hug. "Dr. Wayne is taking a personal interest in this patient, and he's the best physician on staff." Marnie smiled and expressed gratitude for the caring approach by nurse Raines and then turned her attention to the patient in the hospital bed. Kristin was resting but managed to smile when she saw her parents. Her attempt to shift in the bed was accompanied by a painful groan.

"Take it easy, Kristin," Dr. Wayne cautioned. "You've been through quite an ordeal and your body needs to rest." Regardless of his affection for the Sarkisian family, Dr. Wayne was still following professsional protocols. "I'm recommending medication for pain, limited movement, and complete bed rest. That's doctor's orders, young lady." His voice was stern, but the smile that followed was endearing. Kristin's parents waited for the doctor to finish and then went to their daughter's bedside.

"Mom... Dad... I'm sorry." Her words were barely distinguishable.

"It's the medication," Dr. Wayne chimed in a low voice. "She's drowsy and about to drift off. We'd better keep it short."

Marnie leaned close to her daughter and whispered. "It's okay, darling. You're going to be just fine." She gently stroked Kristin's hand and used her handkerchief to wipe a tear from the corner of her daughter's eye. The young woman looked at her father and saw his eyes were filled with tears. She wiggled her finger for him to come closer. Mark leaned forward to hear what she had to say. "How about a smile, Dad?" Her slight groan could not mask the pain she was feeling. "You know, I almost nailed those two goons." She winked at her father, then closed her eyes and drifted to sleep.

"Yes, sweetheart. I'm so proud of you," Mark said as he planted a kiss on his daughter's forehead.

"I believe we've done all we can for now." Dr. Wayne motioned toward the door. "Of course, we can arrange accommodations here if you prefer to stay close to Kristin." The invitation was just what Marnie was hoping for and she jumped at the opportunity.

"Oh, that would be wonderful," Marnie responded. "I'd like to be here when she wakes up."

Suddenly, a voice spoke up. "I'd like to stay, too, if it's alright with you folks." Collin Nichols had been unnoticed in a dim corner of the room during the time Mark and Marnie were comforting Kristin. Now the trooper came forward and politely made his presence known. "I'm sorry; I didn't want to distract you earlier."

The parents greeted the officer and expressed their appreciation for his help. He explained that he planned to write his official report of the shooting incident while at the medical center and preferred to do it while staying close to Kristin. Marnie appeared overjoyed by the suggestion.

"I think that would be really nice," she said to the officer. "I could use the company. Perhaps we could have a nice conversation about Kristin."

"Yes ma'am, I would enjoy that." His response was accompanied with a blush.

Mark was satisfied to have his wife and the young lawman remain at the hospital with Kristin. He had business to take care of with the men who had shot his daughter. Mark knew who they were and where they were likely to be hiding out. There was one other thing that Mark had come to believe based on the events of the last four days. He was pretty sure that the men who had harmed his daughter had something to do with Susan Clark's disappearance.

Sheriff Garrett had arrived at the emergency room and was updated on Kristin's condition. He was headed down the hallway when Mark rushed out of the patient's room.

"Hold on, Mark," the sheriff said, grabbing his friend's arm. "Where are you headed in such a hurry?"

"I don't have time to talk, Larry Ray." Mark pulled away from the sheriff's grip. It was obvious that he was looking for revenge on Jubile Walker and Spook Daniels. Sheriff Garrett motioned to the officers stationed near the emergency room to stop Mark before he made it to the exit doors. Moments later, he confronted his friend.

"Look, Mark, I know you're upset, but taking on Jubile and Spook isn't going to help matters," the sheriff reasoned. "We're already planning to take them into custody just as soon as the sun comes up. It's too dangerous to attempt anything on the mountain in the dark." Sheriff Garrett gave Mark a consoling pat on the back. "It will be daylight in a couple of hours, and I promise you that we'll get them." Mark knew that the sheriff was making sense, but it didn't help to change his feelings for the men who had tried to kill his daughter. He wanted to administer his own brand of justice, but first he had to figure out how to get away from the sheriff and his deputies.

"Okay, I guess you're right," Mark apologized. "Maybe I just need to go home and get a few hours sleep. It's been a really stressful night." The sheriff motioned for the deputies to release their hold on Mark.

"That's okay, buddy." The sheriff tried to lighten the mood. "Look at it this way. Your daughter stopped a robbery and saved the money at the bank. She's got some bruises and a tattered bullet-proof vest, but she's a hero." He laughed and then poked fun at himself. "I've been a lawman in this county for three decades, and I don't believe anybody thinks of me as a hero." The deputies looked at each other and nodded their agreement. Mark was just pleased that he wasn't going to be detained by the authorities. "Now, you go home and try to get some sleep, Mark," the sheriff advised. "We'll probably have those fellows in custody by the time you wake up." Mark thanked the sheriff and indicated that he would go home to rest. He left the lawmen and started for the exit door but decided to make a quick detour through another hallway to see Dr. Wayne. Five minutes later, Mark left the medical center with a syringe filled with insulin safely tucked in his jacket pocket.

Sheriff Garrett had suspicions that his best friend hadn't been completely truthful about going home to rest. "You fellows get ready to head for Buffalo Mountain within the hour," he instructed the deputies. "I've got a hunch we better get there as soon as we can."

Larry Ray's premonition was accurate. Mark's stop at his house would last only long enough to get his gun.

Earlier that evening, a rustling noise came from the other side of the door. Susan feared that the man who had attacked her earlier was returning to finish the job. The sound of a key grating inside the rusty padlock sent chills through her and she closed her eyes. The door opened and a bright light found her huddled in a corner.

"Please don't hurt me anymore!" Susan sobbed and lowered her head, too weak to put up a fight. The man was cautiously shuffling

toward her. He deflected the blinding glare away from Susan's face and used his flashlight to shine a path across the room. His hands were extended as though he were indicating that he meant her no harm.

"Easy there," he said when Susan turned away. "It's me, Toad." He quickly corrected himself. "Aubrey Canterbury, the fellow who helped you on the trail."

Susan was startled by the man's admission of his identity. "You're the creep that brought me back to this hell hole to die!"

Toad lowered his head and mumbled an apology. "Yes, I'm sorry. I never wanted to hurt you. I only threw in with those fellows to make some money." Then, he tried to clear his conscience by telling Susan the story that led to her imprisonment:

Jubile and Spook had approached Toad to be a lookout during their robberies of local places. It was an easy way for him to make some quick money, so he agreed. Their initial heists were successful and the three split the proceeds after selling the loot on the black market. Toad's share of the take was always considerably less than what the others got. Eventually, they got greedy and wanted to expand the operation. None of the three had the smarts to come up with a workable plan until some odd circumstances put them into contact with a new partner who showed them how to make major scores and avoid being captured. The alliance proved to be lucrative and the petty thieves became full-time criminals who always seemed to be one step ahead of the law. A problem arose when Susan happened upon Jubile and Spook while they were stashing the loot from a recent burglary. They figured she would alert the authorities, so they decided she would never get off the mountain alive.

Susan was more interested in getting to safety rather than hearing about the escapades of three criminals. She had unwittingly stumbled into their lives. Her life was hanging in the balance and her only option for surviving appeared to be a frightened bumpkin.

"Please, Mr. Canterbury, it's not too late," she pleaded with the man who was showing remorse for his earlier actions. "Please help me to get off this mountain."

Toad gave a fearful look around the room, trying to muster enough courage to do the honorable thing. He was a weak soul and it showed in his response. "I'm sorry, Miss, but I just can't. Jubile would kill me and sink my body into the quarry lagoon right along with your car."

Susan was startled by the revelation. She had hoped that someone might discover the abandoned vehicle parked near the base of the mountain and launch a search for her on the mountain. Toad's ramblings confirmed the chance for a rescue was slim. No one even knew she was on the mountain.

"I've got to go now. They're expecting me to show up at that school event so that people won't become suspicious." Toad pulled away from Susan's grasp and rushed to the door. A look of fear was plastered on his face when he looked back at the young woman lying on the floor. In a moment of compassion, he left Susan with a glimmer of hope.

"Miss, I'm leaving the door unlocked."

Chapter 26

Two Missouri troopers joined Sheriff Garrett and three deputies when they left Auburn. The band of officers would make a stop at the Aubrey Canterbury home before they proceeded to Buffalo Mountain. It was 4:30 a.m. and the convoy of headlights reflecting off the wet roadway cast an eerie scene across the countryside. The place was dark, with the exception of a dim light filtering through the curtains of a room at the back of the house.

Sheriff Garrett went to the front door after the other officers had taken positions surrounding the house. The loud knock was followed by a command.

"This is Sheriff Garrett; open the door!" He didn't wait long for a response. "Toad, you've got ten seconds to open this door before I kick it in!" The porch light immediately flicked on. Mrs. Canterbury inched the door open and spotted the police vehicles lined up in her front yard. Sheriff Garrett didn't intend to carry on a social conversation. "We need to

speak with your husband, Mrs. Canterbury."
Judging by the expression on her face, Toad's
wife wasn't surprised by a visit in the middle
of the night.

"Aubrey's not feeling good, Sheriff.
He's had the 'runs' ever since we got home
from the school festival." Larry Ray was in no
mood for excuses, especially after having one
of his deputies shot just hours earlier.

"If you think he's sick now, just wait
until I get my hands on him," the sheriff yelled
as he brushed the woman aside and burst into
the foyer. Two deputies rushed the front porch
with their guns drawn and followed the sheriff
through the door. Sheriff Garrett had been at
the Canterbury place on prior occasions and
was familiar with the layout of the house. It
wasn't difficult to locate where Aubrey was
hiding when he heard moans coming from the
bathroom. "I'm coming after you, Toad, and
you better be ready!" the sheriff yelled as he
kicked the bathroom door open. A hideous
stench and the site of Toad rocking back and
forth on the toilet greeted him.

"Oh lordy, lordy, I'm hurting, Sheriff
Garrett. I'm hurting a lot!" The two deputies
stood in amazement as their sheriff was
unsympathetic to the plea and grabbed Aubrey
by his ear, pulling him off the toilet. A strip of
toilet paper was stuck to his rear.

"Toad, you better keep praying because when I get finished, you're going to think you went to hell!" The sheriff twisted Aubrey's ear until he squealed like a pig.

"Aiyee! Aiyee!" Toad screamed in anguish as the sheriff pressed him about the botched bank job and Susan Clark. "Aiyee, please, no more," he pleaded. "Walker and Daniels will kill me if they find out I talked to you." Larry Ray wasn't going to waste any more time. He pulled his .44 Colt from the holster and pressed it against the whimpering man's temple.

"Listen to me, you no-account piece of garbage." The sheriff was bending over, nose to nose with the half-naked man who was squirming on the floor. "You better spill your guts right now, or I'm going to splatter your brains and there won't be enough left of you for Jubile and Spook to identify!" The deputies had never seen their chief in such a rage. Sheriff Garrett was likely violating Aubrey Canterbury's legal rights, but the deputies weren't about to interfere. They had their hands full trying to calm down Aubrey's wife.

"I told him so; yes, I did!" Mrs. Canterbury screamed. "I warned Aubrey that hanging around with those two scumbags would land him in jail!" She stepped into the bathroom and clutched Aubrey between the legs. "Now, you tell the sheriff what he wants to know or you'll be singing tenor for the rest of your miserable life, Aubrey Canterbury." Then she squeezed.

Sheriff Garrett released his hold on Toad's ear; it was obvious that the wife had a better handle on things. He stepped out of the bathroom and joined his deputies. The three lawmen watched a transformation come over Toad. He proceeded to confess how he became involved in the crimes with his buddies and their partner, a person that Toad claimed having never met in person. He became sullen when he got to the part about Susan Clark. Then Toad began to sob as he told how Susan had unknowingly stumbled upon the criminals four days ago. The final piece of his confession shocked the lawmen. "You're too late. I don't think she's alive," he cried. "I'm sorry."

Anger boiled inside Larry Ray Garrett as he worried about his friend Mark having to confront the men who had harmed Kristin and Susan. The sheriff was already speeding toward Buffalo Mountain by the time a deputy pulled out of the Canterbury drive to transport Toad to jail.

———◦———

It had been several hours since Aubrey Canterbury informed Susan that he left the door to the room unlocked, but she didn't have the strength to take advantage of the opportunity to flee. Now she feared that her last chance for freedom was about to slip away. She crawled to the doorway and used the open door to pull herself to her feet. The eight steps leading to the main floor would be her next challenge. She spent the next hour clutching a railing and leaning against the walls of the stairwell as she painfully pulled her body forward, one agonizing step after another. Finally, she made it to the top of the stairs and collapsed to the floor. She remained there, wondering if she could go on.

Susan was lying in a state of semi-consciousness. She was barely aware of her surroundings when a crackle of lightning ripped through a large oak tree near the building. The blinding flash, followed by an earth-shattering blast of splintering wood, was like a shot of adrenalin into her body. She sat up and took in her surrounding. A small lantern was on a table, but it only brought an eerie dimness to the room. Susan hadn't heard any voices for hours. The only sounds had come from the storm—lightning strikes, thunder, and the incessant rain. She worried that the men would come through the door at any moment. The front door was not a good choice for an exit from the building.

Susan noticed that a side window had been left open by a few inches. The floor beneath the window was damp, indicating that the passing storm had found its way into the building.

She scooted to the window, determined to use it for an escape. The water on the floor saturated her running shorts and Susan felt the cold dampness on her bare skin. It made no difference; she had spent four days in a cold, damp dungeon.

The window would be a challenge for a weakened person, let alone someone whose body was being racked by the effects of a diabetic episode. She stretched her arms to reach the windowsill and then gripped the wooden ledge with all her might. Slowly, she pulled herself to her feet and leaned against the window. She saw her reflection. The rain pelting against the window was matched by the tears streaming from her eyes. The pain was too much, and the heartache she had endured was overwhelming. Her body was trying to surrender.

Susan rested her head against the windowpane for a moment and whispered: "I will never give up; I will stay strong in my faith; and, I will win this race."

It took every ounce of strength for Susan to grasp the bottom of the window frame and shove it open. The full force of the storm sent a spray of cold rain and wind cascading through the open window and hit her like a *typhoon, but she held fast. Susan absorbed the initial impact and prepared for her leap of faith. She would escape...or die trying.*

Chapter 27

Mark pulled into the drive at the farmhouse and left the Jeep's engine running. He ran into the house and retrieved the gun he had purchased two years earlier. Its intended use was to ward off wild animals that wandered too close to the residence at night. However, the only time he had fired the weapon was for target practice. He had adapted to living in harmony with nature, even if it meant accepting coyotes, possums, and skunks. He put six bullets into the clip of the .22 Berretta and inserted one into the chamber. Now loaded, it became his lethal weapon.

Mark pulled on his waterproof hiking boots and rain gear. The mountain trail would be more treacherous than usual due to saturation from the storm. His decision to take the old Jeep in order to get better traction into the lower bluffs would be a tradeoff because of its leaky canvas top. Also, there wasn't time to re-attach the flimsy side doors that had been removed during pleasant weather. He stepped out of the house and splashed his way through large puddles that had appeared in the short time it took to change clothes and retrieve his gun. The storm had increased in intensity. Quarter was huddled inside her shelter adjacent to the house but poked her head out when she heard the front door open. "No, Quarter. You stay inside," Mark commanded, worried that the Lab would follow him to the Jeep. She lowered her head and retreated to a dry spot inside the shelter.

Mark cranked over the engine of the Jeep and slowly drove down the long gravel drive. He reached the entrance of the orchard and was startled by movement he caught out of the corner of his eye. A damp pile of fur flew through the opening on the passenger side of the Jeep and landed next to him. Quarter had decided to accompany him in spite of the downpour. She landed in her favorite spot, panting heavily.

"Damn it, Quarter. I told you to stay behind and I don't have time to take you back to the house." Quarter didn't share Mark's anguish as she licked the moisture from her damp paws. Mark drove onto the highway that led to Buffalo Mountain, knowing that Quarter was the least of his worries. His focus was to bring Jubile Walker and Spook Daniels to justice. Quarter would just have to tag along and not interfere.

The trip took longer than usual due to the driving rain. He kept the Jeep at thirty miles per hour to avoid losing control on the slick highway. The old wipers, or at least what remained of them, did little to clear the windshield. They intermittently smeared dead insects across the glass on the few occasions when they were able to slosh back and forth. The highway was void of most other traffic except for an occasional trucker and a few travelers who opted to risk the dangers of driving through a storm in the early morning hours. Mark finally turned off the highway onto the county road for the last leg of the journey. It was almost 4:30 a.m. and daylight would come in less than an hour, but the morning skies would remain dark and overcast. Thirty minutes later he gunned the Jeep onto the washed-out quarry trail at the foot of the mountain. He fought the steering wheel trying to keep from sliding off the muddy path as the Jeep left a half-mile of ruts and tire rubber in its wake. Eventually, the vehicle that had survived two wars and two hundred thousand miles of travel surrendered to the elements. Two blown tires and a smoking engine stranded Mark and Quarter a mile from the quarry.

"That's as far as we go, girl," Mark said, looking at his partner with the matted coat. "We're hiking the rest of the way." A blast of lightning split the sky and was followed by the rumble of thunder as heavy clouds recoiled and smashed together. Mark jumped from the Jeep and sank into three inches of mud. Quarter wasn't anxious to follow and remained huddled in the passenger's seat. "Come on, Quarter, I can't leave you here by yourself. Jump!" The Lab reluctantly took the leap and joined Mark on a muddy path leading to the abandoned quarry. They had traveled for only a few minutes when Mark looked down the trail and caught a glimpse of what appeared to be headlights moving toward where he had parked the Jeep. It was still dark and the sheriff's men weren't expected to make an appearance before daylight. Either Larry Ray's plans had changed, or someone else had serious business on such a nasty night when all the mountain creatures had taken cover. Mark grabbed Quarter by the collar and stepped off the trail. He pulled the Beretta from its holster and waited in the chilling rain under the shelter of a large pine tree. It wasn't long until a flash of lightning revealed the silhouette of someone moving slowly up the trail. Mark released the safety on his gun and waited until the person tromped close to the pine tree.

"Hold it right there. I'm armed!" Mark yelled without exposing himself. The startled person stopped and his eyes pierced the darkness trying to locate the source of the voice. Mark was nervous and not sure what to do next.

"Dr. Sarkisian, is that you?" Mark remained cautious about revealing himself. He kept his pistol ready and queried the man.

"Yes, and who are you?"

"It's me, Jeffrey Williams. I've been trying to catch up to you since you left your place."

"Jeffrey, what on earth are you doing here?" Mark said as he approached the drenched figure holding a tattered umbrella.

"I was returning to Maryville after a business trip and pulled into that truck stop at Auburn for gasoline. That's where I heard about your daughter getting shot." A crackle of lightning stretched across the sky and for a fleeting moment both men had a clear view of one another. Mark pulled on Quarter's leash to bring her closer to his side and calm her from barking at Jeffrey Williams, who was continuing to explain his appearance at the mountain. "I stopped at the medical center and the sheriff told me he might have a lead on Susan's whereabouts. He said you had gone home, so I drove to your place. I was about a half-mile from your farm when I saw tail lights pulling out of the driveway and figured it was you." Mark shook his head, amazed at the story he was hearing. "The storm slowed me down, but I'm here now and ready to help." He reached inside his jacket and pulled out a gun to show Mark that he had come prepared.

The encounter had slowed Mark down, but his mind was still focused on reaching the quarry. There was no question that he needed assistance, but a shaky young person waving a pistol in the air wasn't the answer. Jeffrey would be much safer helping in another capacity.

"Jeffrey, listen carefully," Mark said, taking him by the shoulder to emphasize the seriousness of the situation. "The sheriff will be here soon and someone needs to get him up this trail as fast as possible. That's your job!"

"But, Dr. Sarkisian, I think you better take me with you." The protest fell on deaf ears. Mark wasn't entertaining any options.

"Forget it, Jeffrey." Mark didn't want to waste more time talking. "Now put your gun away and hustle down the trail to meet the sheriff." He handed over Quarter's leash.

"Take Quarter with you. She may not be much help to me at the quarry." Jeffrey took the leash and reluctantly retreated down the trail. Mark watched him lead Quarter along the trail until they disappeared into the darkness.

Mark wondered about the young man that he had met just days earlier. There was something about Jeffrey's story that didn't add up. It seemed odd that he just happened to be passing through Auburn during the early morning hours of an attempted robbery at the Drovers and Merchants Bank. And now, having him show up at the mountain was too much of a coincidence. Too many things about Jeffrey's story didn't make sense, but Mark had been delayed long enough and needed to get on to the quarry.

He had gone a short distance when he heard what sounded like a dog's continuous bark coming from somewhere down the trail. If it was Quarter, then something had riled her into a frenzy. He was about to turn back to check on Jeffrey and Quarter when the yelping suddenly ceased. Now the only sounds came from nature—lightning, thunder, and huge drops of rain splattering through a canopy of foliage.

Chapter 28

A sliver of light peaked over the mountain crest by the time Mark reached the rusty gate leading into the quarry property. The rain had diminished and caused an annoying drizzle to bead on his clothes. He wiped the moisture from his face and surveyed the terrain. The slow-moving storm clouds gradually allowed enough sunlight to expose two vehicles parked near the main building. One was the mangled remains of what had been Jubile's black pickup. Steam billowing from the engine compartment indicated the truck had made its final journey. Spook's red truck was parked nearby, the same one that ran Mark off the road days earlier. Several large boxes were stacked on the lowered tailgate. Mark presumed the two thieves were preparing to load up and make a run for it. He decided to stay put a few more minutes before making his way down the slope. Hopefully, the extra time would allow Jeffrey to arrive with help.

There was stillness in the air. The rumble of thunder had become a faint echo. It was replaced by sounds of mountain wildlife coming awake. A rabbit ceased nibbling and perked its ears as a coyote crept through tall grass. Predator and prey were both on the alert, and Mark was suddenly growing very nervous. He wondered if the animals weren't the only ones stalking on Buffalo Mountain. His imagination played tricks with his mind: *What if the old-timers at the Co-op weren't just spinning tall tales about man-eating animals on the mountain?* Mark unzipped his rain jacket and reached for his pistol. His hand brushed against an object tucked inside the pocket, and then he remembered the insulin that Dr. Wayne had given to him at the medical center.

Movement from behind a scatter of trees caught Mark's attention. Whatever it was moved quickly, darting from behind one tree to another. He peered into the semi-darkness but caught only glimpses of hazy images. He considered firing a warning shot into the darkness but feared the men inside the quarry building would hear it. Mark released the safety on the gun, making it ready to fire at the twitch of his finger. Then he silently waited for an attack. Whoever was lurking in the early morning darkness must have been watching from the time he reached the quarry gate. Now they disappeared: *I've got to get a grip on myself. If I don't go down there now, I might as well give up and turn back.* He took a deep breath and slipped through the gate.

Mark's boots failed to hold a grip on the muddy slope as he skidded to the bottom of the hill and eventually came to an abrupt stop in a clump of shrubs. He immediately saw something that startled him. Someone was inching their way along the outside of the building being cautious not to alert the men inside. Just then the front door swung open and the person in the shadows pressed against the building trying not to be discovered. A lanky man stepped outside carrying a large box that he shoved into the bed of the truck. He hoisted his rump onto the tailgate and lit a cigarette. After a few puffs, he blew a ring of smoke and pitched the cigarette butt into a puddle of water. Then he sauntered back into the building.

The person in hiding had crouched to pass under a windowsill. The glow of light coming from the window helped Mark to identify who it was. Susan Clark was desperately limping to freedom. She struggled to maintain her balance but continued to move in Mark's direction. He needed to take action before anyone else emerged from the building, but a whispered voice startled him before he could make his move. "I'm coming right behind you." Mark spun around as Jeffrey slipped into a position next to him.

"Jeffrey, it's good to see you," Mark whispered. It was a stretch of the truth, but Mark was happy to have the reinforcement, even if it came from a fellow nervously holding a gun. "What about the sheriff?"

"He's on his way," Jeffrey quickly responded. "I came ahead to lend you a hand."

Mark found the communication with Jeffrey to be confusing for the second time since coming to the mountain. He didn't understand why the lawmen hadn't already arrived, but this was not the time to discuss semantics. He was watching Susan now crossing an open stretch of ground and heading in his direction. If either of the men inside the building stepped outside, Susan would be like a deer caught in the headlights. Mark left the protection of the shrubbery and rushed toward her. She was startled, but he placed his hand over her mouth to muffle the scream.

"Shhh, Susan," he whispered in her ear. "It's Mark Sarkisian. Jeffrey and I are here to help you." He scooped her limp body into his arms and carried her to the hiding place. Mark had told Jeffrey to keep watch during the rescue in order to call out a warning if the men came out of the building. Then he removed his rain jacket and cradled Susan in his arms. "You're going to be okay, Susan," He reached inside the pocket of his jacket and nervously retrieved the syringe. Mark hesitated, but as soon as Susan saw the lifesaving insulin she grasped his hand and guided the needle to her thigh. Seconds later the lifesaving medicine was moving through her system. Mark covered Susan with his jacket and gave her encouragement as they waited for the shot to take effect. "Just hang on a little longer and we'll get you to the hospital. You're safe now."

Susan's eyes were closed, yet her smile indicated that she was alert. "Thank God," she murmured. "I never gave up hope that someone would come for me."

Mark's emotions soared. His intent in coming to the mountain was to get revenge on the men that harmed his daughter. Now all of that anger had been replaced with the joy of finding Susan alive. The pleasant moment was short-lived as the door to the quarry building swung open.

"Shhh," Mark cautioned. He placed a finger to his lips to signal that they were not out of danger yet. They watched Jubile walk to a small shed and return carrying a small box marked *Dynamite*. His work at the quarry had given him plenty of experience with explosives and he was about to put it to use.

"If she's hiding inside, there won't be a shred of proof that the girl was ever here after the blast," Jubile said, spitting a wad of tobacco. "That idiot sheriff will probably think we went up in smoke, too."

"I guess there's no sense waiting for your friend any longer," Spook responded. "He's probably more interested in a manicure than splitting the loot." The comment was so laced with sarcasm that it was obvious Spook didn't care much for their "silent" partner in crime.

"Naw, this is peanuts to him. He wants to be a multi-millionaire." Jubile gave a nasty laugh and spit another wad of chaw. "That's why I always called him a big shot."

The ongoing conversation between the two felons fascinated Mark. He wondered if Aubrey Canterbury was the other fellow they were talking about. The "Toad" had never given the impression that he aspired to be anything, let alone a millionaire. Whoever it was, Jubile and Spook were planning to leave him behind. They were loaded and ready to leave. The only thing left to do was to light the long fuse stringing from the box of dynamite.

Mark realized that the blast would likely obliterate everything around the building. He and the others were much too close. He lightly caressed Susan's hand. "Susan, can you hear me?" She nodded her head to let Mark know that she was still alert. "We need to get out of this area as soon as possible." Mark spoke softly trying not to frighten her. "Can you handle it if we carry you to the other side of the slope?"

Susan was hurting, but she realized the urgency of the situation. She opened her eyes and smiled. "I've made it this far, Dr. Sarkisian, and I'm not giving up now."

"Young lady, you have got the right stuff." He lifted Susan comfortably into his arms. "Come on, Jeffrey. Let's get out of here before Jubile blows this place to smithereens." He started to carry Susan, but Jeffrey hesitated. Mark turned to face a gun pointed in his direction. "Jeffrey, what are you doing?" Mark was livid, but he managed to keep his voice low enough to avoid alerting the men standing outside the building. "Put that gun away and let the sheriff take care of those fellows. Sheriff Garrett and his deputies should be here any minute now."

"I don't think the sheriff will be here anytime soon."

"What are you talking about?" Mark fired back as he helped Susan get her feet on the ground. "I thought you showed them the way when you went back to meet him."

"Sorry, but I never saw the sheriff." Jeffrey's tone turned to arrogance. "I suppose it was only a matter of time before a smart guy like you got this all figured out." He kept the gun aimed at Mark while he reached over and confiscated Mark's weapon. His next move confirmed that the junior executive knew more about the mountain than he had let on. "Hey

Walker! Daniels! Get over here!" Mark stepped forward, but Jeffrey let him know that he wouldn't hesitate to use the gun.

"So, you're somehow connected with this criminal operation," Mark said angrily. Then he remembered something he had been meaning to ask. "And, what did you do with Quarter?"

"Oh, the dog," he said with a pained expression. "Yeah, I clubbed the mongrel when we got out of your sight." Jeffrey didn't show an ounce of remorse. "I would have shot her, but I knew you would hear it and maybe double back to check it out." His words were stone cold. "She hobbled into the timber, probably dead by now. I never understood why she growled at me from the first minute she saw me."

Mark lowered his head, holding back tears as he thought about his long-time companion: *I always said Quarter was a good judge of character. Now she may have given her life because of it.*

"Well, you finally showed up, Mr. Big Shot," Spook grumped as he and Jubile arrived with their rifles. "And I see you nailed two of our favorite people."

Jubile's sarcasm wasn't nearly as subtle as he pointed the rifle at Mark. "I think your luck just ran out, Dr. Sarkisian." Susan clutched Mark's arm fearing that Jubile was

305

ready to kill Mark. He lowered his weapon and broke into a cruel laugh. "Naw, it ain't gonna happen that quick, Sarkisian. I want you and the lady to sweat, waiting for the fuse to burn."

"Stop your rambling, Jubile, and help me get them into the building," Jeffrey said nervously waving his gun. Mark had no choice but to carry Susan to the building and help her into a chair. The box of explosives lay only a few feet away. An unlit fuse dangled from the box. Mark remained silent facing the two rifles. Susan's glare revealed her disdain for the former boyfriend as she confronted him.

"I don't understand, Jeffrey. Why would you risk everything and get mixed up in this nasty business?"

Jeffrey's suppressed anger erupted and he fired back. "Well, of course you don't understand! You could never understand! You're Miss Popularity, the Teaberry Girl, and the town's favorite distance runner!" His ranting was condescending. "You never came from a broken family! You never had to scrape to make a living just to get stuck in a company that never appreciated your intelligence or talent!"

"Intelligence and talent," Spook said with a smirk. "Wow, somebody sure thinks a lot of himself."

"Shut your mouth, Spook!" Jeffrey fired back. "I've just about had it with your stupid comments." Spook hunched his shoulders as if the words had no effect on him.

Jeffrey made an aggressive move toward Susan and Mark tried to intervene, but Jubile motioned with his rifle to stay put. Jeffrey bent down until he was sneering into the helpless woman's face. "I finally saw the opportunity, Susan," he said in a vile tone. "Millions of dollars buried in land owned by a couple of Indians that don't have squat, and they're not interested." His voice dropped to a nasty whisper as he continued putting on a show for a captive audience. "Can you imagine that, Susan?" He exaggerated throwing his hands toward the ceiling and screamed, "They're not interested!" He regained his composure and summarized the performance in a slow, mocking voice. "They would rather live in harmony with nature." He bowed his head as though applause was warranted.

"Man, that is one sick dude," Spook mocked, but Jeffrey let him know that he was in no mood for joking from a man he couldn't stand.

"I told you to shut up, Spook, and I'm not going to warn you again." He pointed his gun in Spook's direction. Jubile motioned to his partner to "cool it" with the ribbing. Everyone, including Jubile, was aware that the man dangerously waving his weapon was showing signs of severe instability.

Mark knew it was a precarious situation and tried a different approach. "Look Jeffrey, I can understand your ambition to afford some luxuries, but I'm just baffled at how you ever got connected with these no-accounts." The two people he was referring to took major offense and started for Mark, but Jeffrey waved his gun to keep them in check. His relationship with Jubile and Spook was growing more intense by the minute. It wouldn't be long before each man would regret the business arrangement.

"Now that's a great question, Dr. Sarkisian," Jeffrey conceded, "one that I've asked myself a hundred times in the past few days." He almost sounded remorseful and proceeded to explain how he came to know Jubile Walker and Spook Daniels. "I was making my way down the mountain after my offer to buy the property was soundly rejected by the old Indian woman." He lowered his head and continued to speak about the events months earlier, which had altered his life. "I wandered into the quarry camp," he paused to look at his former girlfriend sitting in the chair, "just like you did, Susan." His eyes teared. "At first, Jubile and Spook thought I was a lawman, but they soon realized I was just a civilian who had seen too much of their theft operation." Jeffrey seemed to be pleading his case when he looked again at Susan and said, "They were talking about killing me."

"It sounded like a good idea to me," Spook said, confirming that he had been in favor of putting a bullet in Jeffrey months ago. The young fellow was too deep in thought and let the comment go for the time being.

"That's when I decided to cut a deal with these thieves," he continued and drew a hateful look from both men. "I knew the SRA satellite system could be used to their advantage during their heists, so I offered my technical expertise in return for my life and their help in framing the Wanatees."

"So, Noah Wanatee finding the Teaberry wrapper was no accident?" Mark asked.

"Heavens no," Jeffrey responded and wiped tears from his eyes. "I had these two scatter the gum and some other belongings of Susan's close to where the Indian kid hunted. Sure enough, the very next morning he spots a piece of Teaberry gum."

"Okay, I think I get the picture, but one thing I still don't understand is how some of Susan's belongings showed up near St. Joseph." Mark was putting the puzzle together in his mind and Jeffrey held the final piece. He seemed willing to clear his conscience.

"That was my idea, and these screwballs went along with it," Jeffrey admitted, and pointed at his partners. "We figured that if the police found Susan's stuff on the banks of the Missouri River, it would keep the search away from Buffalo Mountain, at least for a short time." He lowered his head. "I was so filled with hate after she broke off our relationship that all I wanted was revenge and the opportunity came when she stumbled into the quarry. I pitched Susan's things when I passed through St. Joseph on my return trip to Maryville." He glanced up and the look of distain coming from Susan told him there was no need to continue. "I guess you know the rest of the story, Dr. Sarkisian."

"Yes, I think I do," Mark said with a consoling nod. "You realized that Sheriff Garrett would eventually investigate the Wanatee family during his search for Susan, and you gambled that he would discover something of hers in their possession." Mark was assuming the persona of a detective describing the sequence of a crime. "The Wanatees either get arrested for Susan's suspected death, or they're so shamed by the inference that they decide to vacate the mountain. It would leave the door open for you to finagle a way to acquire their land." He paused long enough for everything to register before he asked, "Is that what you were thinking?"

Jeffrey nodded in the affirmative. "That was pretty much the plan, Mark. I think you got it right." Calling Mark by his first name appeared to be an acknowledgement that Jeffrey's scheme to gain riches was coming to an end.

Susan slumped lower in the chair. Beads of sweat had replaced the drops of rain on her forehead and her skin was pale. She couldn't last much longer if her vital signs continued to drop. The other men had shown no sympathy for Mark or Susan, but a final appeal to Jeffrey might be their only chance for survival.

"Listen to me. It's not too late to turn this around and do the right thing," Mark reasoned with Jeffrey. "You may have made some mistakes, but you're not like these two career criminals." He caught an evil look from the men and knew he was getting dangerously close to a fatal conclusion. "You're not ruthless enough to be a killer." Judging by the change in Jeffrey's expression, the words were having an impact on the troubled young man.

Jubile and Spook weren't buying into Mark's plea. They made an aggressive move toward him but stopped when Jeffrey again threatened with his gun. "Back off, you slime balls! I need time to think." Jubile retreated a few steps, but Spook had reached his limit. He was tired of taking orders from someone who considered himself superior. He wasn't going to let Jeffrey belittle him any longer.

"Why, you little pipsqueak! You're no better than us," Spook wailed. "In fact, you're worse." He stuck his finger in Jeffrey's chest and continued to rant. "You knew the girl was dying in that dungeon, and you went right along with the plan." Susan's saddened eyes focused on Jeffrey. He was shaking his head trying to deny the accusation, but Susan knew the truth.

"Shut up, you imbecile! I must have been crazy to associate with an ignorant hick like you!" Jeffrey scoffed. He stepped back and cocked his gun, but Spook kept coming.

"Imbecile?" The reference was the final straw for Spook. "Jubile stopped me from burying you the first time we met," he said, while ignoring the gun pointed at his midsection. "Now, I'm gonna make up for that mistake."

The verbal bashing had an impact on more than just the intended victim. Susan clutched Mark's arm in fear. She recognized the voice of the man who had tried to molest her in the room when she was held captive. Jubile had shifted his eyes from guarding Mark and Susan to watching the two men quarrel. The temporary lapse gave Mark an opportunity to scan the room for anything that might be used in an attempted escape. The room seemed barren of anything that could be used as a weapon until he spied an old pickaxe with a splintered handle leaning against a wall in the far corner of the room. He kept his eyes on Jubile and inched his way in that direction. Mark might have made it except for Spook's next actions.

Jeffrey had continued to back up as Spook advanced on him. Now, with his back to the wall, he warned the aggressor that he wasn't afraid to shoot. Rather than suffer the humiliation of retreating, Spook's hands caught Jeffrey by the throat and pressed him against the wall. "Time to die, you little bastard," he yelled, while squeezing the life out of his frail adversary. Those were Spook's final words.

The barrel of Jeffrey's gun was pressed firmly into Spook's midsection when he twice pulled the trigger. Mark watched Spook lurch as the bullets ripped through his flesh, and he slumped to the floor. An ugly burst of blood spread from under his body and pooled on the wood floor. The shooting had been at such close range that Spook's soiled t-shirt became shreds of charred material mixed with dirt and blood. A small wisp of smoke drifted from the bullet holes and a rancid smell permeated the room. Mark moved to steady Susan as she turned away from the hideous sight while the other two men stood gawking at the lifeless body.

Mark realized that the reprieve wouldn't last long. He saw anger building in Jubile as he stared at the man holding a gun over his friend's body. Revenge was on his mind and he raised his rifle. If Jubile was willing to kill Jeffrey, then Mark and Susan would be next. Mark made his move. He dove for the pickaxe and rolled once before coming to his feet, grasping the weapon as though he were ready to swing for a homerun. The daring move caused Jubile to fire a wild shot. A bullet barely missed Mark and penetrated the wall. He stood helpless against the rifle and tossed the pickaxe to the floor to signal surrender. Jubile remained incensed and aimed a second shot for Mark's head. He was ready to kill the man who had been his nemesis for years.

"No, please, no!" Susan couldn't stand to see her rescuer about to be gunned down.

Her cries infuriated Jubile even more and he smacked his hand across her face. Jeffrey had stood passive during the action between Jubile and Mark, still trying to gather his wits after shooting Spook. Now the sight of Susan tumbling to the floor brought him into the fray. He anticipated becoming the next target as soon as Jubile finished with Mark.

"That's enough," Jeffrey warned, turning the gun on Walker. "Make another move and you'll be joining Spook in hell." It was a standoff. Each man trained his weapon on the other, just waiting for the slightest flinch. Mark cautiously stepped to Susan's side, hoping to shield her from the eminent gun battle. Seconds seemed like an eternity and neither man uttered a sound. They were caught in a sordid game, searching for that slight edge that would allow one to crack off a shot without catching a bullet in return. Susan pressed her head against Mark's shoulder, fearing the shootout would also claim bystanders. Finally, Jubile broke the silence.

"Spook was right; we should have buried you months ago." The hateful look in his eyes betrayed his thoughts. It was time to settle the score. He didn't care if he died as long as he took Jeffrey with him. He squeezed his finger on the trigger, but a voice from outside the building caused him to hesitate.

"You, inside the building!" Mark was thankful to hear a voice that he easily recognized, but the other two men were panicked. "This is Sheriff Larry Ray Garrett. Come out of the building with your hands up!"

Chapter 29

Jubile Walker and Jeffrey Williams were locked in a standoff, trying to decide whether or not to dissolve their felonious business relationship with gunfire. Now the two set aside their differences long enough to rush to the window of the quarry building where Mark and Susan were being held captive. Sheriff Garrett's posse of deputies and troopers had mastered the mountain's dangerous terrain. The lawmen were strategically positioned in front of the building, unaware of a hidden exit located at the rear. The earlier sound of shots inside the building caused the sheriff to fear for Mark's safety. He issued another order. "Walker and Daniels! This is your last chance to come out of the building." He added a personal message to his final warning. "And, anyone you're holding in there had better be safe, or you'll never walk off this mountain." The other lawmen were surprised at what they heard coming from their leader. Sheriff Garrett saw their reaction and put the issue to rest, "It's no threat, boys. It's a promise."

Jubile wasn't planning on going to prison. He smashed a window with the butt of his rifle and fired several rounds. The bullets slammed into the old machinery and then ricocheted in all directions. The lawmen that were using the equipment for protection ducked lower and covered their heads. "If you want me that bad, Sheriff, why don't you come and get me?" Jubile fired another shot that pinged off of the dozer blade that shielded the sheriff.

"Hold your fire, fellows." Larry Ray was eager to nail Jubile, but not if it meant risking someone's life. "We don't want to be shooting any innocent people that might be in there."

Mark helped Susan duck behind a wooden table that had tipped over when the shooting began. It didn't provide much protection, but it was better than standing around waiting to catch a stray bullet. Jeffrey scuffled across the floor to confront them.

"The two of you better do what I say, or I swear I'll shoot you right now," he threatened. "Now, get through that rear door and head down the stairs." He motioned toward the back of the room with his gun. Jubile was so intent on keeping the lawmen at bay that he never noticed Mark and Susan reluctantly following Jeffrey's instructions.

The stairs led to a series of narrow hallways, one of which contained the underground room where Susan had been held captive four days. Susan could never have made it to the bottom of the stairs without Mark's assistance. She hesitated at the frightening door, but Jeffrey shoved the two hostages down the hallway, while keeping his gun trained on them.

The lower area of the building had originally been constructed with the quarry workers in mind. The men could enter the lowest level of the building by passing through a short tunnel that led underneath the building. It allowed them to access the shower and break room area without having to enter the main floor where the quarry office was located. The tunnel entrance had become overgrown with foliage and wasn't easily noticeable to an occasional hiker. Jubile had started a rumor several years earlier that the tunnel had collapsed and become a haven for poisonous snakes. None of the townspeople had any desire to verify the story and the tunnel eventually ceased to be a topic of discussion at the Co-op. The tunnel and its adjoining hallways beneath the building had proven to be ideal for the theft operation. Jubile and Spook used it to transfer their stolen loot into the building without the risk of being seen by anyone who happened to come near the quarry.

The underground rooms were ideal for storing the stolen merchandise until it was safe to dump it into the black market.

Mark and Susan made the turn down the final hallway, still being prodded by the barrel of Jeffrey's handgun. They reached the connecting passageway, which led to a narrow tunnel with a low ceiling. There was no artificial lighting, but glints of sunlight filtering through foliage indicated the exit was nearby. Jeffrey kept a safe distance and stayed ready to foil any attempt Mark might make to overpower him.

Mark pushed through the briers that covered the entrance and then held back the tall shrubs in order for Susan to exit. He toyed with the idea of allowing the sprigs to swish back into Jeffrey's face, but the young man was skittish and anticipated the move. He ordered Mark to step away before he exited. Mark offered his arm for Susan to steady herself and saw that she was able to stand on her own. Even in the hazy pre-dawn light, he could see that color was returning to her body. The shot of insulin was taking effect. For the first time since finding her, Mark actually thought Susan could survive her ordeal. They still had to deal with Jeffrey, and his sense of remorse appeared to be waning.

"Get on that path and head up the slope," Jeffrey demanded, after checking the tunnel to make sure they hadn't been followed. Mark and Susan had no choice and started on the seldom-used path that led to a steep cliff overlooking a lagoon. A set of tire depressions in the damp ground seemed to be curiously out of place. A vehicle had recently straddled the narrow path, but the single set of tracks seemed to indicate it was a one-way trip to the summit. Mark assisted Susan when she struggled on the slippery path. The show of kindness only heightened Jeffrey's anger directed at Mark. The three continued to hear the intermittent gunfire coming from further down the trail. They reached a small plateau above the quarry and Mark helped Susan to sit with her back resting against a tree.

"She can't go on, Jeffrey," Mark said, ignoring the threat of the gun. "She's exhausted and needs a break." He was surprised not to hear a rebuttal. Years of sitting behind a desk and smoking cigarettes had not prepared Jeffrey for the rigors of mountain trekking. He was breathing heavily and sweating profusely.

"Okay, but only for a few minutes," he stammered, trying to catch his breath. Mark used a handkerchief to wipe Susan's brow. She flashed a smile, grateful for his companionship in spite of the dire situation. Then she shared an inner thought.

"If something happens and we don't make it," she paused, and her eyes saddened, "I want you to know how thankful I am for what you've done."

"It's nice of you to say that, Susan," Mark said, wiping the tears that had begun to trickle down the young woman's cheek, "but I think you're going to be running in a lot more races." The encouragement boosted Susan's spirits. Mark ended the brief conversation with words she had often heard from her father, "Hold onto your faith and don't ever give up."

Jeffrey was on the ground trying to catch his breath. He began making small talk and rambling about his miserable life. Evidently, he had been dealing with personal issues long before his transfer to SRA's office in Missouri. His tone was solemn, even remorseful. Susan realized an opportunity. She rose and moved closer to the troubled man. He shunned away, afraid of making eye contact with the woman who had rejected him. She put a hand on his shoulder and spoke with sincerity.

"I never meant to hurt you, Jeffrey," Susan said in a thoughtful tone. "I hope you believe me because it's true." She moved her hand and touched his cheek. "Please, let us go. Jeffrey's eyes filled with tears, betraying a man longing for a lost love and riches, and now he had neither. Mark watched from a distance and saw that Susan's gentle approach had an effect on Jeffrey. He appeared to be calmer and had even lowered the gun until it merely dangled in his hand. It appeared that he was actually considering Susan's request for freedom. The mood was broken by the sound of rifle fire coming from the quarry. The resting spot provided a vantage point for observing the battle being waged below.

"That Jubile Walker is a maniac," Jeffrey rambled as he looked down the slope toward the quarry building. "He'll never let them take him alive. That's how much he hates the sheriff." Sporadic flashes of gunfire came from the building and they could hear Jubile screaming profanities.

"Come and get me, you miserable S.O.B.s!" Jubile yelled, and fired another shot.

Sheriff Garrett wasn't willing to risk the safety of his men, but his patience with Jubile was running thin. He figured some taunting might induce the gunman out of the building. "Hey, Jubile!" he called out in a melodic tone. "Uh, or is it Jubule?" the sheriff feigned being confused regarding the outlaw's real name. "Sorry, I'm never quite sure what to call you. We've got it both ways on your criminal rap sheet at the jail!" The pun caused Jubile to cringe and fire off more rounds intended for his adversary. Sheriff Garrett decided to push it to the brink. "Frankly, sometimes we just call you that stupid, no-account, good-for-nothing piece of trash!" Most of the deputies nodded in agreement. Sheriff Garrett cautioned them to keep their heads down and maintain a close vigil. "He'll be coming out soon and it won't be to surrender. Everyone stay alert!"

Larry Ray had been sizing up the situation since the beginning of the fray. Jubile was the only person shooting from the building, so he figured Spook Daniels was out of the picture. He calculated that Spook might have been a victim of the earlier gunfire inside the building. Before that, the sheriff suspected that Mark might be a captive, but now he believed that no one else was alive in the building. Otherwise, Jubile would have mentioned having a hostage and tried to negotiate a getaway. Larry Ray's emotions got the best of him as he thought about his long-time friend and the prospect of never seeing him again. He said a silent prayer, *"Lord, please help us all to come out of this safely."*

Susan sat next to Mark and watched the action play out at the bottom of the hill. Jeffrey kept a distrusting distance from the two as he observed his former partner in crime hold the lawmen at bay. He knew it wouldn't be long before the sheriff would get the upper hand, but it provided Jeffrey with some time to gather his wits and weigh his options. The time was shortened when Jubile yelled a final threat.

"Hey, Sheriff, I've got a present for you, and I'm gonna deliver it in person!" Jubile had reached the end of the line. He rested his back against a wall and focused on the box containing explosives. His plan to skip the country with a pile of money had been foiled and his buddy was lying in a pool of blood. He intended to take some lawmen with him if he was going to die in this battle. Jubile pulled a stick of dynamite from the box and struck a match. He watched the initial flame dim to an orange glow before pressing it against the dynamite fuse. The flash filled the room with smoke and a nauseous odor. He knew there were only thirty precious seconds to toss the lethal stick before it obliterated everything within sixty yards of where it would land. Jubile stepped into the doorway and sneered as he waved the sizzling stick of dynamite above his head. Then he began a suicidal charge.

Sheriff Garrett quickly realized Jubile's intention and called a warning. "Hit the dirt fellows; he means to kill us all!" The deputies and two state troopers dove for cover, but only one man remained standing. Larry Ray Garrett had dedicated thirty years of his life to protecting the people of Auburn County, and that included the men and women that worked with him. He had never taken a human life in the performance of his duties. Now he was faced with that decision.

Jubile's crazed ranting echoed off the nearby cliffs as the fuse burned on the blood-red cylinder. A few more seconds and he would be close enough to send it into the pile of boulders and equipment being used to shield the officers. The ripping explosion would not discriminate between rock, metal, and humans. He cocked his arm and stretched to launch the sizzling missile. Jubile hesitated just long enough to scream his final threat against law and order, "You can go to hell, Sheriff Garrett!" Those precious seconds were all Larry Ray needed.

"You might be right, Jubile, but not today," the sheriff yelled and took dead aim.

What Jubile never heard was Larry Ray Garrett's silent prayer as he repeatedly fired his .44 Colt, *"Forgive me."*

Three shots hit Jubile squarely in the chest. He reeled backwards and slumped to the ground. His eyes remained open, fixed on the stick of dynamite still clutched in his hand. The last flicker of spark made contact with powder and the ensuing blast shook the old quarry building's foundation. Huge deposits of dirt and stone flew a hundred feet into the air and then harmlessly fell to the ground. A slight morning breeze helped to dissipate the dust and smoke that spewed from a six-foot deep hole blown into the earth. Jubile Walker had dug his own grave, so to speak.

Sheriff Garrett didn't waste any time giving orders to his men. "A couple of you fellas check the building to see if anyone else is inside." He cautioned the men to be careful since he wasn't sure what had happened to Spook Daniels. It took only moments before the officers reported that Spook had already met his demise. The sheriff wasn't surprised at the news. "One of you fellows head back to where we left the paramedics and bring them up here. We may still need them." Larry Ray had stood looking into the deep hole in the ground when he suddenly switched his attention to the terrain above the quarry. He saw movement on the upper trail. Whoever it was must have heard the blast, but now they were moving out of the area.

"What are you looking at, Sheriff?" asked one of the state troopers.

"I'm not really sure, but I intend to find out," he said, while reloading his weapon. "You fellows finish here while I check on something." Sheriff Garrett headed for the narrow trail behind the building. "Send help if I'm not back in an hour."

Chapter 30

Susan and Mark had watched the ongoing battle at the quarry. They were relieved when the officers emerged unhurt from the shocking blast. Jeffrey appeared to have a renewed spirit, but for another reason. He forced the two captives to continue on the path. His sense of remorse left him when he realized Jubile and Spook were permanently out of the picture. Now only two people knew about his involvement in the crimes, and both of them were walking ahead of him, nearing the top of the cliff.

Sheriff Garrett hurried along the path leading up the slope. He stopped to catch his breath at the spot where the others had rested. He could see that the officers below were busy processing the site, and the paramedics had arrived. He took a few deep breaths and began tackling the last leg of the climb.

Mark helped to steady Susan as they walked on the path. She had trouble maintaining her balance and showed increased signs of fatigue. Jeffrey grew more agitated, sensing that the two were stalling for time. "Get moving; we're almost to the top." He looked down the trail and was startled to see someone moving fast and gaining ground. "Speed it up or I'll kill you right here!" His wild expression showed that he wouldn't hesitate to pull the trigger.

"Jeffrey, don't be a fool," Susan shouted. "You'll never get away with this. They'll find you here and know you were involved in all of this messy business." Her plea fell on deaf ears.

"That's not how I figure it, Susan," he countered. "With you two out of the way, I can sneak my way off this miserable mountain and nobody will be the wiser." He was spouting crazy talk that made no sense. "Who knows, maybe I can still convince them that the Indian family is to blame for your disappearance." Susan realized it was useless to try reasoning with him.

"I don't think you give Sheriff Garrett nearly enough credit," Mark interjected. "He's not one to fall for such a bogus story."

Jeffrey was determined to stick with his plan. They reached the summit and he forced Mark and Susan dangerously close to the edge of the cliff. Behind them was a three hundred foot drop into the lagoon. "Get on the ground and stay there!" he yelled. Another glance down the path sent him into a panic. "That damn sheriff just won't give up." Glints of sunlight reflecting off Sheriff Garrett's badge helped Jeffrey to identify who was tracking him. He knelt behind a boulder and waited until the sheriff was within range. Mark, however, wasn't going to sit still and allow his friend to be ambushed.

"Larry Ray, watch out!" The sheriff immediately stopped and unsnapped the leather strap on his holster, but the warning came too late. Jeffrey fired two shots and the lawman dropped off the trail.

"I don't think your friend is going to be much help to you now." The nasty crack brought a hateful look from Mark. "Maybe I should go down there and make sure I got him." Now Jeffrey wasn't so confident and was second-guessing himself. He started for the path, but Mark's angry sarcasm triggered his paranoia.

"I think that's a great idea. Why don't you just mosey down there and find out just how very resilient our sheriff is, you *esh.*" In his anger, Mark had unwittingly substituted an Armenian term for a jackass. Jeffrey didn't know the interpretation but caught the inference.

"Who do you think you're talking to, Sarkisian? You're just trying to trick me and I'm not falling for it." He continued to maintain a high opinion of himself in spite of being exposed as nothing more than a common criminal. "I'm not some ignorant fool like Walker or Daniels, and I'm not a town yokel like that Toad Canterbury."

"That's true, Jeffrey. You're nobody's fool," Susan interjected, when she realized Mark was messing with Jeffrey's mind. "You go on down there and make sure you killed the sheriff." Her nonchalant attitude confused her former boyfriend. He paced back and forth trying to decide whether to risk an encounter with a wounded lawman.

Susan whispered to Mark. "He's doing the same thing he always did when he had to make a decision at work," she said shaking her head. "He would agonize over simple matters, and eventually hand it over to Paige to make the decision." Mark nodded to indicate he remembered the friendly administrative assistant at the SRA office. Jeffrey became more agitated by the whispering.

"I knew it! Yes, I knew it!" he screamed in a high-pitched voice. "You're trying to trick me too, Susan." He babbled like a madman carelessly waving the gun and strutting with his head lowered. His face was somber as he finally looked again at Susan and Mark. "Well, it's going to end right now." Jeffrey's eyes were forlorn, reflecting a deep sense of hopelessness. They filled with tears and he carelessly pointed the gun at his captives. "No one's ever going to make a fool out of me again."

Chapter 31

Sheriff Garrett groaned once his body came to a stop at the bottom of a steep hill. The bullets had missed him by mere inches. His only hope to avoid the gunfire was to dive over shrubbery and try to avoid breaking his neck as he tumbled to the bottom of the hill. The soggy ground provided some cushioning, but it didn't prevent several cuts and bruises. He remained still for a minute and then sat up to check the damage. The initial examination was encouraging. He appeared to have survived remarkably well, other than some trickles of blood seeping from cuts on his hands and arms; that is, until he tried to stand. The excruciating pain and quirky angle of his foot left no question that his ankle was broken. Help was a considerable distance away. A rustling sound coming from nearby timber caused him to think that the foot injury might be the least of his worries. Someone was hurriedly closing in on him. Larry Ray reached for his pistol, but it was missing. The weapon had jostled from the holster during the fall.

Now it was lying in the dirt halfway up the slope. He scooted on his butt to a nearby tree. Then he rested his back against the trunk and braced for an attack. The sound in the timber grew louder, but the source brought a welcomed smile to the sheriff's face.

"Quarter, you old son-of-a-gun!" the sheriff shouted when he saw his best friend's pet emerge from the timber. His voice turned sympathetic when he saw the canine's condition. "My gosh! What happened to you, girl?" Quarter limped forward and Larry Ray saw blood dripping from a wound above her eye. She whimpered and licked the sheriff's face. "Oh, you poor thing, somebody really did a number on you, girl," he said scratching behind her ear. "I guess we're both really busted up, but how in the world did you find me all the way up here?" His question was answered when Israel and Noah Wanatee came rushing from the timber. Both were carrying their rifles in a non-threatening manner. Larry Ray tried to stand.

"Stay down, Sheriff. We will help you," Israel Wanatee called out as he hurried to Larry Ray's side. "You will cause more injury to the ankle trying to walk on it."

Larry Ray was shocked. He had stood in the Wanatee cabin only days earlier ready to engage in a gun battle with the two Native Americans, and now they were coming to his aid. Israel motioned for his son to search for something to use as a splint.

"I'm sure lucky you fellows came along when you did," the sheriff said graciously. "It's hard telling how long I would have laid here until someone found me."

"It's not luck," the older man replied. "We followed you and the others a good distance." Israel saw the confused look and continued to explain. Israel and his son had remained in the shadows when Mark and Jeffrey arrived separately at the mountain. They were angered to see the younger man club the Lab and tried to help her after she ran from him. Jeffrey had hurriedly backtracked up the mountain and they lost track of him. Later, they watched in the background when Mark staked out the quarry building and then kept their distance when the lawmen battled Jubile Walker. "We were suspicious but did not understand the situation." Israel lowered his head and reflected. "The men in the building were evil. It is good that they will not hurt anyone again." He paused long enough to apply a splint to the damaged ankle with the pieces of wood Noah had gathered. Larry Ray tried not to flinch, but it was obvious that he was in pain. "This should help protect the wounded area until you reach the hospital." The old Native American gave the sheriff a pat on the back and his son continued the story.

"We saw the three people sneak out of the small tunnel from our position on the bluff. Later, we saw that you followed their trail." Noah Wanatee's account was concise. "We wanted to help, but rough country had to be crossed to get here." He paused to smile at Quarter. "The loyal dog followed us all the way." The reference to Quarter prompted the sheriff to focus on something more important than his broken ankle.

"Israel, listen to me." He clutched the old man's arm. "Mark and the girl need help, and I have no one else to rely on." He paused when the old Indian raised his hand to indicate he knew what needed to be done.

"I understand, and I will take care of it." His words were soft and reassuring.

Quarter was licking her wounded leg when she abruptly cocked her head and sniffed the air. The others smelled nothing, but Quarter had caught a faint scent of Mark in the morning breeze. She disregarded her injuries and bounded up the hill to follow the scent.

"You stay with the sheriff and make sure that his men find him," Israel instructed his son. Then he turned to the sheriff and spoke softly. "You can trust us, Sheriff." He grabbed the 45/70 Sharps rifle and followed Quarter to the top of the hill.

Chapter 32

Susan and Mark were defenseless as they stood at the precipice of the cliff. The crazed man with the gun was convinced he had only one chance to avoid prison. If his two captives took a few more steps backward, his problems would be eliminated by a three hundred foot vertical drop. He aimed the gun directly at his intended victims, hoping the threat would force them to take the last few steps. Susan nearly lost her balance, but Mark caught her just as one foot slipped over the edge. She made a final plea once she was back on solid ground.

"Please don't do this, Jeffrey." The words fell on deaf ears. He already realized that neither of the two had any intention of a suicide jump. He would have to shoot them and dump their bodies over the cliff. Mark wasn't giving up without a fight. He broke from Susan and ran toward Jeffrey, but the charge came to a halt when a bullet grazed his shoulder. He fell to his knees as Susan rushed to shield him from another shot that Jeffrey was about fire. Mark used his free hand to apply pressure to the wound, knowing that another attempt to charge would hasten the murder.

"Better stay down, Sarkisian, and take it like a man." The chilling words were filled with hate. Jeffrey put his finger to the trigger once again and Mark turned his head away, not wishing to witness his own execution.

"No, Jeffrey!" Susan's words were the last thing Mark heard as Jeffrey pulled the trigger for the fatal shot.

Quarter had continued on the trail sniffing Mark's scent. Israel Wanatee was a short distance behind but gaining on the wounded Lab. She crested the summit with her heavy coat of fur stained with blood flowing from the wound on her forehead. Quarter bared her teeth and growled at the sight of Jeffrey. In that split second, the Lab launched herself at the man who had unmercifully beaten and left her for dead. Ninety pounds of canine muscle rammed into Jeffrey's back just as he pulled the trigger. The bullet intended for Mark spiraled harmlessly into the sky as Quarter's blow sent Jeffrey sprawling to the ground. He was temporarily disoriented but scrambled to retrieve the weapon that had dislodged from his hand.

The impact of the collision catapulted Quarter dangerously close to the edge of the cliff. She let out a whimper of pain as her body slammed into the muddy ground and rolled toward the drop-off. Her sharp nails jabbed into the dirt to slow the momentum of the tumble. She came to a halt with her backside dangling precariously over the edge. Mark rushed to grab the Lab's thick collar, hoping to pull her to safety, but he was too late. Quarter's claws raked the moist ground as she continued to slide further over the cliff. A moment later, the gallant Lab dropped from sight. Mark reached the precipice and hoped to see that Quarter had somehow managed to land on one of the narrow ledges below the overhang. He saw no sign of her.

A stream of blood was running down Mark's arm. Susan pressed her hand over the wound to diminish the flow, but Mark's full attention was focused on the man who was quickly recovering from the blow delivered by Quarter. Jeffrey was bent on committing murder.

"This time there won't be any second chance for either of you!" he screamed as he rushed the two helpless people lying on the ground. Mark used his body to shield Susan just as Jeffrey started to squeeze the trigger.

The shot was ear-shattering, much too powerful to come from a small caliber pistol. Its report echoed through the mountain. Mark slowly raised his head and faced a shocking sight. Israel Wanatee had reached the summit in time to witness Jeffrey about to fire a fatal shot. The proud Indian cocked his rifle and took dead aim. The blast from the old buffalo rifle bored a two-inch hole into Jeffrey's back. He was practically dead on his feet by the time the huge chunk of metal exited his chest. Mark told Susan to keep her head down to avoid witnessing such a gruesome ending. Jeffrey haplessly staggered toward the cliff as the life drained from his body. He teetered on the edge for a few seconds and then turned to face the two people whose lives he had planned to end. Jeffrey's eyes rolled in his head and he catapulted off the cliff.

Noah reached the summit just minutes after he heard the thunderous discharge of his father's rifle. He was accompanied by para-medics and state troopers. The Auburn County deputies had remained with the sheriff to assist him in getting to an ambulance that waited farther down the mountain. Noah stayed with Susan as one paramedic attended to her. Mark joined Israel Wanatee after having his wound cleaned and bandaged by the other medic.

The storm had moved far into the distance and a sky was filled with white clouds drifting casually across a blue canvas. The two men sat in silence as they gazed at the mountain's most distinct feature. When he finally spoke, Israel Wanatee's words captured a lifetime.

"It is good that the mountain honors the bison. There was a time when they were free to enjoy this land," he said, and then reverently bowed his head. "There was a time when people respected others."

Mark remained silent, soaking in the wisdom shared by a person who had very little formal education. He thought about his trip to the mountain when he had tried to convince the wise man that his son needed to be sitting in school. Something remained to be said.

"Thank you for what you did today. It was a miracle that you found us." Mark extended his hand to the man who had saved his life. The old Indian smiled and then hesitated before responding with words that Mark would remember for the rest of his life.

"I am not the one to thank, my trusted friend." Israel gently held Mark's hand and then looked into a blue sky. "The *Keeper of the Mountain* always holds his people close to his heart." Mark watched the proud man slowly make his way back down the trail and gradually fade into the timbers of Buffalo Mountain.

The medics were ready to transport Susan from the summit, but she asked them to wait. She called to Mark and he knelt beside her. Susan motioned for him to lean closer to hear something intended only for his ears.

"God bless you, Dr. Sarkisian," she whispered with tears in her eyes. "I'll remember you forever." Her lips lightly brushed his cheek.

Mark looked into the eyes of a young woman who had challenged death on the mountain and won. He smiled and gave her a wink of an eye, "Susan Clark, you are going to be a great teacher!"

And, Susan cried happy tears.

The End

Epilogue

Elijah Carneal continued the daily routine of managing the Auburn Co-op. Each evening he checked the butter tub that was intended for contributions to the "coffee fund." Most days it was empty.

Ellen Downing continued in her position as administrative secretary to **Superintendent Dan Williams** at the Auburn School District. Before retiring, she took pride in telling the new kindergarten classes, "I knew your daddy, your grandpa, *and* your great-grandpa when they were in school."

Dr. Andrew Wayne continued to fill in at the Auburn County Medical Center where he was known to inform the young interns, "It's perfectly okay to be a little quirky, as long as you take good care of your patients."

Mary Rose, Carolyn, and Roxy Wilson, the 'Singing Shamrocks,' continued to perform tunes at the annual Auburn Back-To-School Festival. It seems that no one ever noticed the decanter of Irish whiskey stashed beneath their sheet music.

Paige Morgan was promoted to Regional Manager for the SRA Corporation and helped the company be named to the "100 Fastest Growing Companies in the United States."

Aubrey (Toad) Canterbury was sentenced to eight years in prison for his involvement in the crimes. His wife divorced him and began dating the owner of a fast-food restaurant.

Israel and Noah Wanatee declined several lucrative offers to purchase their land in Hidden Valley. They preferred to live in harmony with nature and protect the natural resources of Buffalo Mountain.

Sheriff Larry Ray Garrett announced his retirement after three decades dedicated to protecting the people of Auburn County, Missouri. Three months later, he was overwhelmingly elected to the state legislature. His winning campaign was based on the slogan, "I spent 30 years getting rid of the crooks in Auburn County, and I think I can do the same thing in the state capital!"

Amelia and Wilbur Clark were content to continue working the farm and were pleased that their daughter was happy in her career as a teacher.

Kristin Sarkisian returned to work at the Auburn County Sheriff's Department, sporting an engagement ring given to her by newly-promoted Sergeant **Collin Nichols**.

Mark and Marnie Sarkisian finally got to enjoy a life of retirement at the orchard, just growing fruit and baking Armenian delicacies created from "a pinch of this and a pinch of that."

Susan Clark began her work as a third grade teacher in the Auburn School District shortly after the incident on Buffalo Mountain. During her first day, she stood at the front of the little "cherubs" to conduct the roll call. She paused and smiled when she came to the names beginning with the letter 'S.'

"Hope Louise Sarkisian?" the teacher called out.

"Present," the little girl responded and then politely folded her hands on her desk.

"Chase Sarkisian?" the teacher called, eye-balling the mischievous twin seated next to his prim sister.

"That's me! I'm right here in front of you, Miss Clark," the little boy said while excitedly waving his hand practically under Susan's nose. "Gee whiz, Miss Clark, my Grandpa Mark said you were pretty, but gosh, you're beautiful!" He turned around in his desk and gave a thumbs-up to his classmates. Susan blushed and the entire class broke into laughter.

Life went on in the sleepy town of Auburn, Missouri. Things didn't change much. Well, maybe a little. The **Old Coots** continued to meet daily at the Co-op to enjoy the "free" coffee and spin their yarns, but they had a new tall tale that some folks swore was true. It seems that on those special times when a pre-dawn mist is in the air and a light fog floats through the forests of Buffalo Mountain, a person might catch a glimpse of a large, spirited **Black Labrador** chasing at the heels of white-tail deer as they disappear into the timber. Rumor is, the big Lab never catches them...but then, "she wouldn't know what to do if she did catch one."

Acknowledgements

My thanks to the following people who helped to make this novel a reality:

Marylin Erganian, the real-life Marnie, was always by my side providing cheerful encouragement. She is my best friend and the love of my life. The Lord really does bring angels to earth, and I was lucky enough to marry one.

Julie Casey of *Amazing Things Press* provided her talent as an editor and publisher to turn the original manuscript into a published novel.

Michael Mosiman, my brother-in-law, lent his technology skills to the project and baled me out on more than one occasion when the computer decided to shut down in the middle of a sentence. Sadly, he passed away only a few months before *Keeper of the Mountain* was published.

Susan (Schmidt) Smith brought her expertise as a professional educator to the project in serving as one of my proofreaders. Her encouragement and compassion for the story remained throughout the writing.

Dr. Frederick Kiehl shared his knowledge of medicine and helped to move the story along as it related to Susan Clark's medical condition.

Larry Ray Downing was my *Kemo sabe.* His unwavering friendship and the quality of his life inspired me to create the fictional character Sheriff Larry Ray Garrett.

About the Author

Nshan Erganian was born and raised in St. Joseph, Missouri. His father survived the Turkish massacres of the Armenian people in the early part of the 20th century and came to America as a boy for the opportunity of freedom. He became a well-respected merchant and married Rose Sarkisian. The couple had four children, one of which is Dr. Nshan Erganian, the author of *Keeper of the Mountain*.

The author's life has included successful careers as an educator, public school superintendent, healthcare administrator, and professional consultant. During his career, Dr. Erganian was named as "Missouri's Outstanding Administrator" by the Missouri Community Education Association. At one point, he and his wife, Marylin, a staff assistant to a United States Congressman for sixteen years, decided to leave the hustle-bustle of the corporate and political world and purchased two commercial orchards in Missouri, which they rejuvenated and operated for many years.

Nshan Erganian is a member of the St. Joseph Writer's Guild. *Keeper of the Mountain* is his first novel. His other writings include the short stories *Mom Was A Baseball Legend* and *A Grandparent's Guide to Caring for Twin Toddlers*.

A Message from the author:

Thank you for taking the time to read my book.
I would be honored if you would consider
leaving a review for it on *Amazon*.

Check out these titles from Amazing Things Press

Guardians of Holt by Julie L. Casey

Keeper of the Mountain by Nshan Erganian

Rare Blood Sect by Robert L. Justus

Evoloving by James Fly

Survival In the Kitchen by Sharon Boyle

Stop Beating the Dead Horse by Julie L. Casey

In Daddy's Hands by Julie L. Casey

Time Lost: Teenage Survivalist II by Julie L. Casey

Amazing Things Press

www.amazingthingspress.com

Made in the USA
Charleston, SC
06 October 2014